WHEN SKIES HAVE FALLEN

by

DEBBIE McGOWAN

Beaten Track

www.beatentrackpublishing.com

WHEN SKIES HAVE FALLEN

First published 2015 by Beaten Track Publishing
eBook first published 2015 by MMRomanceGroup
Copyright © 2015 Debbie McGowan

A CIP catalogue record for this book
is available from the British Library.

ISBN: 978 1 910635 50 6

Back cover image: Hammersmith Palais, Spring 1941
Created by the United Kingdom Government
Ministry of Information Second World War Official Collection
Public Domain (expired Crown Copyright)

Front cover image: reworked licensed stock image – usage is not indicative of the models' identities, activities or preferences

Beaten Track Publishing,
Burscough, Lancashire.
www.beatentrackpublishing.com

Acknowledgements

With heartfelt thanks to:

Al and Nige, magnificent beta-readers and damned fine fellows;

Mariah, for cheering/egging me on, and for never giving up;

Patch, for random letter placement;

Andrea, ever my literary champion;

The DRitC team, without whom these stories would not be possible.

Finally, a huge thank you to Tiffany, for a truly wonderful prompt. Here is your story.

Extracts taken from *Aaron's Rod, Lady Chatterley's Lover* and *The Rainbow*, all by D H Lawrence (public domain).

Song lyrics from 'After the Ball is Over', by Charles K. Harris (public domain).

Author's Note

Whilst the characters and settings in this story are fictional, the social and political events are real. The language used is, as far as it is possible to discern, that of the time period in which the story is set. A glossary of military terminology is included at the end of the story.

Dedication

They went with songs to the battle, they were young.
Straight of limb, true of eye, steady and aglow.
They were staunch to the end against odds uncounted,
They fell with their faces to the foe.

They shall grow not old, as we that are left grow old:
Age shall not weary them, nor the years condemn.
At the going down of the sun and in the morning,
We will remember them.

'Ode of Remembrance', Lawrence Binyon

Table of Contents

Ours is essentially a tragic age, so we refuse to take it tragically. The cataclysm has happened, we are among the ruins, we start to build up new little habitats, to have new little hopes. It is rather hard work: there is now no smooth road into the future: but we go round, or scramble over the obstacles. We've got to live, no matter how many skies have fallen.

—*Lady Chatterley's Lover*, D H Lawrence

PART ONE: 1944

Chapter One:
January, 1944

Although the winter had been milder than usual, for a couple of weeks now, the temperature had rarely exceeded ten degrees, and several inches of compact snow made for treacherous excursions. Yet the good people of Buckinghamshire refused to be beaten by the cold spell, and the Palais Dance Hall was as crowded as ever, with not one man in civvies. Many of the women were also in uniform, creating the illusion of a dull sea of blue, green and tan upon which floated the vibrant lemon, rose and turquoise hues of the few girls old enough to go dancing, yet too young for service.

From the standing area at one end of the hall, Corporal Robert Thomas Clarke—Arty to those who knew him—and his fellow RAF servicemen watched the swirling couples ebb and flow in their gentle waltz to the air of the three-piece band onstage. A brazen young woman in flimsy crimson, lips painted to match, spun close, granting the men a flash of stocking-top; some whistled their appreciation, but Arty's attention was elsewhere.

"The WO looks like he's got sticks up his trouser legs," Leading Aircraftman Charlie Tomkins remarked to the group at large, and they all laughed in agreement. Arty shook himself out of his daze and turned to see their warrant officer and his dance partner pass by, both of them so stiff it was a wonder they were able to move at all. Most of the couples danced without sophistication, although perhaps with a greater sense of rhythm and more freedom to their movement.

The WO and his girl waltzed out of sight, and the men returned to their conversations—except Arty, who scanned the dance floor, looking for the American airman he had been watching for most of the evening. The American was broad-shouldered and handsome, with his well-fitting, brown serge tunic and thick, blonde hair, his angular features softened by the relaxed, crooked smile he had offered to the young woman he'd been leading in the waltz. He had moved with such elegance that Arty could have watched him dance forever. Alas now he was nowhere in sight, so Arty settled for watching everyone else. He found it a truly moving experience, almost as wonderful as when he was dancing himself.

"Are you getting out there this evening, Art?" Charlie asked.

"Maybe." Arty kept his focus on the dancers. "If I had someone to dance with."

Charlie acknowledged Arty's words with a nod. He scanned the settees, where those women who were not dancing were seated with their friends, waiting for someone to make the offer. Some didn't bother to wait and instead danced with each other, taking turns to lead, but how it usually worked was the man would politely approach the woman—*may I have this dance?*—and with outstretched arm, she would politely accept and allow him to lead her in the next dance.

"Shan't be long," Charlie said. Before Arty had a chance to respond, Charlie was edging his way around the dance floor towards a slender woman in WAAF uniform: a sergeant. Arty watched the two interact, with Charlie wearing his winning smile, which rarely failed to woo the women he dazzled with it. He pointed Arty's way; the WAAF sergeant glanced over, and Arty's cheeks warmed. He loved dancing, and he was very accomplished, but when it came to asking he was terribly shy. His friends—Charlie in particular—always insisted on finding a graceful young woman to be the Ginger Rogers to his Fred Astaire. Once he was on the dance floor he'd forget about all those eyes on him, and that they were at war, and how unmoved he was by the closeness of the woman in his arms.

After a couple of minutes spent chatting with the WAAF sergeant, Charlie beckoned for Arty to go over; he quickly smoothed his uniform and set off, attempting a confident stride.

"This is Sergeant Jean McDowell," Charlie introduced. Arty offered her a smile, and she blinked up at him with big brown eyes, her tiny pink mouth forming a tiny smile. Charlie raised his hands in a flourish to signal that he was handing over, and departed, leaving the two of them to become acquainted.

"I'm Arty. Would you care for this dance?"

Jean nodded swiftly, and with assertiveness matching the three stripes on her arm, but at odds with her seemingly meek demeanour, she took Arty's hand and led him onto the dance floor. They found a space in the middle of the room, and the music did the rest. In an instant all of Arty's fears diminished, his right arm confidently found Jean's waist and, with her right hand in his left, they stepped off together, joining the throng in their swaying, flowing waltz.

At first, they made small, tentative steps, waiting for openings so they could move around, but then other people started to pay attention and moved out of their way. Arty became bolder and spun Jean, whose skirt should have restricted such graceful kicks, yet did not. They danced as if they had been dancing together for many years, matching each other's stride, anticipating next steps and never losing time. By then, the floor had cleared, leaving Arty and Jean to do just as they pleased. They pivoted and spun, hesitated and reversed—they had extraordinary grace. Jean was as natural as Arty, her feminine curves complementing his strong, lithe physique.

The waltz came to an end and many of those around them applauded. Arty grinned, glancing down at Jean to find that she was grinning too. After a count of four a quickstep began, and Arty saw, over Jean's shoulder, the American airman, standing with two others, his head cocked to one side to better hear his associate. Arty and Jean danced on, the rest now joining them. On each spin where Arty found he was facing that direction, he'd glimpse the American, uncertain if he was imagining the fleeting seconds when their eyes met before other dancers blocked his view.

Following the quickstep, the bandleader gave an even quicker count of four, and the three Americans were immediately surrounded by girls, clamouring to be their partners for the jitterbug. Arty and Jean stayed where they were, soon picking up their pace. Arty swung around and pushed Jean away from him, keeping a tight grip on her hand as she spun and sprang back. They slipped and they slid into chassis and spins, for the most part unaware of the rest of the dancers. Aside from a certain American airman, no one else stood a chance of keeping up with them, although by the end of their jive they, like most, were in need of a breather. The music stopped, and Jean looked up to Arty, her lips spread in a wide smile, her breaths puffing against his chin and neck.

8

"I need fresh air," she told him. He tilted his head towards the balcony, and Jean nodded in agreement. Some of the other dancers voiced disappointment at their departing stars, who paused to bashfully bow and curtsey before dashing hand in hand, up the stairs, along the balcony and out onto the dark terrace, to the far end where there were fewer people. They stopped and leaned on the iron railing, exhilarated and breathless, and for the moment appreciating the cold air on their clammy skin.

"You're quite a dancer," Arty complimented Jean sincerely.

"Thank you for saying so. As are you." It was the first time Arty had properly heard Jean talk, and she was very well-spoken, almost aristocratic. "Who taught you, Arty?" she asked.

"To dance? My aunt—my mother's sister, that is."

"You attended a dance school, surely?"

"No. Did you?"

"Yes." Jean traced her fingers along the railing. "Dancing, deportment and elocution. I hated it when I was a gal, though I'm glad now. When the war is over, I'm going to open a dance school. I'm on the lookout for a dance partner so I can enter competitions and make a name for myself." She laughed as she pondered a thought before adding, "I don't think that's quite what my mother has in mind. She wants her only daughter to marry into high society, but I have no interest in finding a husband." She turned to face Arty, although it was too dark for each to make out the other's features. "Have you ever considered dancing in competitions?"

It would have been far less of a surprise had she asked Arty if he were hoping to find a wife, because it seemed a more pertinent consideration. How could one afford the frivolity of dance in wartime?

9

"I've never given it any thought," he answered, and it was the truth, though he'd considered the other at length, and realised with some misgivings that he, likewise, would be expected to marry at some point in time.

"Would you consider it?" Jean asked. "Dancing with me, I mean?"

Arty scratched his ear, delaying his response. "After the war?"

"No. I've just transferred from Gaskell to Minton. I'm taking over the wages office for both bases."

Jean paused meaningfully, but Arty wasn't sure why. He could see her in profile now, against the clear night sky, her breath creating a transient cloud. She shivered, and in his mind he formed the suggestion that they return inside, but that was not what left his mouth. "If you were to find a husband, I imagine he would not take kindly to you dancing with another man."

"You're right, of course," Jean agreed, "and if you're trying to let me down gently..."

"Well, you are very beautiful, Jean. I just don't think war is a good reason for rushing into marriage, that's all."

Jean laughed, but not to mock. "Arty, this is not a flirtation. You are absolutely right. One *should* wait for the right person, and if that person never appears, then what of it? I am content the way I am. I'm not looking for a husband, just a man who can dance. So what do you say?"

Arty delayed a few seconds longer and then nodded. "Yes. I would very much like that."

Chapter Two:
February, 1944

With all of the tables and chairs stacked against the walls, the mess hall at RAF Minton provided more than adequate space for practice. The group captain had approved it; he was as enthralled as everyone else by the prospect of having nationally acclaimed dancers in their midst, and Arty and Jean's rotas now included officially allocated time for their dancing, simply because it was good for morale.

The captain agreed that on Thursday evenings, Arty and Jean would dance at the Palais, on Saturdays at the base, travelling down to London to take part in demonstrations and competitions as and when they were called upon to do so. They were accomplished in most ballroom, but *their* dance was the waltz and they were quickly becoming RAF favourites.

It was on one rainy afternoon in late February, after they had perfected a couple of variations, that Jean stopped dancing, right in the middle of the barren room, looked Arty straight in the eye, and said, "Those Americans at the Palais were the advance party."

Arty feigned ignorance. "Americans?"

"Oh come now, Arty. Surely you don't think you can fool me?"

"F-fool you? I don't understand."

Jean smiled gently and took his hand. "Come and sit," she requested, though he had little choice in the matter. She led him across the hall and hopped up onto a table, patting the space beside her. Arty reluctantly complied and sat rigidly, staring dead ahead. From the kitchen came the sounds of clanging pans and shouted orders. They wouldn't be overheard, but still, Arty had a good idea what Jean wanted to say, and he was wishing so very hard that she wouldn't.

"The Americans are taking over Gaskell tomorrow," she said.

"How do you know?"

"Gaskell's WAAF have already transferred to Minton. They were moving into our quarters when I went on duty this morning. And the NAAFI have been given their orders for Saturday night. We're to host a welcome ball."

"Oh." Suddenly Arty was sick with nerves, and not on account of knowing he and Jean would be the main entertainment on Saturday night.

"I felt I ought to warn you," Jean explained.

"We've been practising a lot. We won't make fools of ourselves."

She took his hand again and held it in both of hers. "Of course we won't, but I wasn't talking about that. I wanted to warn you, because...well, I saw it, Arty. The way you looked at the American sergeant."

"I... Who?"

"The big man with the impossibly blue eyes, square jaw, fast moves..."

Arty turned away, hoping it might stop Jean from saying anything further, certain his face was hot enough to set itself alight. He wasn't good at bluffing when the stakes were

12

negligible, never mind when his freedom might depend on it.

"Oh, Arty." Jean laughed quietly and squeezed his hand. "It will always be our secret, I promise. I care a great deal for you. God forbid that you should go through...well, you've no doubt read the same things I have, and you deserve love and happiness as much as the next man."

He considered denying everything, telling Jean she'd got it all wrong. He was merely admiring the man's dancing, and she had read more into it than was there. If he offered Jean the lie, she would accept it, and it wouldn't be mentioned again. Yet the longer he delayed, the greater his need became to tell her the truth. They'd known each other for only a few weeks, and they were already close friends. She trusted him, and he trusted her, but this...*abhorrence* of his: he had never spoken of it to anyone other than his sister, genuinely fearful for his life if he were found out.

"Arty? Are you all right?"

"Yes," he said, his voice croaky and tight. He cleared his throat and tried again. "Yes. I am." Mustering all of his courage, Arty turned to face her and lowered his voice to a volume barely above a whisper. "I've never acted upon it, Jean, I swear to you. Indeed, until now I've never met anyone with whom I'd want to. How would I approach him? I'd risk imprisonment, at best, if I made a mistake."

"If you're asking my opinion, I don't believe there is anything wrong with you following your heart. All this nonsense of not acting upon it. Why should you not? That they would turn a man into a criminal for his love of another, well, *that* is criminal, Arty, and I would say as much to anyone who dared to suggest otherwise. I do understand that one must be discreet. However, I don't believe you've made a mistake. He was watching you too. I saw him."

"I don't know..." Arty sighed and rubbed his forehead.

13

"I do. Arty, he liked you. I'm convinced of it."

"What if other people noticed?" The fear made Arty's throat tighten again and the knot in his stomach grew more painful. "If you saw it—"

"We were dancing together. Your cheek was pressed to mine." Jean raised an eyebrow and smiled mischievously. "Your very *hot* cheek, whenever he was in sight."

"And you're certain no one else noticed?"

"Quite certain."

"If they found out—"

"We'll make sure they don't," Jean said firmly. She gave him a moment to gather his thoughts and then wrapped him in a warm, tight embrace. "You know, Arty, our dancing together might just be the perfect masquerade."

"There's still the small matter of what happens when you meet someone you decide you want to marry."

"*If* that ever happens, then I'll keep him a secret, just like you and Jimmy."

"Jimmy?"

"Oh, didn't I tell you? Technical Sergeant Jimmy Johnson, United States Army Air Forces, twenty-seven years old." She released Arty and placed a motherly kiss on his head. "Take a chance," she whispered. "You deserve to be happy."

Chapter Three:
March, 1944

The mess hall floor had been polished until it gleamed like glass, making it a little slippery for normal operations but perfect for the evening's dancing. The band had set up onstage and were tuning up, with most of the Minton service people already in attendance; only those on duty were absent, although they were covering each other in order to put in an appearance. Boosting morale was everything right now; just that morning Charlie had told Arty that the American airmen were all about morale. They'd formally met their counterparts at Gaskell the day before, and they were pleasant chaps, if not a little slack, with their rolled-up sleeves and caps worn on the backs of their heads. A sloppier drill Arty had yet to see, such as he was paying attention, his eyes straying to every man wearing sergeant stripes. None were Technical Sergeant Jimmy Johnson, and it was probably just as well.

Several WAAF entered the mess hall, all smiles and best frocks, but Jean stood out from the rest in her long, white dress with a feathered hem that lifted delicately and swished from side to side as she walked, revealing dainty white shoes and a flash of smooth, shapely legs, the dim light reflecting off her nylon stockings. The Americans had brought plenty of booty with them, including the stockings, and Jean had confided that she was delighted: no more drawing on seams and worrying whether they were straight, or fretting about rain making the gravy browning run.

"You're going to shame them tonight," Charlie said, watching Jean and her fellow WAAF drift across the hall; some stopped to chat to airmen, others continued on to get drinks.

"You do a mean foxtrot yourself, Charlie," Arty said.

"Not a patch on you though, eh?"

"I don't know about that."

"You could waltz across the Western Front and still return home unscathed," Charlie joked, always trying to make light of their losses.

Arty shook his head but laughed anyway. "The waltz I can manage. The jive is an entirely different matter."

Charlie waved his hand dismissively. "Oh, the Americans know how to do all that showy business, but you and Jean…" He smiled and his eyes sparkled.

Arty nudged his friend knowingly in the side. "She's an extraordinary dancer," he agreed.

"And you and she?"

"Just friends."

Charlie nodded thoughtfully. He was evidently seeking Arty's approval, though Arty was loathe to give it. Who was he to permit or deny such things? Jean had firmly stated that she had no interest in courtship or marriage; Charlie, at twenty-six, was the middle son of three, the youngest killed in Belgium, the eldest still fighting over there, hence his glib humour, for it tempered the reality. No doubt Charlie felt the loss keenly, and he was under duress to carry on the Tomkins family name, but there were many more women on the base and in town. *Surely any of those would be more than willing to court Charlie?* Arty chastised himself; what a preposterous notion, that Charlie could pick and choose whom to like when Arty had endeavoured and failed to do the same.

"What do you think, Arty? Do I stand a chance?"

"Better than most, I'd say. If you want to dance with her tonight—"

Charlie laughed. "Captain Taylor would have my guts for garters. Maybe next time." He clapped Arty on the shoulder and stepped off towards the bar. "She's all yours tonight, my friend."

Arty watched Charlie weave his way through the small groups standing and chatting casually, noticeably more floor space between the British and the Americans, but that would change, once each recognised that they were not so different from the other, and their enemy was the same. The Americans seemed brash, boastful of their victories to date, in contrast to how reserved the British were. There was a great deal of arrogance, but they were in a strange country; their ways were young compared to the rich history of the British Empire to which they had once belonged.

Arty had been born the year after the Great War ended, nine months to the day from his father's return. It was a common occurrence, and he was one of many children born around that time, their understanding of war being one of adventure with no notion of death to blacken its majesty. Their fathers and uncles did not speak of what they had endured, nor of the lives lost, until war broke out again, and Arty often wondered if a peaceful agreement might have been reached had those returning home spoken out sooner. War was not glorious; war was not proud. What victory was there to be had in so many losing their lives? It did not stop history repeating.

These thoughts, like the other thoughts he had, Arty kept to himself. It would do no good to share with anyone how strongly he disagreed with warfare, but he would fulfil his duties in the war effort, and fulfil them well. As for his other thoughts: they could be just as dangerous, and it worried him tremendously that Jean had read him as if he were an open book, like *that* book his sister Sissy held dear. Being some ten years older, Sissy had been in service to a wealthy gentleman in London for most of Arty's living memory, and she had evacuated with her employer to Kent, only to be ousted when he was forced to return to his native Italy. Poor Sissy went home distraught, for she loved everything about her job, not least the gentleman's collection of fine art and literature. His claim that he had been a friend of the author D H Lawrence was well substantiated by his library, which boasted a complete set of Lawrence's works, including a certain publication deemed too obscene for general consumption.

Lady Chatterley's Lover, Sissy's employer refused to let it leave his house, but, being the sort of man he was, an artist and intellectual, he agreed to Arty visiting with Sissy, and he did so, many times. Those nights, huddled together in the vast, lumpy reading chair, embers glowing in the hearth, while they pored by candlelight over page after page of Lawrence's words... Such wonderful memories; Arty clung to them with every part of his being, though it was not the recounting of Lady Chatterley's pursuits that stayed with him, but those of Aaron Sisson.

> *Robert went with the bicycle lamp and stood at Aaron's side.*

> *"Shall I show you a light to the road—you're off your track," he said. "You're in the grounds of Shottle House."*

"I can find my road," said Aaron. "Thank you."

Jim suddenly got up and went to peer at the stranger, poking his face close to Aaron's face.

"Right-o," he replied. "You're not half a bad sort of chap—Cheery-o! What's your drink?"

"Mine—whiskey," said Aaron.

"Come in and have one. We're the only sober couple in the bunch—what?" cried Jim.

Aaron stood unmoving, static in everything. Jim took him by the arm affectionately—

"Did you read that, Sissy?" Arty whispered. "A man affectionately taking the arm of another man."

"Indeed. That is why I wished for you to read Mr. Lawrence's work."

"What do you mean?"

"It occurred to me, Arty. Most young men of your age are interested in one thing alone."

"One thing?"

"Yes, brother. Young ladies."

Arty's eyes fell and his shoulders rounded. "I am not worrying unduly then. There is something very wrong with me."

Sissy set the book down in her lap and tugged Arty close. "No. There is nothing wrong with you, dear brother. Come, read with me some more."

When Jim woke in the morning Aaron had gone. Only on the floor were two packets of Christmas-tree candles, fallen from the stranger's pockets. He had gone through the drawing-room door, as he had come. The housemaid said that while she was cleaning the grate in the dining-room she heard someone go into the drawing-room: a parlour-maid had even seen someone come out of Jim's bedroom. But they had both thought it was Jim himself, for he was an unsettled house mate.

There was a thin film of snow, a lovely Christmas morning.

"Good evening to you, Corporal."

His voice, a slow, deep rumble, startled Arty from his remembering. His breath caught in his throat as he fought to reply. "A good evening to you also, Sergeant…Johnson, isn't it?"

"Sure is." The man held out his hand for Arty to shake. "Technical Sergeant Jim Johnson, at your service."

Arty reciprocated: "Corporal Robert Clarke." The palm against his was big, rough and cool to the touch.

"Robert, Bobby, or Bob?"

"None, actually. Arty is what they call me, on account of my initials. My middle name is Thomas."

"Arty," the American airman repeated with a wide smile displaying straight, white teeth that made Arty hide his own behind tight lips. "Great name, Arty. Has a good ring to it. They call me Jimmy, but I prefer Jim myself. You'll be wooing us again this evening, I take it?"

"Wooing?" Arty's vocabulary had abandoned him, along with his propensity to take in air.

"You and Sergeant McDowell."

"Oh, yes. The waltz." What an absolute fool he must seem.

"Looking forward to it," Jim said. The smile remained in place, as did the firm yet gentle grip of his cool fingers on

Arty's own. "Well," he drawled, bringing the other hand up to sandwich Arty's, momentarily increasing the pressure and then releasing, "let's talk later." He looked Arty in the eye, capturing him with a piercing blue gaze.

Jim departed, and Arty quickly turned away, fearful that someone had seen their exchange. It was, to all purposes, an innocent introduction, but the look Jim had given him offered much more than words. Arty's heart was thumping hard and he was panting like a dog on a hot day. He closed his mouth and drew air through his nose, slowly, deeply.

Love is the soul's respiration.

When you love, your soul breathes in. If you don't breathe in, you suffocate.

"Are you feeling unwell, Arty?" Jean asked.

"No, no. I'm quite well." He attempted a smile of reassurance.

She pursed her lips, her finely pencilled brows arched high. "We are to commence the dancing in five minutes," she said.

"I'll go and get, er, a...a drink." Arty nodded to confirm that's what he'd do. "Yes. A drink. Would you like..." He stopped and took another deep breath, releasing it slowly. "Oh, Jean."

"Get your drink. You can tell me while we dance."

Arty nodded again and did as she suggested, blinkering his vision against Jim and his friends standing together at the end of the bar.

"Arty," Charlie greeted him with a clap on the back and a cheery smile. "Here." He handed him a pint of beer. "I thought you were on your way over, until I saw you talking with Sergeant Johnson."

"Ah, yes. He was…wishing Jean and me luck."

"Luck?" Charlie laughed too loudly. "That was decent of him."

There was a gleam in Charlie's eye that betrayed his true feelings, and whilst Arty wanted to placate his friend, he was relieved to sense envy coming from Charlie, rather than suspicion. But could he be certain Jim wasn't interested in Jean? That was the problem: how did one communicate about such dangerous matters?

Keep mum, she's not so dumb.

Arty glanced over to where the poster hung on the wall of the mess hall; it was a mildly amusing premise, that the one person apart from his sister he had confided in looked like the attractive woman in the poster cautioning against careless talk. An RAF mess hall was a place where it felt safe to speak with a little more candour. Yet for almost all of these people, and he estimated there were eighty or more present, there was only one enemy. Tonight men and women would dance together, perhaps drink a little too much, share a moment of affection, a kiss, even. Where usually this state of affairs did little more than sadden Arty, he was feeling something far more powerful than sadness this evening. *They* did not face imprisonment simply for following their heart, so why should he?

As Arty's indignation rose to anger, Jean beckoned him from across the dance floor. He took down a mouthful of beer and handed his glass back to Charlie before meeting Jean halfway. They moved together as would new lovers, a slow step towards each other; Arty offered his hand and Jean accepted. Nervousness temporarily took over Arty's senses so that he barely heard any of the bandleader's announcement, welcoming the USAAF servicemen from Gaskell, nor his and Jean's introduction. But with the count

22

of three, the buzzing in his ears ceased, and he and Jean were swept up in The Blue Danube waltz.

Moving slowly at first, the flow of the melody lifted their heels and then let them drop. They spun to the left, and slid to the right, so they now could traverse the length of the floor. As the tempo picked up, Jean's skirt twirled around, caught in eddies that she and Arty had made. At the end of the room, as they spun, Arty glanced past Jean and gasped.

"You are making me bold, Jean," he whispered through almost closed lips.

She leaned near to his ear and whispered back, "I know. You feel different tonight, Arty. Charged, full of vigour. Is he watching now?"

"Yes."

Jean used her body to steer Arty around so that she caught a glimpse of Jim Johnson. She hummed knowingly and smiled.

"I'm more certain than ever that he likes you."

"Perhaps he likes you," Arty speculated.

Jean laughed and leaned back. Arty smiled at her. He was going to do it. He was going to take the chance, and if he landed in prison? Well at least he wouldn't have to be part of this blasted war.

***

The night wore on, and people danced and drank and found their common ground. The Americans were either very generous or possessed great cunning; they had come armed with promises of the plentiful gifts from their supplies back at Gaskell—chocolate, sweets, gum, cigarettes and, of course stockings, which was almost as powerful an allure as them hailing from the land of movie stars. Even the most independent WAAFs were swooning at the fine young men, most of whom were also highly accomplished dancers.

"I think it's their more relaxed posture," Jean observed from the settee where she and Arty had crashed, having danced for a solid hour. They had gladly given over their prime spot to the jitterbug, particularly as it meant Arty could watch Jim without rousing suspicion that it was driven by anything other than artistic interest. Jim was not a small man, easily as tall as Arty and much broader, but it didn't hinder him in the slightest. The woman he was dancing with was an AC2, little more than a girl, really. When Jim slid her along the floor between his legs, turned and grabbed her around the waist, she positively flew into the air, the thrill of the dance pinking her cheeks and painting an enormous, enchanted smile upon her face.

"Daphne has got the hots for your friend," Jean said with a laugh. The girl was certainly enamoured with the handsome American, and he was charming her most convincingly.

"Are you sure?" Arty asked Jean again. "He seems to delight in dancing with every girl who asks."

"Just like you, eh?" Jean grasped Arty's hand and gave it a tight squeeze.

"Yes." She was right; just like his own enthusiasm, Jim's was all about the love of dancing, but still Arty felt anxious. "Are you all right here? I need some air."

Jean nodded and smiled in reassurance. "Yes. I'm fine."

Arty stood and, after being intercepted by well-wishers several times, made it across the mess hall to the outside. The evening was cool, but the weather of late had been mild, and the breeze was refreshing, seeming to clear his muddled thoughts. In the heady exhilaration of their dance, the notion of approaching Jim hadn't troubled him at all. Now, without Jean to goad him on, he was becoming more and more certain that saying nothing would be the wisest thing to do. Arty leaned back against the wall and stared up into the dark, overcast sky. Had there been stars he could have whiled away the moments counting them. Instead, his traitorous mind filled with wonder, of what it would be like to comb his fingers through Jim's thick, blonde hair, to feel the sturdiness of those shoulders against his palms, press lips to lips... It was a sin to think of touching a woman in such lustful ways, but a man?

"Beautiful night."

That same deep baritone he had just imagined whispering tendernesses tore him from his thoughts. "Yes. No stars though."

"No," Jim agreed. "Other than you and I."

Arty turned his head to his companion. Jim's smile shone through the darkness.

"You're quite the celebrity, Arty Clarke."

Arty chuckled bashfully. "I suppose so. As are you. You dance very well."

"Thank you. I sure seem to be a winner with your gals."

"Yes, I noticed that."

"You sound like you're..." Jim paused, as if to consider his choice of words.

"Envious?" Arty suggested.

Jim laughed quietly, and Arty detected an underlying tremor. "Yeah. That's a good word for it."

The air next to where Arty's left palm pressed to the wall became slightly warmer. He spread his fingers to investigate, making contact with skin. He decided bravely to leave his hand where it was and see what happened.

Jim continued, "So, would I be right in thinking your envy is not of my jitterbug?"

"That would be correct, Sergeant."

"All right."

A finger bridged Arty's little finger. His heart was pounding so hard he was certain Jim could hear it.

"You know what'd be really great?" Jim said. "If there were somewhere on the base that two guys could talk without fear of being overheard."

His words prompted Arty to lean forward. He could see no one else. Jim breathed out heavily and grasped Arty's hand.

"Arty, I…"

"Yes, I know." Arty was having the same fight to keep his breathing steady. "I think there are a couple of places, I'd need to conduct a reccy, but not tonight."

"That's fine. Just… Don't take too long, will ya?"

Now it was Arty's turn to laugh with nervous excitement. "No. I can promise you that."

Chapter Four:
March, 1944

To the east of the base, about three-quarters of a mile along a disused service road, were three small hangars. Built in 1915, the buildings were too small and far away from the main base to be of any practical use. They were checked daily for any traces of occupation, but had otherwise been abandoned to the elements.

The Sunday afternoon of the weekend following the dance to welcome the USAAF, Arty, who was off-duty, borrowed a bicycle and rode out to the hangars. The reason he had prepared for the event of anyone asking, though no one did, was that he had noticed several species of butterfly he did not think he had seen before. Since childhood, butterflies had fascinated Arty and he was confident his knowledge was sufficient to waylay any suspicion that his interest in that particular area of the base was anything other than butterflying.

It was quite a windy afternoon, and changeable, with the windsocks billowing every which way. As the wind's direction shifted, the creaking of the corrugated metal sheets constructing the three hangars momentarily became louder before fading into the distance once more. Indeed, the foreboding groans were no louder up-close than half a mile away. Arty dismounted and walked his bicycle in between two of the hangars, leaning it against the side of one and stopping still for a few minutes to slow his racing heart. He was in good shape, but the purpose of his mission both excited and frightened him.

When he eventually recovered his faculties, Arty explored each of the hangars in turn, discovering that not one of the three was completely empty: in the first were corroded parts of biplanes that had been out of service since the end of the Great War; the other two housed dribs and drabs of metal crates long since rusted shut. Hay, which had blown in through the gaps, coalesced into loose balls and tumbled around the debris, and it was cold now Arty was out of the weak spring sun. Thoughts of huddling close together against the chill made him shiver all the more. Yes, this place was perfectly suited to their requirements.

The wind was behind him all the way back to the base, where he returned the bicycle and went straight away to the wages office, to tell Jean of his find.

"Wonderful!" Jean hugged him so tightly that her bosoms were squashed flat to his chest. Behind her a couple of the WAAFs were whispering slyly.

"What are they talking about?" Arty asked.

"Oh, don't worry about them," Jean said. She released him and straightened his shirt. "Last Saturday, after you left, I danced with Jim so I could gather information for you. They've been whispering ever since and no doubt think I'm a floozy."

"Don't ruin your reputation on my account, Jean."

"Who cares what they think? What happens next with…" Jean mouthed, "Jim?"

"I need to get a message over. I'm not really sure how."

Jean patted Arty's arm. "Leave it to me," she whispered and then continued to speak normally, "Thank you,

Corporal. Please tell Captain Taylor we need..." She turned to the one of the other women. "Two more clerks, would you say, Betty?"

"For the USAAF wages?" Betty asked. Jean nodded. "Aye, Sarge. But one'd do."

Jean turned back to Arty and winked. Try as he might, he couldn't stop himself from chuckling at Jean's cunning.

"I'll go and see the captain right away, Sergeant McDowell." Arty returned the wink before leaving straight for their group captain's office to make 'Jean's' request.

Captain Taylor was no one's fool, but he'd arrived at Minton soon after a raid that had killed five servicemen, including his predecessor, and spirits had, understandably, been low. Thus Arty, like everybody else on the base, knew that all one needed to do to get the captain's authorisation was to convince him that whatever was being asked for would improve morale. Even so, he only agreed to one additional wages clerk until the number of USAAF airmen at Gaskell had been officially confirmed. Arty duly returned to Jean and told her what Taylor had said.

"There's a transport wagon in need of a good run out." Jean was already at the door. "I'll be back within the hour, Betty."

"Right, Sarge."

Arty trailed behind Jean, as always stunned by her gall. They entered the garage where three transport wagons were parked in a line, the one to the left brand new. From behind it stepped Charlie Tomkins, his mouth widening into a grin before he came to attention in front of the two NCOs.

"Sergeant McDowell, Corporal Clarke."

"As you were, LAC Tomkins," Jean said. "Arty's offered to accompany me to Gaskell to organise the USAAF payroll. I thought perhaps I could kill three birds with one stone."

"Three birds, Sarge?"

"Take your new wagon for a spin and collect some of the promised supplies."

"Sounds good to me, Sarge. Do I need to clear it with the captain?"

"All taken care of."

Arty's eyes widened. Captain Taylor knew nothing of Jean's plans.

"No problem, Sarge," Charlie said.

Ten minutes later, they were out on the open lane, heading towards Gaskell with Jean behind the wheel of the enormous green transport wagon.

"Where did you learn to drive one of these?" Arty had to shout to be heard over the engine.

"Up in Lincoln. I drove the crews to their bombers." She glanced Arty's way, her smile softening with sadness. "I was the last gal a lot of those boys saw," she added.

Arty stayed silent after that. Theirs was a training base, and only the technicians and engineers were permanently stationed there. Pilots and crewmen would complete their training and move on before they took part in any campaigns. Of course, they all knew what lay ahead, but it was less immediate than delivering half a dozen young men to what might be their final flight.

"Do you drive, Arty?" Jean asked.

"I've never tried. My sister said she'd show me how sometime."

"Ah," Jean said with a knowing smile.

"What?"

"Not once have you talked down to me, or tried to take over, and I'd decided it was because of…you know."

In spite of the wind blowing in Arty's face, he still felt his cheeks becoming warm. Jean glanced his way again and laughed.

"But now I see it's just that you are well used to strong women. Tell me more about your sister."

And so Arty told Jean all about Sissy, who was christened Mary, but had never been known as such. Sissy was smart and had she been born a boy, she would have studied at Oxford, but their father, who had studied there himself, refused to allow it. Instead, Sissy left the grammar school and went out to work, first as a maid to a wealthy London couple, who were friends with the Italian gentleman, Antonio Adessi: the supposed acquaintance of D H Lawrence. At a dinner hosted by Sissy's employers, she impressed Adessi so much he offered her the position of housekeeper, and she accepted without hesitation. Now he had been sent back to Italy, Sissy was once more living at home and loathing every single second.

"She and your father don't see eye to eye?" Jean asked.

Arty chortled. "To put it mildly."

They had arrived at Gaskell and as soon as their details were checked they were ushered straight through the gate. Jean, who knew the base well, took a shortcut to the main barracks, which was hidden behind two enormous hangars, both wide open. At the far end of the runway a bomber landed and a group of men started walking to meet it. Everything seemed so laid back: men worked with pipes, cigars and cigarettes hanging from their mouths; some were even sprawled on the grass at the side of the runway. It was a world away from Minton, and Arty wasn't sure he liked it.

Jean stopped the wagon and jumped down to the ground. Arty stepped a little more carefully. It was a very long way down, and he was feeling jittery. What a fool he would make of himself were he to accidentally miss his footing, and how glad he was that he'd been so cautious, for when he looked up, Jim was already on his way over, a big smile on his face.

"Well, fancy seeing you two here! If I knew you were coming, I'd have cleared some space for a demonstration."

"We're here on WAAF business, Sergeant Johnson," Jean explained. "I need to speak with your commanding officer." She leaned closer. "And I've come for more of those stockings."

The deep boom of Jim's laughter sent a shiver through Arty that he wasn't quick enough to disguise, and Jim's eyes fleetingly met his.

Jean turned to Arty. "Perhaps, Corporal, you could give Sergeant Johnson a hand with loading the supplies onto the wagon?"

"Yes, Sarge," he replied, not entirely sure his sweating hands would be of any use.

"Great," Jim said. "Sergeant McDowell, I'll take you up to Major Johnson—no relation—and then we'll get those supplies together."

Arty watched Jean and Jim march to the control tower and go inside. He leaned against the truck and closed his eyes, his ears tuning in to the sounds around him, American voices, so many different accents all mingling together until he could not discern a single word they were saying. These men, and they were all men, were so far away from home, their families, their loved ones. How hard that must be. Arty had always insisted he would never marry, though not for that reason. He much preferred the prospect of a life alone to one of lies. Not even Jean, for whom he cared a great deal and considered very beautiful, could tempt his passions in that direction, and she was the only one who had ever come close.

A life alone. Now he considered it properly, could he stand to follow that path? He felt so uncertain, afraid, and yet he could not walk away. He imagined what Sissy would say if she were here now, at his side, waiting on Jim's return.

She would be with Jean; *take a chance*, she'd say. *Follow your heart.*

"Corporal R. T. Clarke is a thinker and a dreamer."

Arty opened his eyes, squinting against the sun. Jim stood in front of him, still smiling, always smiling, his blue eyes sparkling.

"And a man of his word," Jim added.

Arty nodded and found he too was smiling.

"Come with me," Jim said. "We'll grab a few things and talk while we load them on the jeep."

"Jeep?"

"It's new, isn't it?" Jim asked, setting off at a slow stroll, which Arty at first assumed was to give him a chance to catch up, but Jim seemed in no rush, and as they walked across to the hangar, Arty observed that they all moved at the same slow pace.

"What's new?"

"The truck."

"Ah! Yes. I believe it is. Is it always so..." Arty stopped short of suggesting the Americans were lackadaisical, but by British standards they were exactly that.

"We can jump to it when we have good cause. Ain't you seen us dance?" Jim tormented, and Arty laughed. Yes, he had seen that this was true.

To the left of the hangar there was a large, single-storey building, to which Jim indicated. "It's full of junk, so everything's stashed in here for the time being." Jim opened the small door in the back of the hangar and beckoned Arty to follow him inside, which he did. The through draught was tremendous and the door behind them slammed loudly, echoing for several seconds. Arty's eyes had not yet become accustomed to the relative darkness of his immediate surroundings, although he could make out the silhouettes of

33

two bombers against the light streaming in from the front of the hangar.

"This way," Jim instructed. Arty turned and followed the sound of Jim's footsteps, deadened by what Arty could now see were boxes and crates, the stacks getting taller the further they were from the door, creating a corridor, with the wall on one side and the stacks on the other. In places the passageway was so narrow Arty had to turn sideways, all the while aware of his heart thudding harder and faster as he registered the partial privacy afforded by their location. But he was a coward with no assurance Jim's intentions were anything more than loading him up with American swag to take back to Minton. Surely if the man failed to make his move now, Arty would have his answer. On the other hand, he might be feeling just as Arty did, and for fear they would miss what might be their only chance.

Jim was almost at the end of the narrow clearing when he drew to a halt, turned back, and, without word or warning, grabbed Arty by the shoulders and kissed him firmly on the lips. It happened so quickly that were it not for Jim's continuing hold on him he may well have decided it was nothing more than wishful thinking. In the moments that followed, neither man moved, but then Jim pulled his hands away and coughed nervously.

"I…er…I guess I—"

"Don't be sorry," Arty whispered.

"Oh, thank God. For a second I thought I got you all wrong." Jim advanced again, and this time their mouths connected in a kiss that was like the hunger of the starved, craving the feast they had been denied for so long. At first, their lips stayed tightly closed, as each fought to control their urges, until Arty could stand it no more. With his palms on Jim's cheeks, his instincts took over, his lips relaxing, softening as both men opened their mouths, each stealing

34

the other's gasped breath, while their bodies hardened. It was what Arty had been waiting his whole life for. This one kiss.

Jim's tongue poked playfully at Arty's, which surprised him at first; he had never kissed anyone before, save his sister, aunt and mother. Jim did it again, and Arty poked back. They laughed in silence, nervous, delighted, needing more, and when Jim's tongue entered Arty's mouth a third time, Arty married their lips so that Jim could not so easily escape; nor did he try to.

Beyond the barricade of boxes, tools clanged and men called out to each other, a distant reality blurred by this stolen moment that could have lasted forever and still have been too short. There would be many more to come, unless they were caught in the act now. With a great deal of reluctance, Arty and Jim slowed their kiss and finally withdrew, both too frustrated to feel bashful.

"Take these," Jim said, passing across a box of stockings. "I'll bring the cigarettes out in a second."

Arty nodded and squeezed his way back to the door, the effort of holding the box of stockings above his head enough to temporarily take his mind away from the pulsing ache between his legs. Out in the open once more, and blinded by the brightness, he loaded the stockings onto the back of the wagon, remaining where he was while Jim passed him the boxes of cigarettes.

"We'll get the candy next," Jim said.

"Sweets?" Arty asked.

"Yup. And chocolate. This hasn't been cleared, by the way, but it won't be a problem. You comin'?"

"Yes." Arty jumped down from the wagon and followed Jim back to the hangar, beyond disappointed to discover they no longer had the secluded space to themselves.

35

"Aw, shoot," Jim said as he led the way through that same narrow passage. He put his hand behind his back and his fingers made contact with Arty's thigh. The tingle zapped straight to his privates, and he coughed to cover his reaction. He heard Jim give a low chuckle.

Loaded up with boxes of sweets and chocolate, they carried them out and then sat together on the back of the wagon, legs dangling. Jim lit a cigarette and passed it to Arty, who rarely smoked, but liked the idea of sharing a smoke with Jim. He liked the idea of sharing everything with Jim.

"How long are you here for?" Arty asked. "Do you know?"

"It's classified, but I can tell you that it's for the foreseeable future."

"That's tough on the people back home."

"Yeah. How about your folks? Do they live close by?"

"Not far. About fifty miles from here. I get home more often than most."

Jim sighed deeply, and Arty noticed his gaze become distant, thinking of the people that mattered to him. It occurred to Arty that Jim might have a girlfriend or wife, and though he wasn't sure he wanted to hear the answer, he had to know.

"Is there anyone special, back home?"

Jim continued to stare into the distance, but he was smiling now. "No. Only Mom and Pop. My little brother, Joshua, is stationed in England too." Jim turned both the smile and the question on Arty. He shook his head.

"Dad, Mum, and Sissy, my older sister. My uncle also lives with us, but he's fighting in France."

"Jeez." Jim said no more on it, instead giving Arty's arm a friendly squeeze. Arty nodded sorrowfully: yes. It was hard on all of them with family at the front line, and they'd had

36

no word from Uncle Bill in months, but better that than a telegram from his CO.

They finished the cigarette, and there was still no sign of Jean.

"I ought to get back," Jim said with notable reluctance.

Arty didn't want Jim to leave yet either. He was sorely tempted to suggest they try sneaking another kiss, but it could wait until they met at the old hangars. Checking no one was close enough to hear, he quickly muttered, "I've found us somewhere. Three disused hangars, three-quarters of a mile due east of Minton."

"When?"

"Tuesday afternoon or Friday morning."

"Tuesday." Jim considered. "I can do Tuesday."

"It's a date then."

"You betcha."

Chapter Five:
March, 1944

"Corporal Clarke. A moment of your time, please?"

Arty was riveting a panel to the underside of a Wellington's wing, and he'd been so far into his thoughts that he startled and almost fell off the stepladders. Wiping his hands on a rag, he descended to the ground.

"Sergeant McDowell," he acknowledged Jean formally, though the joy twinkling in her eyes told him this was not a formal RAF matter.

"Have any of your men remarked on receiving extra in their pay packets this week?" she asked.

"No, Sarge, can't say they have, though I doubt they'll be rushing to mention it."

Jean smiled. "Yes, indeed. When you come to a suitable pause, call up to the wages office, please?"

"Yes, Sarge."

Jean nodded once and marched away, her heels clacking against the asphalt. She stopped to briefly converse with a group of young airmen who puffed their chests and stood tall in her presence, only relaxing when she continued on her way. Even at a distance, Arty could see their delight at the good-looking WAAF sergeant taking the time to say hello. Jean was very beautiful and received a great deal of attention from men of all ranks. She knew how to play their game, convincingly acting the part of the shy young thing if it worked in her favour, as she had when Charlie first introduced her to Arty at the Palais. Since then, Arty had come to realise she was confident and independent; she enjoyed men's company, but she was neither floozy nor the kind of woman who needed a husband.

"Got a three-quarter-inch spanner there, Art?" Charlie called.

"In the right-hand tray, Charlie. Try not to lose this one, eh?"

"I'll bring it straight back."

"Hm. That's what you said when you borrowed my oil can. And my bradawl."

"I wondered where I got that from," Charlie said, dodging a playful cuff around the ear. He departed with a grin. Arty shook his head and chuckled to himself. Charlie was forever borrowing his tools and rarely returned them without being reminded, assuming he could find them to return at all. On this occasion, however, Charlie was true to his word: five minutes later he was back, waiting at the base of Arty's stepladders, spanner in his hand and a thoughtful frown on his face.

"Just stick it in the toolbox," Arty told him.

"Hm?" Charlie said without moving.

Arty continued tapping rivets along the left edge of the panel, occasionally glancing unnoticed at his friend.

"What's on your mind?"

Charlie shrugged his shoulders. "Everything and nothing. I received a letter from my brother this morning with a bloody great hole in the middle so all it said was 'Dear Charlie, love Walter'. I'm sure our mother dropped him on his head."

"Twice, if you're the sensible one," Arty tormented. He descended the ladder and clapped Charlie on the back. "At least you know he's alive and well."

"But for the grace of God. No news about your uncle?"

"Nothing. Sissy says Mum is staying hopeful, but Dad is assuming the worst. Apart from that they're all quite well. Sissy got hold of a couple of hens. That was her main news. They've been having eggs for tea every night."

"A cause for celebration," Charlie said, his tone partly mocking, but the small things were worth celebrating, and there had been no real eggs at Minton since the previous September.

"I hope we're home by this time next year. It's Mum and Dad's ruby wedding."

"Forty years married." Charlie shook his head. "Can you imagine it?"

"Yes, I can," Arty replied wistfully. Had Charlie asked that question even a fortnight ago, Arty's answer would have been a definite no. Now he dared to imagine a lifetime shared with another.

"I'll let you get on," Charlie said, already walking back to the garage. "And if you can squeeze in a good word for me with Sergeant McDowell—you know? That I'm reliable, look after myself, take good care of my equipment, never lose anything…"

Arty laughed and threw an oily rag at Charlie. It missed.

Since he was already stopped, Arty decided to go and see what Jean wanted to talk to him about. When he'd told her about meeting Jim, she'd been just as excited as if she were going herself. She more than likely wanted to give Arty a pep talk; it was all she'd done for weeks, and it was as annoying as it was endearing.

The wages office was Jean's domain and she kept it spick and span, not a paper out of place, not a speck of dust, and

41

daylight poured through the sparkling-clean windows. Usually there were four women in there, eyes trained on the sheets of numbers in front of them, speedily typing on their comptometers whilst conversing with each other about all manner of things. It made Arty wonder how they didn't make mistakes. In fact, they so rarely cocked up he was certain Jean's remark about the men being overpaid was a ruse.

"Where is everyone?" Arty asked, peering through the door of the office, deserted apart from Jean. She beckoned him in and greeted him with a peck on the cheek.

"Betty's gone to a funeral and the other two are in the mess hall."

"Oh," Arty acknowledged. He walked past her and looked out of the window, towards the distant hangars where he would be meeting Jim in less than an hour's time. Jean came over and stood next to him.

"Have you washed behind your ears?" she teased. She tugged at his earlobe, squinting and pulling funny faces as she gave him a once-over. Arty raised his eyes and waited out the moment. She grinned up at him. "You're nervous?" she asked. He nodded. "About someone seeing you, or being with Jim?"

"Both."

"You're not going to chicken out, are you?"

Arty shook his head rapidly, but the cat had got his tongue.

Jean gave his hands a squeeze of reassurance. "I'm proud of you," she said. "Love is brave."

"And foolish."

"Yes. It makes a fool of most of us at some point in our lives."

"Speaking of which, I'm to tell you that Charlie is a good, honest man."

42

Jean started to laugh. "He's a relentless man. Next time you and he speak, tell him I'm thinking of him. In the meantime, Corporal Clarke, don't you need to be somewhere within the hour?"

"Yes, Sarge," Arty replied. He gave her an American-style salute and headed for the door.

"Have fun," she called after him.

"I'll do my best," he promised.

Chapter Six:
March, 1944

Arty wheeled his bicycle around the back of the small, deserted hangars, where he carefully lowered it to the ground and stepped back to check it was well concealed. The black grip of one handle stuck up over the long grass, but he doubted anyone would notice unless they were specifically looking for it; certainly they wouldn't see it from a distance. The entire area was overgrown: the low, barbed wire fence was hidden under the brambles, and stray wheat spilled from the farm fields beyond the perimeter of the base.

Shielding his eyes with his hand, Arty looked out across the open expanse of green: it was still too early in spring for the wheat to have changed colour, or for there to be many butterflies, but a few keen brimstones flitted along the hawthorn hedge and red admirals were out in force. From Arty's current viewpoint, the farmhouse stood almost central on the horizon, the only civilian building for miles around. Squinting into the sun, he observed the movement of a dark form as it became isolated from the buildings. Possibly, it was a man, but they were too far off for Arty to even know if they were moving closer or further away. Minutes passed, and their attire changed from a dull brown-black to khaki, their gait and shape came into focus: broad shoulders, bright blonde hair glowing in the afternoon sun. Arty didn't think he'd been so happy and relieved in his life.

"Afternoon, sir," Jim called as he neared the hangars.

"A good afternoon to you also," Arty replied. "A lovely day for it."

"It sure is," Jim agreed.

This first meeting would be a pantomime of politeness, playing out whilst they assessed the safety of their meeting place.

"As far as anyone is concerned, I'm spotting butterflies," Arty explained quietly, once Jim was close enough to hear.

"Butterflies, huh?" Jim halted at Arty's left side and turned to look back across the field he had just traversed.

"See over there?" Arty pointed to a pair of brimstones dipping and soaring over the swaying wheat. "Those little fellas are the reason we call them *butter*flies."

Jim followed the movement of the dainty butter-coloured insects across the field. "Fellas?"

"Those two are males. The females are paler, almost white. Brimstones are one of very few species that hibernate, which is why they're around so early in the year. They're the longest lived of British butterflies."

Jim nodded his understanding. "Fascinating," he said.

Arty chuckled bashfully. "You're just being kind."

"Not at all. I'm eager to know more about your hobbies. And you."

The brimstones disappeared through the hedgerow into the next field. Jim indicated to a butterfly with red and black wings. "You have monarchs here?"

"Occasionally," Arty said. "They're not native, but a few brave souls make it across the ocean. That one, though, is a red admiral. Very similar colouring and patterns on the wing tips."

"How interesting," Jim said. It wasn't the first time someone had made that comment about Arty's hobby, but it was the first time since his childhood that it had not been issued in mockery.

"Where did you tell them you were going this afternoon?" Arty asked.

"Nowhere. If anyone wanted to know, I'd just say I was exploring the area. That's what we all do in our free time. England is a beautiful country."

"You like it here."

"Very much. Particularly the fine company." Jim glanced Arty's way, and they both smiled.

"How are you finding the weather? Warm enough for you?"

Jim raised an eyebrow. "Have you ever been to Miami?"

"No, can't say I have," Arty said with a laugh. "The farthest I've been is Cornwall." At Jim's frown, he explained, "South-west coast. Are you from Miami?"

"West Virginia, but they sent us to Miami for training, and then shipped us over to cold Gaskell. It's thirty degrees cooler than a Miami spring. Quite a shock."

"Hence the winter fatigues," Arty realised.

"Yep. I guess we'll get used to it. For now I'll try to suffer the cold hands in silence."

"How can your hands be cold when you've just walked five miles?" Arty teased.

Jim held his hand out in front of him. "You don't believe me?"

Arty touched his palm to Jim's, the contact insufficient to establish whether it was cold or not. He glanced sideways, noting Jim doing the same. He closed his fingers around Jim's hand.

"It is a little on the chilly side, yes," he said.

47

Jim laughed quietly in response and vented a long, slow breath. Arty didn't need to ask why, for he could feel it: the connection between them that neither could hide or deny.

With hands still joined, they lowered their arms to their sides and remained close, watching the butterflies and talking freely. What a relief it was to share with someone who understood the doubt and confusion, the fear of being alone, of being persecuted, and yet they had each been so fortunate in finding allies in their family and friends.

"I've never told a soul," Arty admitted. "My sister worked it out for herself," he shook his head, "just like Jean."

"Yeah, she's a wily one, that sergeant of yours," Jim agreed.

"She is. It worried me at first—that she and Sissy knew just from looking at me—but Jean says it's because she and Sissy both enjoy the company of intelligent men, yet they have no interest in marriage. They can tell apart the men who will accept a woman's friendship from those who are after a bit of how's your father."

A deep rumble of joyful laughter erupted from Jim. "How's your father? We've heard that a few times since we got here. At first we were wondering why y'all were asking after our pops. But your Jean put us straight real quick."

Arty laughed too and nodded. "She's a wonderful woman. Charlie, my friend, is very fond of her. Funnily enough, she'll play coy with the other airmen, RAF or American, but not with Charlie."

"Sounds like she might be persuaded," Jim mused.

"Yes, that may be. Though she's very much like my Sissy, is Jean."

"You mentioned your sister was older?"

"By ten years. Our mother keeps telling her she's cooked her goose now. She's an old maid."

"So you're what? Twenty-three, twenty-four?"

"Twenty-four."

Jim hummed. "Thirty-four's not so old."

"I suppose not, and she's thick-skinned. Mum and Dad love us, and we never wanted for anything as children. We both went to grammar school, and Sissy could have gone to Oxford to study, but Dad refused to permit it. Sissy tried everything to persuade him. She begged, pleaded, threatened to leave home. He told her he'd lock her in her room if she didn't let it be.

"So she stayed quiet and miserable. The day of her eighteenth birthday she found a job in London and she left home. Mum cried for a month, and Dad insisted Sissy would be back once she realised independence wasn't all it was cracked up to be. He's not the sort to admit he's wrong, but Sissy didn't come home. She was offered the position of housekeeper to a rich Italian—an intellectual and an artist— and she never looked back, until they evacuated during The Blitz, and then he was forced to return to Italy. Sissy went home. Fifteen years, she'd been away, and the first thing Dad says is, 'I told you, didn't I?' The man is so damned stubborn."

"Yeah, my pop's just the same," Jim said. "The day they came for Joshua and me, Mom cried buckets, but Pop? He just went off to work as usual. The last thing he said to us was, 'Guess I won't get to be a grandaddy after all,' like Joshua and me wouldn't be coming home."

"Oh, Jim," Arty said, squeezing his hand in sympathy. "I'm sorry."

After that, Jim remained quiet and thoughtful, and Arty thanked God for his own parents; however stern and distant they might be, and in spite of sharing Jim's father's disappointment for the lack of grandchildren, they didn't intentionally hurt him or Sissy. Whether that would be true if they knew their son was, at that very moment, falling for another man, Arty wouldn't like to say.

Sissy had advised Arty never to tell their mother and father, and he had no intention of doing so. It was his business, not theirs, and for as much as he loved and missed them, he'd set his sights on moving to London after the war. Those excursions to visit Sissy were his favourite memories, the only times he could truly be himself, and it had given him a love of the place that left him grieving for what Jerry had taken from them. There would be much work to be done to rebuild the city, and Arty's skills would serve him and his country well. So whether he chose a life of solitude, succumbed to marriage, or followed his heart, it was unlikely his parents would ever discover his secret.

"My pop doesn't know about me," Jim said, as if he had read and was replying to Arty's thoughts. "My mom…" Jim chuckled. "These two old guys had a ranch right up in the hills, kept to themselves, just came to town on business. Of course, everyone knew, or *thought* they knew. Mostly it was just talk, but this one time they got chased right out of town. It turned violent and those guys? They couldn't fight back. And so my mom, she's in the yard and she sees them coming her way with the townsfolk hot on their tails, and she hollers to 'em, 'Hide in the barn!' She takes their horses and releases them into our paddock. The townsfolk go right on by, think they're chasing the guys all the way home.

"They stayed with Mom a few hours, told her they'd gone to buy provisions but fled empty-handed, in fear for their lives. When they were leaving, she sent Joshua and me to keep lookout. They were long gone when Pop came home from work. Next day, Mom and I got their groceries and took them up to the house, but they'd cleared out, horses gone, windows boarded.

50

"Mom was the angriest I ever saw her. All the way home she kept on saying how the townsfolk didn't understand and their ignorance had chased off two of their own. I thought she knew them, maybe they were friends of Grandpa, but when I asked she said she'd never talked to them before that day. I wanted to know why she'd helped them. She said she'd explain when I was old enough to understand. I think I was about eight or nine years old at the time.

"She didn't need to tell me in the end. She'd seen it in me when I was a youngster and she loved me just the same. Joshua's got a girl now, so Pop will get to be a grandaddy after all. I'm happy for him, truly, and I told Mom I was sorry I couldn't give her that. You know what she did? She hugged me tight and told me she prayed every night that I would never come up against the hatred those two old guys did, or be forced to hide away and be someone I'm not. But you know, Arty?" Jim looked him right in the eye and said, "I'd rather be dead."

Chapter Seven:
Spring–Summer, 1944

Arty and Jim met regularly at their secret liaison point, in the middle hangar of the three, where there were enough crates to conceal their presence, should anybody happen their way. The four-inch space below one of the corrugated panels provided an excellent lookout, though it also created a terrific draught. As the weather turned warmer, the blankets they had stowed in between the crates were no longer required, and in any case the heat they produced when huddled together, venting the heat of their passion through their kisses, was quite sufficient to stave off the chill.

Arty, who was much closer to the hangars, usually arrived long before Jim, which gave him an opportunity to inspect their hideout and make sure it had not been tampered with. He checked for disturbances, and there was always something, although thankfully never caused by human beings. They often had the company of smaller rodents, and the bigger ones: rats, mice and rabbits were their constant companions, seeking shelter from rainy days, or from the many stray cats who fancied them for dinner. There was nothing quite so startling, for man and beast alike, as a cat suddenly leaping from its hiding place and pinning its prey to the ground, although more often than not the cats would flee as Arty entered the hangar.

There was, however, one cat that did not flee. At first, Arty and Jim thought the animal had come to the hangar to die. Its dull fur rippled over its bony spine and ribcage, and it was listless, turning circles on the blanket they had spread on the floor for it. Neither man could stand to see it suffering, and Arty immediately set off back to the base, returning twenty minutes later with scraps of meat and a canister of water. The animal ate hungrily, but still it did not leave.

Not wanting to return to a corpse, Arty and Jim settled in on their other blanket to mind the poor, brave beast. Their chatter was inconsequential, a means to pass the time and ignore the ache each felt in his heart for how that little cat endured.

But it, or rather, *she* did not die. Both men shed silent tears as the skinny stray birthed her three kittens, and openly sobbed when her nursing failed to revive the smallest of the litter. When the mother cat left briefly to hunt for food, Jim took the kitten from its brothers, and he and Arty buried it in the field behind the hangars. For all the human tragedy of war, it was the loss of this one tiny beast that seemed to hurt the most, at the same time strengthening the bond between the two men.

Over the weeks that followed, Arty and Jim always brought food scraps for their cat family, rightly proud of their role in assisting the mother to care for her kittens. Now young cats, they were typically boisterous and forever putting themselves in harm's way, but they were learning as fast as they were growing, and they were fine, handsome animals. Like their mother, the smaller of the two was black with a white belly and three white socks; the larger was pure black and both were sleek as silk. Soon after they were weaned, the mother left, and Arty and Jim never saw her again, but her sons came to visit regularly, knowing there would always be scraps to be had.

"Think I'll get me a cat after the war," Jim told Arty one evening, while their feline friends chased after the balls of dried grass tumbling around in the warm draughts.

"We've always kept dogs," Arty said, "though I must confess I've grown attached to Socks and Soot."

"Me too," Jim admitted. He lay back, leaning on his elbows, his eyes still trained on the cats' activities. "I'd like to stay in England," he said. "It's not just the cats I've grown attached to."

Arty raised an eyebrow, uncertain how to respond, though the meaning of Jim's words was clear enough, and the feeling was mutual.

"It's not just me, is it?" Jim asked.

Arty shook his head. "No."

"All right!" Jim fairly yelled.

"Shhh!" Arty hissed, but he was laughing.

"C'mere." Jim tilted his head back to beckon Arty closer.

Arty shuffled backwards on his bottom until he was level with Jim's shoulders, and Jim turned and rested his head on Arty's lap, his golden-blonde hair catching the last wisps of the setting sun spilling through the open front of the hangar. Arty brushed his fingers over the red-orange glow, and Jim sighed in contentment.

They remained just as they were until long after the sun had dipped below the horizon, waiting out the dark and the time when their return to their respective bases was more urgent than their need to be together. When that time arrived, they reluctantly pulled each other to their feet and embraced, neither wishing to let go. At least a dozen times they kissed good night and tried to move apart, each kiss taking them a step closer to the outside, before finally Jim sighed and stepped out into the open.

"Tuesday afternoon?" he confirmed.

Arty nodded. "Yes. I'll be here."

Jim waved and set off across the fields for the five-mile run back to Gaskell. When Arty could no longer distinguish him from the darkness, he collected his bicycle and rode home in a glorious daze.

***

The following Tuesday afternoon, Arty arrived at the hangars, and at first glance it appeared that he was still alone. Thinking nothing of it, he wheeled his bike into the field beyond and carefully set it on its side, loosening the handlebar and twisting until it was hidden by the golden wheat, grown to the height of Arty's hip and ready for harvesting. Standing up straight, he rotated, scanning the vicinity to make sure no one was watching before he moved off again. He had taken no more than three steps when he felt a tightening around his ankles and was suddenly tugged to the ground.

Jim rolled Arty onto his back and kissed away his surprise, pushing his tongue into Arty's mouth and then trailing his lips over Arty's chin, down his neck to his collar. They hadn't yet ventured any further than that; it was far too warm inside the hangar for one thing. For another, they would get so caught up in talking, or watching Socks and Soot's antics, that the time passed as fast as the blink of an eye, and then they would each leave independently, ever cautious of rousing suspicion. It always seemed an absolute age to wait for the next time they could meet, though in reality it was never more than a few days.

Now here they were, out in the open, kissing under the warm summer sun, hidden by a screen of sweet-smelling wheat, while all around them, butterflies and bees went about their business. Never had a moment felt so perfect, and yet, Arty sensed a weightiness to Jim's frivolous disregard for consequence. For the time being, he pushed it from his mind, revelling instead in the firm gentle touch of the man who had captured his heart on that very first night at the Palais Dance Hall.

How difficult it was to protest that they should refrain from doing this, for each time Arty drew breath to do so, Jim's mouth stole it. His shirt was now unbuttoned all the way down to his waistband; Jim's warm palms smoothed his sides, drawing him closer. Arty clung to him, returning the ever more passionate kisses, withdrawing for only as long as it took to unfasten Jim's shirt. With the first touch of skin against skin, the desire tore through Arty's body with a heat that, were it naked flame, could have turned the wheat to stubble in seconds.

Jim gasped breathlessly, "Gee, Arty, have you any idea what you do to me?"

Arty tried to form a response, but all that left him was a groan. Oh, what he wouldn't give right now to remove every last piece of Jim's clothing and feel that hard, naked body on his own.

But it was more than desire that had kept them coming back here, to the hangars, for the past five months. They had so much in common: their beliefs about the futility of war, what they wanted to do with their lives once the war was over, a love of dance, thoughts on equality for women, and God. They discussed politics and religion, philosophy and art. And they talked frankly about their feelings—how much they enjoyed each other's company, how safe they felt in each other's arms—and their uncertainty regarding what came after the kissing and cuddling. They talked about missing home, and the romances blossoming all around them, but they had yet to talk of whatever it was they had, almost as if it had only existed in the moments they shared in the hangar, until now.

"Arty, I know we've kinda not…er…what I mean is…"

"You want to go all the way?" Arty asked.

"Well, yeah." Jim laughed and ran his hand through his hair, flustered by his yearning. He rolled to Arty's side. "That's a foregone conclusion, ain't it? We both want that."

"Well, I know I do."

"What I was trying to say is…we've had so little time together, but I don't want it to end."

"Nor do I, and why should it?"

Jim cleared his throat, offering neither answer nor reassurance.

Arty turned on his side, leaning on his elbow and staring down into Jim's face. Jim's eyes flickered his way and a tear rolled from the corner, disappearing into his hair.

"Jim?"

"Yeah. I know." Jim reached up and brushed his thumb along Arty's cheekbone. "I've never felt for anyone what I feel for you. It's like you and I are two halves of a whole. Without you…"

More tears fell, and Arty couldn't stand it. He tugged Jim close and held him fast, kissing each tear, the salty taste a balm that dammed his own tears, for the time being at least. He did not know what this was, did not want to know.

"There's talk of us moving to Norfolk," Jim said; his voice was muffled against Arty's shoulder. "It's not that far away, but it might as well be back in the States, for what it will do to us."

"When?" Arty asked. "When will it happen?"

"If it happens, it'll be soon. But I needed you to know how I feel about you. I want us to spend our lives together."

"I don't know how we do that, Jim."

"Nor do I, or even if it's possible. I just had to tell you, because we might never see each other again."

Chapter Eight:
October, 1944

"The post's here!" Jean said, barely hiding her excitement. She raced across the mess hall to Arty, grinning as she passed him 'her' letter. With shaking hands, he unfolded it. "Oh, I thought we might dance a little first," Jean joked. Arty gave her a quick smile and began to read.

My darling Jean,

I'm counting the days now. Twelve more until we see each other. That's a total of fifty-nine days since we said goodbye and not one has gone by without you filling my thoughts. I love you so much.

I must say, Norfolk here is nothing like Norfolk back home, but I prefer this one. Last week a few of us went to "The Broads" on a fishing trip. The landscape is magnificent, and we found a beautiful secluded lake. I didn't catch a single fish, mind you, but it didn't matter. I just imagined you were at my side.

I'll be twenty-eight years old when next you see me. Will you still have me when I'm an old man? I've been thinking a lot about us finding a place together in the city, getting married, setting up home together with our kids. I'd like to open a workshop, fix up people's cars and bikes. What do you think? Would you be my business partner?

How are Socks and Soot getting along? I know you tell me every time, but I miss them almost as much as I miss you, darling, and I'll never forget the little one we lost. Give the guys a cuddle from their poppy.

See you at the dance hall.

All my love,
Jim

Arty folded the letter in half and put it inside his shirt, pressing it to his heart. He couldn't stop smiling.

"Betty's told everybody that Jim and I are getting married," Jean complained.

Arty laughed. "Oh dear. What did you say?"

"Nothing at all. What could I say? But I don't mind one bit, Arty. I promised you I'd do whatever you needed, so let them gossip. Besides..." Jean leaned closer, "a gal could do worse. Jim Johnson is quite a catch."

Arty pushed her away, and they both laughed.

"So we'll travel down to London on Wednesday morning," Jean continued. "Jim's going to meet us at Tottenham Court Road station. Did you hear from Sissy?"

"Yes," Arty confirmed. "But she won't arrive in London until late in the afternoon. She's very eager to meet you and your fiancé-to-be."

"I'm excited to meet her, also."

Arty nodded and took a big airy breath, overwhelmed with emotion. In just over a week's time, he and Jim would be together again, if only for a few short hours, but he was grateful to have as much as that. Without giving it another thought, he embraced Jean and hugged her tightly.

"Thank you," he whispered. "Thank you for everything."

"Your happiness is all the thanks I need, Arty."

***

The sirens sounded as they emerged onto the street; Arty and Jean stopped and frantically searched the hordes rushing to enter the station they had just exited.

"Over there!" Jean shouted, pointing across to the other side of the street.

Arty saw an arm wave, the flash of blonde hair, the happy blue eyes, the enchanting smile he had missed so much.

Fighting against the current of people, Jean and Arty made it to Jim; Jean hugged him and kissed his cheek.

"The shelter's this way," he said, grabbing both Jean and Arty by the hand and leading them along the street. As they turned the corner, Jim's gaze met Arty's. "Missed you," he mouthed. Arty managed a smile and a nod in response. He had missed Jim more than words would convey, and if these turned out to be their very last moments on Earth, then he would be grateful they had spent them together. But in this chaos he could barely think; there were many air raid warnings at Minton, but they were orderly and controlled, not like this riot of panic, where one was as likely to be crushed underfoot by one's fellow countrymen as be blown to smithereens by the *Luftwaffe*. In Minton, everyone knew

63

what to do and where they should be. Here, in the midst of the city Arty no longer recognised, with sirens blaring and people running in all directions, the shouts of the ARP wardens, and the distant *ack-ack* of anti-aircraft guns, the only thing keeping him from falling to his knees in fear, was Jim.

Jim led them through a door and into a dark passageway, pausing only to warn them of the stairs ahead that fell steeply into the pitch-black.

"Where is this?" Jean's breathless question resounded in the darkness.

"An underground installation of the United States Signal Corps."

"Should we be in here?" Jean asked.

Jim offered no response to Jean's question, but instructed, "When you reach the bottom of the stairs go left."

The handrail slipped away and Arty's knuckles connected with the cold, wet wall. The next step he took with his left foot hit level ground, jarring his knee, hard. He inhaled sharply, hobbling after the sound of Jim and Jean's footsteps. There were other people further ahead, their hurried chatter indistinguishable from its echo.

"Arty?" Jim called back.

"Keep going," Arty urged.

"Hold on. I'm coming to get you."

The three of them had been in the dark long enough for their eyes to adjust, and Arty noticed that Jean had stopped ten yards in front of him. Jim ran back and with a large, strong arm gripped Arty around the waist. Air raid or no, Arty had never felt as safe as he did in that moment.

"I think I can walk unaided," he protested.

"That may be so," Jim agreed, but he didn't move his arm away. "Can you stand?"

Arty straightened his leg and pushed his foot to the floor. He yelped and clenched his teeth. "Hell's bells," he muttered. "What are we going to do about the contest?"

"It'll fix itself, I'm sure. You just need to rest."

"And if it doesn't?"

Jean had made her way back to the men. Without a word, she hooked her arm around Arty's other side and the three of them set off again, slowly. With each hop, Arty's knee jolted painfully, and he bit on his bottom lip to save crying out. As they neared the end of the passage, Jean released him and walked ahead to open the door.

"Romantic reunion, huh?" Jim murmured into Arty's ear, sending a shiver right through his body.

"Sorry," Arty said.

"Not your fault. I should've warned you."

"You did."

"Hey, just humour me, all right?" Jim laughed.

High above them at street level, the all-clear sounded.

"Damn it. Don't tell me I've got to climb those bloody stairs again," Arty grumbled.

"Well, you do, but not quite yet. I want to introduce you to someone. That's why I suggested we meet where we did."

"Oh?"

"My brother is an aide to the general."

"Joshua is here? In London?"

Jim nodded. "He's been here since Operation Overlord began."

"He's high-ranking?"

"No. He's a civilian. A gifted mathematician." Jim gave a self-effacing shrug. "He got all the brains."

Arty raised an eyebrow. "You didn't do so badly for brains either. But I'd wager you got all the good looks."

Jim's smile was unusually bashful. "Are you ready to move on?"

With a nod of agreement, Arty once more leaned on Jim's shoulder, grateful for his support, and the chance to be in his arms, albeit in far from ideal circumstances.

Stepping through that door was like crossing from one world into another. Where the corridor had been dank, dark and oppressive, with oily puddles from the ground water trickling down the curved walls, the room they stood in was bright, spacious and warm. Two felt-topped tables placed next to each other formed a large square that took up most of the room, and every wall was covered in maps of Europe. Aside from the door through which they had entered, there were two more, and each time one opened, the buzz of activity followed the new arrival into the room. Soldiers and civilians, both men and women, came and went, perhaps as many as a dozen passing through, whilst Arty, Jim and Jean watched.

As soon as the next person came into view, there was no mistaking that he was Joshua Johnson. As tall as Jim, though nowhere near as broad-shouldered, Joshua had the same golden blonde mane as his older brother, and the same bright blue eyes that twinkled with joy as he looked from Jim, to Arty, to Jean. An unlit pipe rested in the corner of Joshua's thick-lipped mouth and in his tan cardigan and brown serge slacks he looked every bit as if he had just stepped away from a relaxing afternoon in his drawing room. He strolled lazily with hands in pockets, taking his time to reach their location. Not a word passed his lips as he inspected them up-close, just that same easy smile around the pipe.

"Joshua, these are my friends, Jean and Arty," Jim introduced.

Joshua removed his pipe from his mouth, dropped it into his cardigan pocket, and held out his hand to Jean. She accepted and they exchanged a handshake and a kiss on the cheek. Joshua repeated his silent greeting with Arty, but with a nod and a smile rather than a kiss. He looked at his brother, and then back to Arty. Jim nodded.

"Joshua's coming to watch you dance tonight," Jim said.

Even though the words were directed at Arty, Jim continued to face his brother as he spoke. Joshua looked at Arty and Jean and nodded enthusiastically.

"If I can still dance," Arty said. He tried shifting some of his weight to his left leg and winced in pain.

Joshua's brow immediately creased in sympathy, and he beckoned to Arty, at the same time pulling a chair out from under the table.

Arty grabbed the back of the chair and hopped around the side, gingerly bending his right knee whilst trying not to bend his left. Joshua pulled out a second chair, positioning it close enough for Arty to rest his injured leg on.

"Thank you," Arty said.

Joshua nodded an acknowledgement and looked up to where Jim was standing behind Arty's chair. Joshua tapped his left wrist and shrugged.

"Not sure," Jim said. "When Arty can move again."

Arty peered over his shoulder at Jim, who glanced down and smiled.

"Joshua is deaf and dumb," he explained.

"Ah." Arty turned to face Joshua again. Joshua smiled and with another carefree shrug pointed at his ears.

"Dumb," he said, the word only partially formed in sound, but very clearly shaped by his mouth. Joshua pointed at his head: "Not dumb."

Arty laughed. "Jim said you got all the brains," he confided.

Joshua nodded again and pointed at his brother. "He's a dumb hoofer."

"Oh, here we go," Jim groaned.

Joshua went slack-jawed and made a few shuffling steps from side to side. "You," he mouthed at Jim.

"Arty and Jean dance too, don't you forget."

"They're not dumb," Joshua argued.

Jean and Arty were both laughing hard at Joshua's impersonation. Jim pretended to glare at them angrily, but he was also laughing.

"Get outta here," he said, flicking his hand at Joshua.

Even though the danger had passed, they stayed a short while longer, hoping it would give Arty time to recover. Joshua was good company: he was a very clever and humorous man, and for all of his mockery, his love and admiration of his older brother shone through.

When the time came for them to leave, Joshua hugged Arty and said, "See you later, brother."

Overwhelmed, Arty managed only a tearful smile in response. Soon they would meet up with Sissy, and he just knew the second she set eyes on Jim she'd fall in love with him. But Joshua's blessing was something Arty would treasure for the rest of his days.

Chapter Nine:
October, 1944, London

Arty, Jean, Jim and Sissy had arrived at the dance hall early, which was as well: Arty's knee was still causing him considerable trouble, and it looked like he would not be able to dance after all. Fortunately, their early arrival meant they were able to claim a settee to themselves, and they had chosen one near the door so they didn't miss Joshua's arrival.

Whilst Jim and Sissy went to purchase drinks, Jean took the opportunity to share her thoughts with Arty.

"It's perfectly all right if we don't dance tonight. I would much rather you rested up for now than cause yourself permanent damage."

"Thanks, Jean. I wish I could say you are fussing over nought, but I can barely stand, let alone waltz. However, I had a thought. If the organisers are amenable to the idea, why don't you and Jim dance tonight?"

"I couldn't do that to you, Arty."

"Why not?"

"It wouldn't be fair. You and I are partners."

Arty laughed and took Jean's hand in his. "Perhaps if it were anyone else, I would feel differently about them dancing with you in *our* contest. But this is Jim. The man I intend to spend the rest of my life with, even if that means going to prison, or being subjected to medical treatments. I hadn't realised how much I'd missed him until today. I love him, Jean, and nothing would delight me more than watching the two of you dance together."

Jean's smile could have lit up the entire of London, blackout curtains be damned. "You know there will be no stopping them back at Minton when they hear Jim and I danced together?"

"We could really throw a spanner in the works and have him dance with Sissy. Would you look at the pair of them?"

Jean and Arty both glanced over to the bar, where Jim was laughing at something Sissy had said. They were already thick as thieves, and now Arty knew he and Jim had both Sissy's and Joshua's blessing, it made anything seem possible. Indeed, just a few hours of Jim's company stole away all the troubles of the world, and Arty could almost forget they were at war.

When Jim and Sissy returned with the drinks, Jim met Arty's gaze and held it, with no recourse to words, for each understood the other well enough without.

"How would you feel about taking my place this evening?" Arty asked.

"The waltz? I don't know if—"

"Please, Jim?" Jean interrupted. "I'll even jitterbug with you later." She blew him a kiss.

"Who ever could refuse a beautiful woman?" Jim laughed. "I'll go talk to the judges."

Jim temporarily excused himself, leaving Arty at the mercy of his older sister.

Sissy sat down next to him and gave him a big delighted smile. There was quite a crowd in by now, and she turned towards him and leaned close so that she could speak more freely.

"Jim is wonderful, Arty. If I could have picked a man for you, my choice would have been just as yours."

"So you approve?" he asked, fighting to contain his grin.

She hugged him. "Most definitely. I have a present for you both, incidentally."

Arty eyed her suspiciously. "What kind of present? If it's another of your signor's distasteful publications…"

Sissy laughed at that. "Well…" she said, continuing the joke a little longer, although she had only once sent Arty a book from her employer's collection, and it was quite tame. Tedious, in fact, he'd concluded, before reaching the end of the first chapter, and he'd instantly forgotten everything about it, including the title and the author; suffice to say, it was not one of D H Lawrence's. Nor was it the wonderful story of Oswald and Imre, which he secretly preferred to all of D H Lawrence's works put together, though he dared not tell Sissy that.

While Arty had been musing literature, his sister had become quite thoughtful and serious, feigning interest in the couples taking to the dance floor.

"Bad news, Sissy?" Arty prompted, for he could see she wished to tell him something that she thought he would not like.

"Not bad news," she assured him. "I have moved back to Signor Adessi's."

Arty remained silent. Sissy glanced his way. From her expression she seemed to be expecting some kind of telling off, but he knew how much she'd hated having to return home. Their father was a difficult man. Still, Arty was none too happy to hear his sister was living in London, of all places.

Compelled to defend her decision, Sissy justified, "There have been no air raids over that side of the city since forty-two."

"Well that's something," Arty said. "Do Mum and Dad know you're here?"

Sissy shook her head. "They think I'm in Kent. Antonio is paying me an allowance to look after his houses. It's not much, but it's sufficient for my needs. I have only to feed myself."

"Hmm. Antonio now? Not Signor Adessi?"

"Oh, hang it all." Sissy covered her face with her hands and giggled girlishly.

It both amused and delighted Arty, for he'd always thought his sister and her employer would make a wonderful couple. Signor Adessi saw the best in Sissy, and he treated her well. Even with a home as grand as his, he did not need a housekeeper, cook, gardener and two chambermaids, but he refused to let Sissy perform the more menial duties, choosing instead to put her keen mind to good use. Visitors already called her *la signora*; to Arty, the prospect of Antonio and Sissy becoming wed one day was worthy of celebration, and he reached for his drink to offer a toast. His knee shifted painfully, making him curse.

"Stay there," Sissy said. She passed him his beer, and he held it up in front of him.

"To the future Signora Adessi," he said.

Jean had been listening quietly to their conversation, and she and Sissy raised their glasses, the three of them clanging together, just as Jim returned.

"We celebratin'?" he asked.

"We are indeed," Arty confirmed.

Jim shrugged and picked up his glass. "Here's to…"

"Sissy and her signor."

"All right!" Jim tapped his glass against Sissy's, and then Jean's, and finally Arty's. "And here's to us," he murmured.

"To us," Arty whispered. "Sissy's got a present for us, she says."

"You do?"

"Yes," Sissy confirmed. "It's a surprise. Just wait and see."

Jim gave Arty a questioning frown.

"Who knows?" Arty said. Knowing his sister it could be anything. However, for now they were to be left in suspense, as the contest was about to begin, and Jean and Jim made their way onto the dance floor. Joshua arrived in the nick of time, and Arty quickly introduced him to Sissy. The waltz began, with the three of them watching in nervous silence, keeping their eyes on Jean and Jim as much as was possible. Arty was enraptured, but it was difficult to see from the low-down settee. With a struggle and a lot of support from Sissy and Joshua, he got to his feet, leaning on Sissy's shoulder, with Joshua's arm supporting his back.

"It's dreadfully swollen," Sissy observed.

Arty looked down at his knee, so enlarged the fabric of his trousers formed a taut band around his leg. "I'll see the doctor when I get back to Minton," he promised, returning his attention to Jim and Jean.

They danced very well, especially for a couple who had only rarely danced together in the past, but even Arty's love-blinkered eyes could see there were others far more accomplished out on the dance floor.

"You're a better dancer," Sissy told him, as if she had been privy to his thoughts.

"At the waltz, perhaps. Wait until you see him jiving."

The waltz came to an end, and where Arty and Jean would usually have continued into the next dance, on this occasion a foxtrot, Jim and Jean left the dance floor and returned to the settees. The Johnson brothers greeted each other with a warm embrace and a silent conversation. To whatever Joshua said, Jim nodded and then eyed Arty's knee, his face showing his concern.

73

"How's it holding out?"

"It's not." Arty attempted to hop backwards and get closer to the settee in order to sit down again, but lost his balance. Jim instinctively grabbed him, holding on until he was safely seated.

"One day I'll get to waltz with you, Arty Clarke," Jim whispered close to Arty's ear.

Arty breathed in deeply, suppressing the wave of desire resulting from Jim's proximity and his scent. It left him in something of a daze, which was brought to a timely end by the dangling of a key right in front of his face. He turned to his sister and frowned.

"What's the meaning of this?"

"The present I mentioned. Which hotel are you staying in? I'll take your room."

"I beg your pardon?"

Sissy sighed in exasperation. "This—" she took Arty's hand and pressed the key to his palm, folding his fingers around it "—is the key to the Dalton Place. You have it all to yourselves."

"You…" Arty's voice failed him as excitement and embarrassment overcame his senses. Part of him was utterly terrified by what Sissy was conspiring to bring about, and he felt as if all of his desires were exposed to the entire patronage of the dance hall, but he wanted this. He wanted a night with Jim in his arms. He took the key and wrapped Sissy in a tight hug. "Thank you," he said, doing his best not to cry. "I love you, Sis."

"I love you too, Arty," Sissy said, patting his arm maternally. She looked up at Jim's statue-like form. "Sergeant Johnson, I believe you're needed on the dance floor."

Jim blinked a few times, as if shaking himself from a trance. Only then did he and Arty notice Jean was no longer sitting with them. She was already up and waiting for Jim to join her. Jim looked back at Sissy and nodded once in thanks, before dashing across to Jean, arriving just as the band began to play, and all of a sudden the room sprang to life.

Women flew into the air, or slid across the floor on their backs and were swept to their feet only to do the whole thing over again. The vantage point from the settee was, on this occasion, excellent, with a clear view of Jim and Jean's antics.

"Gracious me!" Sissy laughed. "I'm breathless just watching them."

Arty nodded, transfixed once again by the handsome blonde American airman who had captured his attention ten months ago and would keep it forever.

Chapter Ten:
October, 1944, London

Dalton Place—Antonio Adessi's residence—was a magnificent three-storey mansion house, situated in a well-to-do area of the city, far enough from the docks and munitions factories to be as safe as anywhere in London could be.

The war had cast in stark relief the extremes of wealth and poverty that the people of Britain enjoyed or endured, for war cared not for money or privilege. In war, princes and paupers fought side by side, united by a common enemy. Indeed, rationing had improved the quality of life for the very poorest by ensuring that no man went hungry.

Arty, whose family were neither rich nor poor, had never wanted for food or shelter. His father was a historian, an esteemed scholar who could command a salary that had, before the war, afforded a motor car, annual holidays and a good education for his children. The world inhabited by Signor Adessi and his associates was one far beyond Arty's means, although he had never coveted the exuberance and luxury of Adessi's lifestyle; quite the contrary. He felt privileged to have been granted access to Adessi's house, with its vast rooms filled with books and sculptures and paintings. To his young eyes, everything about Dalton Place had seemed enormous and grand, and the images in his mind were still as vivid and breathtaking as the very first time he saw it.

Thus, it was something of a shock to behold now those same vast rooms, devoid of their splendour, blackout blinds where previously heavy red damask drapes had framed windows that extended from floor to picture rail, and the sparse remaining furniture cloaked in white sheets. Pale rectangular ghosts haunted colourless empty walls that answered Arty's sorrowful sighs.

"I wish you could have seen it before Signor Adessi was sent back to Italy," he said to Jim, a step behind him as they traversed the halls and rooms of the enormous, lifeless manse.

"Are you sure your sister is staying here?" Jim's question echoed up into the ceiling and faded away to nothing.

Arty nodded soundlessly in reply. The house had always been too big for one person, and in any case there was little point in trying to heat and light all twelve rooms when Sissy only required the one. Knowing precisely which room she'd choose, and in spite of how painful his knee was, Arty led the way upstairs to the first floor, past the master bedroom, sitting room and bathroom, to the library. He braced himself, turned the door knob and entered.

The warm air welcomed the two men into the small room, dark but for the gentle orange glow of embers in the hearth. Arty hobbled across and gave them a prod, breaking the shell of smouldering coals to release small yellow flames. Next, he checked the blackout curtains were fully closed before lighting the lamp on the table beside the reading chair. For a moment he stayed where he was, with his back to Jim and the rest of the room. Out of the corner of his eye he could see the empty bookshelves, and suddenly it was all too much.

Perhaps because he was barely a man when the war had begun he had not thought of it beyond believing it was wrong. Hitler had to be stopped, with that much he agreed, and he and Jim had talked of it often during their stolen hours in the disused hangars: of treaties reached through reasoned discussion between learnéd men and women. It was an illusion of peace they sustained in order to ignore the terrifying reality beyond the hangar doors. Of course Arty understood that his uncle and other men were missing, presumed dead. Of course he understood the terrible cost of the D-Day landings. He shared the joy of the other men in the small victories, the sorrow of defeat, but only now, in this moment, in the room that had been the sanctuary of his youth and in the presence of the man he loved, did Arty fully realise the frailty of life.

Were it not for Jim's impeccable timing, Arty would have fallen apart right then and there. Jim encircled him with his arms, and Arty leaned back against that strong, broad chest, each thud of Jim's heart penetrating his ribcage and becoming one with the beats of his own heart. Warm breaths on his neck soothed away his troubled thoughts, a gentle touch of lips to skin quelling his fears and fuelling his desires. Arty turned within Jim's embrace, the smile that usually greeted him absent, in its place manifest passion he was unable to resist.

As their lips came together, so did their tongues, advance, retreat, advance, retreat, a dance or a war, it was all the same now. Arty cupped Jim's face with both hands while his body sought purchase, the hard flesh of Jim's arousal digging into his pelvis, a firm grip on his buttocks ensuring he could not escape, as if he would even try.

In the burning heat of the unstoppable kiss, Jim muttered something about moving to the bed. Arty had not noticed there was one in the room, but accepted the reality when his lover lowered him onto the soft mattress and slowly worked his way down Arty's body, unfastening each button and pushing his shirt fronts to the sides. When he reached Arty's waistband, Jim tugged the shirt free and unbuckled Arty's belt, at the same time ascending his torso and despatching a trail of kisses from his belly to his chest, across from one nipple to the other, before descending once more. With the care of a mother tending her infant, Jim eased Arty's trouser leg past his damaged knee, pausing to look upon it, his eyes softening in concern.

"It's not hurting me," Arty assured him, and it was the truth. His now naked body was so overwhelmed with desire he could no longer feel the pain.

Jim stood to remove his own clothes, all the while studying Arty and smiling. "You are so beautiful, Arty. So long have I yearned just to look at you."

Jim inhaled deeply and exhaled slowly. He too was naked now, and Arty wasn't sure which he wanted most: to look or to feel those hard muscles against him. It was, after all, the first opportunity he'd had to see a filled, hard penis other than his own. The pale brown-blonde hair around it was much darker than the hair on Jim's head, which had begun to lighten in spring, and had turned lighter still during the summer months they had been apart.

"What liars poets and everybody were," Arty mused. Jim frowned, not understanding. "It's from the book I told you about, the one by D H Lawrence. It was in this very room that Sissy and I read it." Arty smiled as past and present conspired to answer the question he and Jim had so often asked of each other concerning how they might consummate their intimacy. Arty recited from memory: "What liars poets and everybody were! They made one think one wanted sentiment. When what one supremely wanted was this piercing, consuming, rather awful sensuality. To find a man who dared do it, without shame or sin or final misgiving!"

"What in the heck were you two reading?" Jim teased, pretending he did not know of Arty's love for books of that kind. Jim's laughter caused his penis to bob up and down, and Arty watched it in desirous fascination.

No further words were spoken then; Jim returned to the bed and leaned over Arty, the taut muscles in Jim's left shoulder bearing his weight while his right hand tended to Arty's needs, exploring each crease and curve of his body, learning it, preparing it. Arty's body strived for more, and he arched without thought, his legs rising, the painful knee all but forgotten to his desire to possess and be possessed. Just the touch of Jim's fingers upon him, within him, awakened new, incomprehensible sensations that spread through his entire being. He reached out and grasped Jim's solid penis, squeezing it in his fist, the first daub of seed warm and slippery against his circling thumb tip. Jim's hips swayed back and forth, matching the motion of Arty's hand, stroke for stroke.

"Every night, Arty Clarke, since I first saw you across the dance hall, I've dreamed of this moment. You were standing with your chums, and there was a woman flirting with y'all, but you—"

Jim paused to change position so that he was lying on top of Arty but leaning on his forearms. Arty placed his palms on Jim's hips, thrusting up against the probing pressure that seemed to have captured his capacity to speak.

"I knew you had no interest in that gal," Jim murmured. His voice, close to Arty's ear, sent trickles of sensation in every direction. This room, being together, it was their chrysalis; safe, snug and warm. Jim nibbled at Arty's earlobe, his neck, his chin, interspersing his words with kisses. "I couldn't keep my eyes off of you. And I wondered…does he know? Can he possibly be feeling like this?"

"I was," Arty gasped. "I do."

"Yeah," Jim said. "I kinda figured."

Arty laughed breathlessly. He felt giddy and quite unlike himself. His heart was working too fast, he forgot to breathe, and his body moved to its own rhythms, just as it did when he was dancing.

Each could now feel the readiness of the other, and Jim allowed Arty to lead so that his entrance was not stark, but a slow gliding of thighs against thighs until their bodies coupled in their divine union. The burning, consuming passion that filled Arty rendered him soundless, breathless, and yet how he wanted to cry out. Jim's eyes clouded with worry, and he began to retreat. Arty shook his head in frantic urgency, clutching at Jim's buttocks, forcing him deeper still. Jim's mouth captured the cry that escaped as Arty gulped and gasped in desperation for more, for less, he no longer knew which.

As Arty relaxed, Jim chanced some gentle movement, and Arty nodded to reassure him all was well. The combined pain and pleasure made it impossible to do more than that. He did not want Jim to stop, but equally he was unsure he could stand to continue. In his mind, words formed and disappeared like footsteps in wet sand; he had wanted this, nay needed it.

> *But how she had really wanted it! She knew now. At the bottom of her soul, fundamentally, she had needed this phallic hunting out, she had secretly wanted it, and she had believed that she would never get it. Now suddenly there it was, and a man was sharing her last and final nakedness, she was shameless.*

Arty's final thought was a revelation. *This* was what it was like to be shameless, to be joined with another in a moment of perfect intimacy. *This* was love, pure, unspoiled, instinctual. For the first time in his life he was complete, but as he began to wonder how that could be, the ecstasy carried his mind to another place, beyond this moment and yet a part of it. The heat of the room and their exertion made him febrile, and he teetered on the edge of his orgasm, gorging his senses on Jim's gleaming body: the violent thrust of his hips, and the ugliness of pure pleasure distorting his handsome features. Arty's seed burst from him like gunfire, striking Jim's chest.

"I'm there too, Arty," Jim panted, and he came into him, crying out, again, and again. Unable to hold his weight any longer, Jim fell down on top of Arty, kissing him over and over, tears pouring from his eyes as he declared his love, lest Arty doubt it.

For a long time after, they remained as one, neither wishing to break the heavenly connection. It would not be their last, perhaps not even their last on this night, but their joint inaction served to keep it a while longer. When the world came into view once more, Jim found a final reserve of strength and slid to Arty's side, their arms and legs still entwined.

"What a gift this is," Jim murmured sleepily. He pressed his lips to Arty's sweat-damp shoulder.

"Yes, it is," Arty agreed. He braced himself and straightened his knee, pleasantly surprised to find it didn't hurt anywhere near as much as he'd anticipated. He sighed in relief and contentment. "Tell me more about this idea of yours."

"The workshop?"

Arty nodded.

"You wanna talk, not sleep?"

"I want to listen to you talk," Arty clarified. "Just the sound of your voice…" He turned to Jim with eyebrow raised. "It'll help my knee mend sooner."

Jim chortled. "Well, all right. I guess I got no choice, if it'll help your knee, an' all. So, I was thinking about us, what we're good at, how we're gonna get by when the war is over. I'd like to stay in England, but if you wanted…"

"Go to America?" Arty asked. Jim nodded. "I haven't given it any thought."

"Wherever we decide to be, I figure between us we could pretty much fix up any old jalopy. All we need's a box of tools and a yard. We find us a place to live…"

"You do mean together, don't you?"

"Yeah, I mean together. Are you sayin' you don't want that?" Jim leaned up on his elbow. He looked so serious, and confused, that it made Arty laugh. He grabbed Jim around the neck and pulled him down again.

"Come here, you daft hoofer."

Now Jim laughed too.

"That does mean dancer, doesn't it?"

"Yeah." Jim rested his arm across Arty's chest. It was a heavy, reassuring weight. "Tell me what you want, Arty."

"You tell me first."

"I already did."

Arty rolled onto his side, gazing at Jim in earnest. "Then tell me again."

"All right." Jim cupped Arty's cheek and looked him in the eye, first the left eye, then the right, then the left…Arty smiled and then started to laugh. Jim stopped fooling around and took a deep breath. "I want us to be together. I want you to wear my ring and I'll wear yours. Nothing fancy—we can tell everyone we're just a couple war widowers who loved our wives so much we swore we'd never remarry. But we'll know in our hearts that we're married to each other. And we'll have lots of kids together."

"Ah, that might be a problem," Arty said. He lifted the edge of the sheet and peered under it.

"You know what I'm talking about. I've missed our little Socks and Soot more than I ever imagined possible."

"And they miss you," Arty said. "Jean and I check up on them every few days, and they love Jean, of course. But then they'd sit by the door, watching across the field, waiting for…" Arty closed his eyes, determined to enjoy this precious night together, but it was hard to pretend his heart had not ached for all those months, watching the two young cats slowly realise that Jim was not coming.

"Hey," Jim whispered. "I'm here now. And when the war is over, there ain't gonna be nothin' to keep us apart. I wanna show you somethin'."

Taking great care not to disturb Arty's knee, Jim climbed over him and picked up his pants from where he had dropped them on the floor. From the back pocket, he took a folded square of paper and his Zippo, bringing both back to bed with him.

"It's from my momma. She and Joshua got this clever code they use so they can correspond freely. I write, Joshua turns it to code, sends it to Mom, she replies to him, he decodes it and saves it till we see each other."

"Blimey, that's a lot of hard work for a letter."

"It started out as a game she played with Joshua when he was small. Pop wanted nothing to do with him, said he was an idiot. He doesn't think that now, but Mom had to fight to keep Joshua with her. She always knew he was special, and I don't mean him being deaf and dumb. She played all these games with him, finding different ways to communicate, and he was real good too, 'specially with numbers. Play cards with him sometime and you'll see what I mean. This is the letter I got last week." Jim handed the letter to Arty and lit the Zippo so he could see to read.

Dear Jimmy,

You cannot know how happy I was to receive your last letter. Your words carried such joy. I am so glad you have found someone. Do you plan to stay in England after the war? If it's better there for you, then you must realize you have my blessing.

You'll be pleased to know that the two old coots are back home. They returned in August under cover of night and came by next day. Poor Tom was heartbroken to hear about their old mare. I think I told you she passed away last fall. She was a real old lady and Billy tried but his Tom wouldn't see reason. In the end they left the surviving mare with us on account of fearing what the townsfolk will do to them next time.

I won't stand for it, Jim. Pop thinks I make my own trouble and I'm sorry to say we fought and I told him about you. He said you wouldn't be welcome here no more and I told him it was none of his business. You're my son and if I say you're welcome, you are. Now he's telling anyone who'll listen England is the new Sodom. You know what your pop's like but don't you worry about him.

I look forward to meeting the man who has brought my boy such happiness.

Your ever loving Momma

Arty held the letter long after he'd reached the end, words here and there continuing to draw his eye. The letters from his own mother were far more reserved and, whilst he never doubted that she loved both him and Sissy dearly, it saddened him that she would never accept his love for Jim. Still, he was fortunate to have the support of those who mattered most: Sissy and Jean. Yet he was also afraid that Jim's proposal, or what he believed Jim's proposal to be, was foolish at best. How long would it be before police were breaking down their door and dragging them off to prison, all because they had dared to love one another? Who would care then, that they were good, honest men who had played their part in the war against Jerry?

Reading between the lines, Arty concluded that Jim's mother, brave and generous soul that she was, had instilled in her son false hopes for a happy future, where men could love one another freely, without fear of persecution. However much he wanted it, Arty could not bring himself to truly believe it was the life that awaited them after the war. Yet nor could he find the strength within to shatter Jim's dream, not least because he shared it.

"What's on your mind?" Jim asked.

Arty wordlessly folded the letter and handed it back. Jim watched him intently, waiting for him to share his thoughts.

"Come on," Jim goaded. "Talk to me."

"Would I be right in thinking you want to tell everyone about us?"

"Jeez, Arty, I wanna shout it from rooftops—this is the man I love and don't you tell me I can't." Jim laughed as he wrapped Arty in a tight embrace and kissed him with dramatic passion. When he released him, the laughter was gone, replaced by a gentle, reassuring smile. "I'm not saying we should do that, darlin'. But if anyone asks I won't deny how I feel about you."

"We'd be dishonourably discharged. They'd send us to prison."

"I don't expect you to do the same."

"I know. But I won't deny you either. I love you, Jim. Yes, I'll be your business partner. And I'll wear your ring."

Jim rolled onto his back and, with a smile on his lips, shut his eyes and sighed deeply. Arty's injured knee meant it took him a while longer to get comfortable. With his head on Jim's chest, and Jim's arms around him, he drifted into dreamless sleep.

PART TWO: 1945

Chapter Eleven:
March, 1945, RAF Minton

Dawn had barely breached the horizon, yet RAF Minton was already a frenzy of activity. A night raid on western Germany, whilst successful in taking out its targets, had seen squadrons returning home with around one hundred Junkers 88s on their tails. Crossing the English coast just after midnight, the Ju 88s infiltrated returning bomber streams and shot down at least two dozen aircraft. When the scram order was given, Minton went to emergency protocol and immediately prepared to take incoming craft. All personnel worked through the early hours, the sky above punctuated by gunfire and explosions, a man-made thunderstorm that ravaged the tranquillity of the cool, English spring night.

Damaged Lancasters and Halifaxes spluttered down onto Minton's runway and limped to a stop as soon as they cleared it, so that others could land. Crews were pulled to safety, shell-shocked but most having suffered only minor injuries. Those with more serious injuries were immediately transported to the hospital. Miraculously, all of the airmen who landed at Minton survived, although there were reports of crashes along the entire east coast, and, in fact, a Lancaster had crash-landed near the disused hangars that only a year ago had been Arty and Jim's secret meeting place.

Now a sergeant, Arty and his men—the aircraft maintenance crew and six technicians in training—were put in charge of the newly installed FIDO. It consisted of two pipelines, running the length of the runway, into which petrol was pumped from three large tanks. It was a highly effective though fuel-thirsty system, which ensured damaged bombers were able to land in any weather conditions. At 0100 hours, Arty's crew opened the valves and started the pumps, although it was Jean and Charlie who drove along the runway to ignite the fuel pipes, and then remained close by in case they burned out at any point during the three-hour emergency landing operation.

By first light the FIDO had long been extinguished and there had been no landings since 0415, yet the air remained thick and heavy with fuel and exhaust fumes. With one last check that the pumps and pipelines were clear, Arty sent his men to get some rest and wandered over to join Jean and Charlie, who were sitting on the back of a wagon parked twenty yards or so from the runway, both having a smoke. Arty's head was banging, and it felt like his cap had suddenly shrunk by two sizes.

"How are you doing, Art?" Charlie greeted him.

"Not bad. You?"

"Same, aye." Charlie subtly shifted his head in Jean's direction. Her eyes were bloodshot and her face was pale and drawn. Charlie jumped down from the wagon and brushed some of the dirt from his trousers. "I'll leave you to it," he said, a yawn escaping as he clapped Arty on the back and set off towards the barracks.

Jean watched him leave and then turned to Arty, offering a smile that crumpled as the tears began anew. Arty put his arms around her and comforted her in silence. She'd told him many stories of her first posting in Lincoln, transporting crews to their bombers: the bravado and forced joviality as she drove them out to the airfield, smiling and waving as they took off, the fear of never seeing them again, and her unspeakable relief at their safe return. It stood to reason that she would know many of the crews that had taken part in the raid, thus also those who had perished.

Her cigarette had burned all the way down to her fingers and she quickly dropped the butt. Arty stamped on it and gave her his handkerchief. Jean dabbed at her eyes and attempted a laugh.

"Do you want to talk about it?" Arty asked.

Jean cleared her throat and shrugged, hopeless and defeated. "I've lost my boys, Arty. Lost so many of my boys. Flight Lieutenant Howard Caffrey, shot down over Filey, no survivors. Squadron Leader Knowles, Lieutenant Harris, Flight Sergeant McCormack—they're all gone." The tears took over again, but Jean talked through them. "Up in Lincoln, Caffrey was one of those sorts who treated his crew as equals and they worshipped him. To the end he'd have been cheering them on, telling them they were almost home. 'Come on, lads. Final push!' That's what he used to say every time they set out." Jean sighed sorrowfully. "Hitler's last stand. That's what they keep telling us, believing it keeps our spirits up when in reality it means they gave their lives for nothing."

Arty quietly listened, understanding Jean's need to voice her anguish without judgement or placation. They had known each other for more than a year, and in all that time not once had she looked to him for support, though he had leaned on her often enough. She was strong, forthright and sensible, taking the usual ups and downs in her stride. But to have lost so many of her friends in one night? It had depleted all of her reserves. And yet, even as the news came in, she had continued with her duties, doing what was required of her without complaint. She was an extraordinary woman, and Arty felt privileged to be counted among her friends.

He had his own worries, of course. The diversions had required a great deal of coordination between the bases on the east side of the country, so Arty was aware that Jim's base had come under attack from one of the Junkers, which fired on a landing Halifax before flying into power lines and killing all of its crew. The most recent communication, received after the last of the bombers had landed, reported no Allied casualties, and Arty's relief was immense. However, his other concern was for Socks and Soot's well-being: it wasn't clear how close to the old hangars the Lancaster had crash-landed and Arty couldn't think of a pertinent way to ask the question. The Lancaster's crew were alive and well; their aircraft was damaged but salvageable. In a few hours' time, his men would go to retrieve the wreckage and he would have a reason to search the area. In the meantime all he could do was hope and pray the cats were safe.

"What are you thinking about?" Jean asked.

"Oh, nothing really." Arty smiled to cover his lie. "Are you ready to take the jeep back?"

"Jeep?" Jean repeated.

"Wagon," Arty amended, kicking himself for letting his thoughts escape unchecked.

"Come on." Jean slid down from the back of the wagon and beckoned Arty to follow her. "Let's get this back and call Jim's base."

"We can't do that."

"Why not? As far as everyone's concerned, Jim and I are engaged to be married. As his wife-to-be, I'm worried sick."

"But we already know there were no casualties." Arty was arguing even though he was already in the wagon. Jean started the engine.

"For *my* own peace of mind, Arty," Jean said, and that was her final word on the matter.

With the wagon returned to the garage, Arty followed Jean to the empty wages office and listened as she placed the call and waited for it to connect. Several more minutes passed before the call reached its intended recipient.

"Jim?"

"Jean. Hey. Everything all right over there?"

"Yes, we're all safe, but I lost a lot of good friends last night, Jim."

"I'm sorry to hear that."

"Thanks. Clear channel?"

"Clear enough," Jim confirmed.

Jean handed the receiver to Arty.

"Hello?" Arty said. His hand was shaking so much he could barely keep the phone to his ear.

"Hey. It's so good to hear your voice."

"Yours too. Are you all right?"

"I am now. How's Jean holding out?"

Arty glanced her way. "Same as always."

"She's in good hands. I guess you won't be dancing tonight, huh?"

"No. Probably not," Arty agreed. Even if they hadn't received a warning from on high to expect it, everyone was of the same mind that a follow-up attack was likely. It made sense that the *Luftwaffe* would take the advantage, knowing British bases would still be recovering from the first wave. The damage on the ground was minimal, but they'd be working straight through to clean up and prepare for another night of emergency landings, so the Palais Dance Hall would have to manage without them for a week.

Arty heard the door open and glanced behind him; it was Betty, one of Jean's wages clerks. She mouthed an apology and left again. Arty sighed.

"I've got to go. I'll quickly put Jean back on." Arty handed the phone to her.

"Jim, it's Jean."

"You take care of each other, all right? I love you so much."

Jean locked eyes with Arty and replied, "And I love you, Jim."

Arty nodded and whispered, "I miss you."

"And I miss you," Jean said.

"Same here. It won't be long now. Give my regards to Charlie."

Jean managed a small laugh, knowing the last part was directed at her. "I will," she said. "Bye."

"Bye."

Jean put down the receiver and smiled at Arty.

"What did he say?"

"To give his regards to Charlie."

Arty chuckled and shook his head. "Always the joker."

Jean nodded and looped her arm through Arty's. "Yes, indeed. Your fiancé is a hoot. Shall we go for breakfast, Sergeant?"

"A very good idea, Sergeant. I could eat a horse."

"They're not rationed, so we could certainly ask."

Arty shoved her playfully. She laughed and took his free hand in hers, leading him towards the door.

"Thank you," she said sincerely.

Arty squeezed her hand. "No. Thank *you*."

Chapter Twelve:
March, 1945, RAF Minton

At midday, Arty and his men headed out in the chilly mist and drizzle to retrieve the wreckage of the Lancaster, which had, fortuitously for Socks and Soot but not so much for the farmer, landed a good two hundred yards away from the hangars, in the middle of the wheat field. The two young cats were nowhere to be found, although it was their napping time of day and they were likely taking shelter. For the time being, Arty chose to assume this was the case and returned to the base with his fellow airmen, his plan being to visit again when he went off-duty that evening.

The atmosphere at Minton was very subdued—no doubt the same was true across the country—and it made for an arduous day, with no let-up from the foreboding grey sky. The men worked on in cold, damp silence, physically and emotionally drained by long hours of hard graft, and by a war that looked set to never end. *Come on, lads. Final push!* The words of Jean's lost flight lieutenant rang in Arty's ears. In his exhaustion, his sorrow for Jean's loss threatened to overwhelm him, and in some respects talking to Jim had made it worse. Much as it was a relief to hear his voice, Arty was now missing Jim more than ever, but he would get through this; *they* would get through this.

In spite of the rain and their damp spirits, by 1800 hours the base was ready for another night of emergency landings, and the group captain ordered recreation time for all except those on guard duty. Arty met up with Charlie and their friends for dinner, where they were joined by Jean and the other wages clerks. The conversation was light and flirtatious and not entirely a façade. Arty listened to Charlie complimenting Jean's hair, which was, as always, shining like the shell of a chestnut. When she was on duty, her hair was pinned in a tight roll just above her collar, but she let it down when they were dancing, and it was that vision inspiring the sentiment presently gushing from Charlie. *Like waves washing against golden sands, the delicate flutter of rose petals on the breeze...* Arty had never heard the man wax so poetical, and he received a fair bit of ribbing for it from the other men in their company.

After they had eaten, Charlie and the others set off for the NAAFI bar, but Jean noticed Arty's delay and hung back.

"Don't you fancy a beer?" she asked.

"I'll come for one later," he said, stuffing leftover scraps of rabbit into his handkerchief. "You go on. I won't be long."

"I'll take you out there in one of the wagons," Jean offered.

"You'll get yourself in bother."

"And you'll catch your death. Come on, let's go and visit your boys."

Arty knew better than to argue with Jean once her mind was made up and followed her out to the garage, where she walked straight past the three transport wagons, to the group captain's Humber.

"Jean..." Arty beseeched, but she was already in the car. She started the engine and looked at Arty expectantly. With a reluctant sigh he climbed in beside her. "We'll get court-martialled for this."

"Only if they catch us," Jean said with a grin as she steered around the wagons and took the car out into the open. A guard drew to a halt, saluted, and then peered through the windscreen, his jaw dropping when he saw Jean and Arty inside. Jean put her finger to her lips and winked at the man. He shook his head and laughed. Arty hid behind his hands.

"You're a dreadful influence, Sergeant McDowell."

"Life's short, Arty, and it's meant to be lived."

How could he argue with that?

Jean drove out onto the disused service road, the Humber's suspension taking quite a battering from the potholes and cracks in the ancient surface. Arty cringed each time a loose stone hit the car's sleek, dark green bodywork. It was a beautiful vehicle, with a powerful six-cylinder engine, capable of speeds of up to eighty miles an hour. Thankfully, Jean was taking a much more sedentary thirty miles an hour, which was still a little too fast, given the poorness of the road, although they were at the hangars before Arty had time to voice his concerns. Jean slowed the car to a stop and left the engine running; the light was fading fast, and they couldn't stay long.

As soon as Arty opened the car door, Socks and Soot came sauntering towards him, their hungry, gravelly mews bringing tears to his eyes. He was so glad to see them alive and well.

"Evening, chaps," he said. They weaved around his ankles, purring and rubbing their faces on his trouser legs. Taking the handkerchief from his pocket, he divvied up the rabbit meat, half on each palm, and crouched down with hands cupped. The two cats guzzled the meat in seconds but stayed for Arty to fuss them. To his shame the tears pricked again and there was nothing he could do to stop them. Socks and Soot brushed their backs against his palms, and he quietly sobbed, feeling wretched and guilty for the indulgence. He didn't hear Jean approach, but there she was, crouched beside him, an arm around his shoulders. She didn't speak; she just stayed at his side, waiting for the tears to cease.

It was quite a fight, but Arty pulled himself together and slowly straightened his legs, wincing at the pain in his knee, still not fully recovered from the jarring it had received in London. Most of the time it gave him no trouble, but he'd been crouched in the fine rain long enough for his shirt to have stuck to his back and he was achy all over. He shivered.

"We should go," Jean said. Arty nodded but delayed a moment longer just to watch the cats trot back to the shelter of the old, tattered hangar: their home.

***

For all of their preparations, the night passed uneventfully. Fighter Command sent Spitfires to intercept the handful of Ju 88s before they reached British airspace, and a new day dawned, still raining, but perceptibly brighter than the one that had preceded it.

Every day, news came of another country joining the war against Germany and Japan, the Western Allies advancing further, Jerry in retreat. Germany was under attack from all sides, and still Hitler refused to surrender. V-2 rockets continued to hit the south of England, killing indiscriminately and without warning. Arty wrote to Sissy, imploring her to leave Signor Adessi's house; she remained resolute.

As March drew to a close, the group captain called Arty and the other NCOs to his office to prep them for the next batch of new recruits, due to arrive in a few days' time. High

Command had decided that Minton would no longer train air crew, and the captain's dismay was palpable as he explained that from there on, the base would provide technical training only.

"What that means, men," Captain Taylor said stiffly as he rose from his chair, "is that all those of you who are not ground technicians and engineers will be transferred by the end of the week, which leaves us with you lot." The captain peered down his nose at Arty, Charlie and the other NCOs who were ground crew. He exhaled sharply. "But never fear, the Yanks are here."

Arty's heart was a leap ahead of his thoughts, and he gasped before he had a chance to check himself. The captain returned to his desk and sat down. Charlie glanced sideways at Arty and back at their captain.

"Yanks, sir?" Charlie enquired.

"Hm? What was that, Tomkins?"

"We'll be working with the Americans, sir?"

"Is there a problem, Tomkins?"

"No, sir."

"We're on the same side."

"I am aware of that, sir."

"And I believe you're already acquainted with the chaps from 383 Squadron?"

"From Gaskell, sir?"

"Indeed, Tomkins."

"Smashing," Charlie grumbled under his breath. Arty's neck hairs bristled.

"They'll be bringing their B-17s with them, so you'll need to work out the logistics of where we put the blighters. That's all for now. Dismissed."

The NCOs departed. Not a word passed between Arty and Charlie as they walked back together, barely acknowledging each other when they parted ways to return to work: Charlie in his garage and Arty in the hangar next to it, seething in silence but powerless to do a thing about it. Next to Jean, Charlie was his closest friend, and it pained him that Charlie disliked Jim so intensely, particularly as it was born of jealousy. Arty had seen it a year ago, on the night of the ball to welcome the Americans. It didn't matter to Charlie that they were all on the same side; Jim was competition, and not just because he and Arty were evenly matched on the dance floor. Even back then, Charlie had been well on his way to falling in love with Jean, and now it seemed she had rejected him in favour of Jim.

As far as everyone on the base was concerned, Jean and Jim were together. They wrote to each other, they met up whenever they could, with Arty playing 'chaperone', of course. When Jim had let slip his intention to remain in England after the war, he stole Charlie's one last hope of winning Jean's heart. Never had Arty faced such a great dilemma. He loved Charlie as if he were his own brother, trusted him with his life. He wanted Charlie to have his chance at happiness, and telling him the truth would give him that, although there was no guarantee that Jean would accept his advances. She didn't want a husband, after all. Nevertheless, Arty had a feeling she liked Charlie, but her supposed engagement to Jim was stopping her from doing anything about it.

So on the one hand, Arty could not reconcile his future happiness being at the cost of Charlie's, while on the other, there was his fear, and the tremendous risk associated with telling Charlie the truth. It was the sort of revelation that could destroy their friendship in seconds, taking his and Jim's liberty with it. Perhaps, then, it would be better to discuss it with Jim first, given that it involved them both and they were partners. Relieved to have a reason to delay acting, Arty got back to work on the Wellington he'd been prepping for a training exercise before the meeting with the captain. He collected his tools and slid underneath the plane to access the front wheel assembly.

"Don't suppose I could borrow that spanner again?"

Arty briefly peered up at Charlie's solemn expression. "In the toolbox," he said. He continued with what he was doing, listening to his friend searching through the spanners, each clang of steel on steel further heightening the tension between them.

After a few minutes, Charlie came back over and sat on the floor, leaning against the plane's front wheel. "I know you and him are friends..." he said.

Arty waited for more, but there didn't seem to be any. "But?" he prompted.

"There isn't one. No doubt Jimmy Johnson's a marvellous fellow. He knows his job, that's for sure. I just wish I could be a man about this. Mind, I don't have any choice, do I? Seeing as he's my oppo."

"True enough," Arty agreed. "I think if you give him a chance you'll be pleasantly surprised."

"And find it in my heart to forgive him for stealing my woman?"

Arty laughed. "Best not let Jean hear you say that. She belongs to no one, Charlie."

"Figure of speech, Art. That's one of the things I like about her. She's got gall, has Jean. Real fight. And she's a great little mover."

"Why don't you talk to her about it?" Arty suggested, thinking on his feet, so to speak, as he was still lying on his back under the Wellington's fuselage and keeping his eyes on the task rather than Charlie.

"Are you suggesting I try and take her from Jimmy?"

"Not as such. Just...I have a feeling that things are not quite as they seem."

"Where there's smoke, Art…"

"Yes, but perhaps Jim's fire burns elsewhere?"

"What, you mean he's got a girl back home?"

"That wasn't quite—"

"So what's all this talk about staying over here then? If he's spinning our Jean a yarn, I'll knock his ruddy block off."

Arty quickly recanted. "I'm not saying he has, Charlie. I'm merely suggesting that the gossip may have got a little out of hand."

Charlie huffed and puffed in anger, and Arty wished he'd stayed quiet instead of trying to find a workaround, because it was backfiring horribly.

After several minutes of Arty pretending he was still occupied, whilst his friend snarled, Charlie muttered, "Well, according to Betty the Yanks'll be here the day after tomorrow, so I might just ask Jimbo myself."

"Good idea," Arty agreed. With any luck he'd have been able to talk to Jim by then, although Charlie was gunning for him so he'd have to get in there quickly.

"Right." Charlie got to his feet and waved the spanner at Arty. "I'll bring this back in a bit." He stomped out of the hangar, leaving Arty to wonder if cowardice meant he'd just let the perfect opportunity pass him by.

"Oh well, no point worrying about it now." Arty slid out from under the Wellington and patted it with affection. There weren't so many flying as there had been before the four-engine bombers came into service, but they were handy for training the lads in the basics. Most wanted to be flight mechanics rather than ground crew, lured by Bomber Harris's promises of glory and the prospect of returning home a hero. If Arty had ever doubted it, Jean's stories of the crews she had loved and lost were confirmation that those young men who sacrificed their lives to the defeat of evil *were* heroes. But he had never understood their way of thinking. Perhaps he *was* just a lowly coward; if not, then why couldn't he tell Charlie the truth?

"I've done the props, Sarge. Is there anything else?"

Arty turned and smiled at the eager young AC2 standing behind him: one of his six lads who would be training in the tethered Wellington.

"That should be everything," he confirmed. The AC2 nodded, and went to join the others loitering outside the hangar, awaiting further instruction. It would be the last time Arty oversaw tethered training, and the last time he listened to young men lamenting the absence of Lancasters, which was what they were doing now, and what they always did. He fully appreciated how disappointing it was to be stuck with an out-of-service Vickers Wellington with its piddly two engines, when they wanted to be marauding the skies in an Avro Lancaster powered by four Rolls Royce engines. Who could fail to be impressed by those mighty machines of war?

But what Arty was going to miss most of all was the crewing up. He'd seen so many groups of lads through their training, and whilst they were under his instruction they were his crew. Some were easier to let go than others, but his current group had been there through the emergency landings and they were outstanding. They'd pulled together, looked out for each other, and they'd worked until they were fit for nothing, all without a single complaint. Every day they turned up and got on with the job, occasionally chancing a remark about when they were air crew instead of 'planks like Sarge', to which Arty would give them the usual ribbing about chasing glory and forgetting where the real work happened. It had become a constant source of tormenting on both sides, yet all the while they'd be grafting away, as efficient as the machines they tended.

105

It was this lot of lads, more than any other, with whom Arty felt the bond air crews talked about. In a few days' time they'd be crewed up, and it was going to be tough to hand them over to their flight sergeants, but Arty knew he'd done all he could to prepare them, so he wasn't sad. There was something rather wonderful about watching those hopeful yet bewildered young men stare like frightened rabbits as the hangar doors closed with them on the inside. They'd enter as individuals—brave, lone adventurers at the start of their voyage—and leave as brothers, for those bonds were as good as blood and would serve them well through the ordeal that lay ahead of them.

Quite why Arty was feeling so morose he couldn't say. By the end of the week he and Jim would be reunited, and for more than just a few stolen moments. They'd be working side by side, eating and drinking together, and he should have been overjoyed. But the reorganisation wasn't all good news: a change of tactics, another bombing campaign—if bombing could win a war, then why was it not yet won? What else was to be done?

Arty yearned for more than just Jim's presence at his side; he needed the sanctuary of knowing Jim was safe. So this it would seem, was love, where one's very survival depended on that of another. Everything Arty had ever believed, every feeling, every thought, every breath he had taken, was meaningless without Jim. *He* was meaningless without Jim, and his conviction that war was wrong waned in the realisation that he would take to the skies himself to stop Hitler if that was what it took to keep Jim safe.

With his spirit replenished, Arty strode to the front of the hangar and shouted, "Right, lads. Let's get this war won!"

The young heroes-in-the-making answered Arty's call to action with a resounding cheer, and as they walked the

Wellington out into the open they started to sing, to the tune of *Mine Eyes Have Seen the Glory*:

> *I took a Flying Fortress up to thirty thousand fe—*
> *(How far?)*
> *I took a Flying Fortress up to twenty thousand fe—*
> *(How far?)*
> *I took a Flying Fortress up to seven thousand feet but I*
> *only had a tiny little bomb.*

Arty didn't join in, but he did laugh heartily at their mocking of the USAAF airmen. There was nothing 'tiny little' about Jim's bomb; he could personally vouch for that.

"Is that right, Sarge?" one of the AC2s asked, making Arty splutter with contained laughter, for the question had followed directly his less-than-pure thought. "The Yanks are taking over Minton?"

"Where did you hear that?"

"Sergeant Tomkins, Sarge."

"Oh, right." Arty glanced back at the garage, where Charlie stood, watching them tow the Wellington. Even from a distance, Arty saw the grin on his smarmy friend's face. Charlie waved his spanner-bearing hand in the air. Arty chuckled and turned back to the junior airman. "Did he teach you the song as well, perchance?"

The AC2's face glowed crimson, and he quickly rejoined the singing, which had now become *We're flying Vickers Wellingtons at zero zero feet*, but their spirits were soaring high. Arty walked up ahead to check their position, and all was well, but as he turned back he heard the drone of engines, flying low and close by. He glanced to his left, along the runway: a Lancaster was coming in fast, and the Wellington was still straddling the asphalt.

"Right, lads. Quick as you can now. Let's get her onto the grass."

Arty dashed to the rear of the plane and joined the effort to push the Wellington clear, the Lancaster's engines now a deafening roar, although it was only running on two and it wasn't decelerating. There was no time to do anything other than bellow, "Run for it!" and follow his own instruction.

"Bradley's down, Sarge!" one of the junior airmen shouted. Arty glanced over his shoulder and saw the AC2 scrabbling frantically to get to his feet. The Lancaster was less than fifty yards from the Wellington. Arty ran back, grabbed the lad by the hand and hauled him upright, yelling, "Run, damn it!" but he couldn't even hear himself. As he shoved Bradley forward and down onto the grass, there was a deafening crash as the Lancaster collided with the rear of the Wellington and sent it spinning around like a top. A tail fin hit Arty in the side of the head and he dropped and rolled. The last thing he saw was the Wellington's front wheel sliding his way; he closed his eyes and waited for impact.

Chapter Thirteen:
April, 1945

Arty lay there, staring up at the Wellington's undercarriage, all around him the frantic yells of men calling for help, calling out to their friends. Someone shouted his name, and he responded that he was all right: in shock, and his heart was racing, but he was, by some small miracle, alive. He rolled onto his front and crawled out into the open. A few sharp scraps of glass and metal had penetrated his uniform, and there was a dull ache in his thighs, but otherwise it seemed he had escaped serious injury, although the cuts would need medical attention. Feeling a little wobbly, he got to his feet and did a quick head count of his crew: all six were present, in body if not in mind.

"The Lancaster, Sarge," one of them uttered. The lads were staring past Arty, their eyes wide in horror. Arty turned to see.

"Oh, my God. Charlie."

The bomber, still in one piece, had crashed into the garage and demolished it, before coming to a stop, nose in the air, leaned up against the now collapsed side of the hangar. The wreckage was still shifting and as it settled, the sound of metal screeching against metal splintered the air. *Charlie was watching us. He was outside. He was watching us. He wouldn't have gone back in.* Arty kept his thoughts on that as he marched unsteadily towards the garage, but the pain in his legs was worsening with every step he took. He staggered across the runway to the nearest group of airmen, mutely waved both hands, and collapsed, unconscious.

***

Later, when Arty came to, he was lying in the midst of hushed, urgent conversation. The bright, round light overhead hurt his eyes, and he was encased in something...sheets, a bed. He tried to sit up and found he couldn't. Both legs, from the hips down, had gone completely to sleep, and the pain...he couldn't bear it. He forced a word up his throat, past his dry, swollen lips. *Help.* A doctor and his staff stopped talking and all turned his way. *Help*, Arty mouthed again, *my legs, please help, my legs, I can't...*

***

Later still, when he came to a second time, the blurred vision confirmed the doctor had given him some kind of sedative, and the bright light was gone, as was the pain. Arty blinked a few times and lifted his head, trying again to focus on his surroundings: a hospital ward, five beds spaced along the opposite wall, all occupied. To his left lay Corporal Arkwright with a bandaged stump where once was his left arm; to his right, LAC Phillips stared blankly at the ceiling.

"Ah, good. You're awake, Sergeant." The matron appeared next to him, her smile compassionate yet stern. "How are we now?" she asked. Arty had no time to reply before she closed in and poked a thermometer between his lips. He compliantly parted his teeth and let the glass tube settle under his tongue. Matron gripped his wrist and lifted her watch, humming under her breath. Arty closed his eyes. He wondered if he was brave enough to attempt to move his legs. The recollection of his previous awakening was dreamlike, but doing as much as wiggling a toe would confirm it. If it were real, then he did not wish to know.

The thermometer was tugged from his mouth, pulling the skin of his lips away with it. Arty flinched and opened his eyes.

"A little high," Matron said, shaking the thermometer down. She returned it to her breast pocket.

"May I…" Arty croaked and swallowed dryly. "Water, please?"

"Certainly, Sergeant." Matron moved off, looking to the end of the ward as she shouted, "Nurse Brownlow. Water for Sergeant Clarke, please, thank you."

"Yes, Matron," came a timid, rushed response.

The matron moved on to Phillips, and Arty closed his eyes again, drifting, remembering…*Charlie*…

"Here we are, Sergeant."

He felt something warm and soft slide under his head and the gentle pressure of the nurse's hand, he assumed. With her assistance he tilted his head forward and sipped at the cup being held to his lips; the water trickled down the sides of his neck. He coughed and spluttered.

"Oops, too much. Sorry."

Arty squinted up at the young nurse. She smiled gently, kindly, *sadly*.

"Can you remember what happened?" she asked.

"La—" Arty stopped and swallowed again. "Lancaster crash. Charlie Tomkins? Is he…" He couldn't finish the question.

"I don't think anyone by that name was brought in, but I'll ask Matron for you."

Arty smiled his thanks.

"Bit more water first, eh?" the nurse suggested.

He had little choice but to comply, and between them they got most of it in his mouth this time. When the nurse decided he'd had enough, she wiped away the spillage and left the cup on the table next to the bed.

"I'll be back in a moment," she said.

The click of heels against linoleum faded into the far distance, as if the nurse were walking for miles and miles. *That's a hell of sedative*, Arty thought. He chuckled, he wasn't sure why. It was no laughing matter. Would they discharge him before Jim arrived? *Unlikely*, a little voice in his head scoffed. It made Arty chuckle some more. *This is no laughing matter. That's what I thought. So what in God's name are you laughing for, man? I couldn't tell you. I think you've—*

"Sergeant Clarke? Are you…"

Arty squinted up at the fuzzy double outline of the nurse standing over him, her concerned features momentarily in focus. She looked frightened out of her wits. She became blurry again, and Arty stopped laughing.

"Can you hear me?" she asked.

Arty nodded as best he could. His neck was stiff and the pillows were restricting his movement.

"Matron said there's no one by the name of Charlie Tomkins been brought in, alive or dead. She's going to contact your CO to see what she can find out."

"Thank you, Nurse. May I sit up?"

"Ah. I'm afraid not. Doctor's orders are for you to stay lying down until he's had a good look at you."

"I understand," Arty said. "Perhaps I might turn on my side?"

The nurse frowned. "I'm not sure. I'll ask Matron."

She trotted off down the ward again and Arty eavesdropped on her conversation with the matron, who harrumphed and grunted, but agreed to Arty lying on his side. The two women came back together.

"Left or right side, Sergeant?" the matron demanded.

"Either," Arty said. He didn't care. The pain was flaring up again and he thought changing position might help. It certainly couldn't make it any worse, or so he thought until they started to roll him onto his side. "Oh, no! No! Stop!" It felt like his lower body was being ripped in half. He vomited and choked on it.

"Get the doctor, now!" Matron shouted.

The nurse's shoes clacked at speed. Arty's chest tightened. He couldn't breathe. He was dying. He was dying...

After the swingboats, they went on the roundabouts to calm down, he twisting astride on his jerky wooden steed towards her, and always seeming at his ease...

D H Lawrence is reading to me. What a lovely way to welcome a fellow.

...on the whirling carousal, with the music grinding out, she was aware of the people on the earth outside, and it seemed that he and she were riding carelessly over the faces of the crowd, riding for ever...

Though I must confess I thought he'd sound a lot posher...less...American.

Arty fought to open his eyes, but the lids fluttered uselessly and stayed firmly shut. *Jim! I can hear you! Jim...*

"...buoyantly, proudly, gallantly over the upturned faces of the crowd, moving on a high level, spurning the common mass."

Arty gave up trying to get his eyes open, deciding it was a dream, or maybe it was heaven, it mattered not. He just

113

wanted to listen to Jim's voice, reading to him. He recognised the story, but he couldn't recall the name of it. *If Sissy were here...of course, Sissy must have given the book to Jim. Can I think her into being too?*

"Everything seemed wonderful, if dreadful to her, the world tumbling into ruins, and she and he clambering unhurt, lawless over the face of it all. He sat close to her, touching her, and she was aware of his influence upon her. But she was glad. It excited her to feel the press of him upon her, as if his being were urging her to something."

"You..." *can't read that in here. They'll have your guts for garters.*

A hand grabbed his. It was big, rough, familiar, and squeezing so hard he would have cried out if he could have garnered the wherewithal to do so. And then a soft, gentle touch to the back of his hand, the two sensations so at odds they were utterly overwhelming, for surely that could not be warm breath disturbing the hairs and giving him goose pimples? *So it was indeed a dream*, Arty concluded, *or else Jim would not be kissing his hand like that, and sobbing.*

Or if it is not a dream, and I am not dead—the lingering pain suggested he was still very much alive—*then I must nearly have died, or am I nearly dead?*

"Sergeant Johnson, please restrain yourself. I do not tolerate such...behaviour on my ward."

"Arty's awake, Molly. He said something to me."

"That's as may be. However—"

"Ain't you gonna check on him?"

Arty's left eyelid was prised open, his muscles battling against the force pinning it back, and not of his doing; he wanted it to open, but his body refused to comply with either his will or the matron's.

"Hm. He does appear to be conscious. Sergeant Clarke, can you hear me?"

Arty tried to answer, *yes, I can hear you*, but the sound would not form.

"He's squeezing my hand," Jim said. He sounded so desperate, like the man at the gallows still pleading his innocence.

"You shouldn't have your hand there for him to squeeze, Jimmy. I'd have thought you'd know better."

Cold air wafted over Arty's chest and then there was a sharp pain right under his ribcage. He tried to buck away from it.

"Responsive," Matron said.

Arty gasped and gulped down air. *Stop! Please, just stop!*

"Was that necessary?" Jim asked angrily. "I told ya he was squeezin' my hand."

"Sergeant Johnson, if you insist on being disrespectful, I will ask you to leave."

"Sorry, Mol—Matron."

"I'll go and see if Doctor is available."

Footsteps retreated, in their wake a silence as thick and heavy as the blankets pinning Arty to his sickbed.

Jim sniffed loudly and moved one of his hands away, but kept hold of Arty with the other.

It's easier to use a hanky with two hands, Arty willed himself to say.

"What'd you say, darlin'?"

"Hanky…"

"Yeah. I, er…" Jim took a deep breath. "Man, you gave me a scare."

Jim was fighting to contain his emotions; Arty could hear it in his voice, could feel it in the shaking of his hands that were usually so strong and steady, but he needed to tell him. Something was very wrong. Before, the pain was a dull, heavy ache that stopped just below his hips, almost as if the bottom half of him was missing. Now it had gone. He felt nothing, just a strange sensation of floating, of leaving his body behind, peaceful, painless, drifting away... *No!* He wasn't ready to die. Not if he had any choice in the matter. But if he didn't...he needed to tell Jim, before it was too late. With great effort, Arty forced out the words, "Love you."

"And I love you, but you're going nowhere, you hear? We got a good life ahead of us, Arty. So much has happened in the past few days, I can't begin to tell you. You ain't going nowhere, because I ain't letting you."

What do you... "Mean?"

"It can wait. You just rest and heal, all right? That's your number one priority. Get better."

All the tension left Arty's body. Jim would not let him die. "Read?" he requested.

"You want some more of this debauchery, huh? All right. I can do that."

One-handed, Jim flicked through pages until he found his place and continued to read. For how long, Arty didn't know, for when he next awoke it was night-time and he was alone, or alone as anyone can ever be in a hospital.

Chapter Fourteen:
April–May, 1945

Over the weeks that followed, Arkwright, who had been trapped under hangar debris which mangled his left arm, was sent to a convalescent home near his family, whilst Phillips was moved to a different kind of hospital. He'd lost the sight in both eyes, and Arty had overheard the doctor say there was no medical reason for it, but he came up with one so Phillips wasn't discharged with the hideous 'LMF' on his papers. Whatever horror Phillips had witnessed that took away his desire to see—there was no lack in Phillips' moral fibre so it must have been something pretty hellish—he wasn't telling. Tragic, also, that it should happen now, with news pouring in from Berlin, where the Soviets had a 'nervous and depressed Hitler' surrounded, and the Third Reich seemed to be rapidly disintegrating.

From Italy came rumours of surrender, though Arty only caught snippets here and there; he was still sedated for most of the day, with a brief reprieve at visiting time. The doctor had told him the sedation was to help with the pain, and in truth the only time it didn't hurt was when he was unconscious. Nevertheless, Arty resisted asking for medicine as long as he could, eager to make the most of those few precious minutes of company, particularly when it came to

Sissy, whose six-hour round trip to visit every weekend left him in no doubt about the seriousness of his condition. Had he still questioned it, the visits from his parents made it crystal clear.

It seemed everyone from Minton had been in to see him at least once, and his men took turns to visit in pairs, as was the rule set by the firm but fair matron. Jim, Jean and Charlie had also devised a rota, which, along with the officially designated hours for visiting, Jim flagrantly ignored. More remarkable still, he was getting away with it and visiting at all hours. If Arty could have stayed awake long enough, he might have been able to figure out how Jim could so easily wrap Matron around his little finger.

Jean came every other day, doing her utmost to keep Arty's spirits up by telling him funny stories, not that he'd confided to her or anyone else just how frightened he was. He could tell she knew something, and the longer she kept it to herself, the more frightened he became. He still had no proper sensation in his legs. Indeed, with the blankets and cage over them, which he was not permitted to touch, for all he knew both legs had been chopped clean off. Each morning the doctor came on his rounds, asked the same questions, took his pen from his pocket and said, "Can you feel anything?" to which Arty would answer, "No," before deciding the doctor was a damned good liar. If that pen had touched the soles of his feet, Arty would have known about it.

"And you're still getting pins and needles, Sergeant?"

"Yes, Doctor."

"Good, good."

And on to the next poor fellow. *Pins and needles*—if they'd been heated to the point where they were glowing white-hot, maybe. At first it only happened in the early hours, when he was due for more pain-killing medicine, but it seemed to be

118

occurring more and more every day. It was the worst pain Arty had experienced in his life, and when it came on during Jean's next visit, he ended up screaming in agony and begging for her help to end his suffering. In that moment he'd meant it, but as the pain slowly subsided and he watched her break down, he realised just how hard it was on everyone else. Like Charlie, for instance, who would begin each visit by offering his excuses for why he couldn't stay long. After twenty minutes or so had passed, he'd rise to his feet and smile an apology, and Arty would joke, "I'd see you out, but the beds here are fit for kings." Charlie would fake a cheery smile and promise to get the beer in once Arty was discharged.

So, along with the physical pain and the furnace-heated pins and needles in his potentially phantom legs, Arty had the guilt of frightening the life out of poor Jean and subjecting his best friend to enduring the company of an invalid. Indeed, he'd convinced himself it would be better if people didn't visit him, if it resulted in guilt and pain for all concerned, particularly if he was already destined for the knacker's yard.

***

"A little bird told me you're ready to go AWOL."

Arty's fitful snoozing came to an abrupt end at the sound of Jim's voice.

"I said, '*My* Arty? Nah. Can't be!' And you're still here, so I guess I was right." Jim pulled a chair close to the bed, but before he sat he leaned over and gave Arty a gentle kiss.

"Jim," Arty whispered, aghast.

"I don't care. If that's what it takes to…" Jim drew in a long, shaky breath. "No matter what they say, or how hard you beg, I'm gonna do everything I can to keep you with me. D'you hear?"

119

Arty's eyes filled with tears, and he nodded.

"I love you, Arty Clarke. Don't you dare think of goin' anywhere without me." Jim caught one of Arty's tears with his fingertip and rubbed it against his thumb, his eyes trained on that small motion as he continued. "I know you're scared. You got every right to be. And I know you're in a lot of pain…" Jim met Arty's gaze and smiled gently. "Jean said I shouldn't tell you, but you have a right to know."

Arty watched Jim carefully, waiting for him to say more. This was about his medical condition, and from Jim's expression it was clear things were very grim.

"Am I going to die?"

Before Jim got to answering, the dreaded pins and needles shot down into Arty's legs, and he yelled out.

"Jesus Christ! Oh God, Jim…"

"All right, darlin', I'm here."

Arty gripped Jim's hand, trying not to squeeze too hard.

"Take a big breath for me, real deep, come on."

Arty tried to do as Jim suggested, breathing in as deeply as he could, whilst Jim moved a little way down the bed and, with his free hand, reached under the blanket and cage.

"What are you doing?" Arty gasped.

"Just trying something. Do you trust me?"

Arty nodded and closed his eyes, focusing on each breath in, holding it for as long as he could before breathing out again. It might have just been wishful thinking, but he was sure he felt a tingling in his right thigh.

"Jim, what are you doing?" he asked again.

"Tell me what you think I'm doing."

"Tickling my leg."

Jim raised his eyebrows suggestively and grinned. "How about now?"

Arty felt it straight away. "You're tickling the other one."

"Kinda. Gimme my other hand." Arty let go and Jim moved down to the other end of the bed, reaching right under the blanket with both hands. "I'm rubbing pretty hard."

"I can feel it, but it's still…" Arty's body tensed. "You know I'm ticklish," he said, a reflex chuckle escaping with the words.

"But it's easing the pain?"

"Yes, it is." Arty smiled at Jim in gratitude, although he'd also spotted Matron heading their way.

"Sergeant Johnson. What on Earth do you think you're doing?"

"Physical therapy, Ma'am."

"Physical therapy?"

"Yeah, see, I been reading about polio and paralysis and I figure Arty's got the same kind of thing going on here. The books say firm, smooth pressure helps stimulate the muscles and gets the blood flowing."

Matron grunted. "A likely story. I'll let it go—this time."

"Thanks, Mol, you're a peach." Jim gave Matron a cheeky wink and her nostrils flared, but that was all; she returned to her station at the end of the ward.

"How do you do it?" Arty asked.

"What?" Jim queried innocently.

"You know what. Charm the birds out of the trees, you could."

"Er…yeah." Jim nodded with faked modesty. Arty laughed and settled back into his pillows. The pain was still there, but it was nowhere near as severe, and for the first time since he was hospitalised he was properly warm.

"You going to sleep on me?" Jim teased.

Arty shook his head but kept his eyes closed, all his troubles dissolving like sugar in warm water. The pins and needles had gone. He thought he probably ought to tell Jim that, but to feel something in his legs after all those weeks of feeling only pain or numbness was blissful.

"Better?" Jim asked.

"Much, thank you."

Jim stopped what he was doing and shifted the cage half a foot to the left.

"Move over," he said.

"Jim, you—"

"Do it."

Against his better judgement, Arty put his hands either side of his hips, hoisting himself a few inches to the left, while Jim lifted his legs for him. Once he was comfortable, or as comfortable as he was getting, Jim lay beside him, taking his hand once more.

"In answer to your question," Jim said, "they don't know if you're gonna die."

"Oh." Arty sighed. "Well, I suppose that's better than an outright 'yes'."

"No kiddin'! A few hours after they got you here, your legs turned black, and the doc diagnosed gangrene. He said it would spread upward, and it was gonna be slow and painful, so he kept you under, hoping you'd go in your sleep, I guess."

"Bloody hell," Arty said quietly.

"Yeah. He went as far as to say it would be more humane to shoot you, but after a while the black started to fade to blue, to purple, to yellow…"

"Internal bleeding."

Jim nodded. "Doc thinks the Wellington crushed all the blood vessels in your upper legs, the pressure built, arteries ruptured. You should've bled to death."

"But I didn't."

"No. You didn't." Jim laced his fingers with Arty's. "Guess God was listening to me, huh?"

"You prayed for me?"

"Oh yeah, I prayed for you. Think I pretty much used up my lifetime's quota. But I'll tell you now, in case there's any doubt, I love you and I'm staying with you, come what may."

"If I lose my legs—"

"You ain't listenin', are ya? *Come what may.* Legs, no legs…hell, who needs legs anyway?"

Arty attempted a smile and pushed away the other fear he had, the one he couldn't bear to think about.

"We'll get that waltz one day, I promise," Jim said, almost as if he could see right into Arty's brain.

"I doubt—"

Jim's kiss stopped him from going any further, and it was a long, slow kiss which Arty thought he should probably resist, but it was an age since they'd kissed, and it wiped out his resistance in one fell swoop. Just to have this physical contact, the warmth and security…it made everything seem perfect, and Arty could've stayed there forever.

As Jim slowly released him, Arty remembered where he was, and why. Surprised by the lack of complaints, he lifted his head and glanced around the ward.

"Where is everyone?" he asked.

"In the canteen."

"The patients too?"

Jim nodded. "Yep. Patients, doctors, nurses, porters…"

"Why? What's going on?"

"Hitler's dead."

Chapter Fifteen:
May, 1945

The moment hung like a scene in a photograph while Jim's statement sank in. Arty's heart was beating so hard and fast he could even feel it in his dead legs. Dozens of questions clamoured to be asked—Was it official? Had it been confirmed? Did it mean the war was over, or was Germany fighting on?—but the answers to all of those questions were overshadowed by his need to know one thing.

"Why didn't anyone tell me?"

"Doctor's orders," Jim said.

"Don't tell Arty the Führer's dead?"

Jim laughed. "Not quite. Doc said it was important you stayed calm—no excitement, no shocks—to give your blood vessels time to heal."

"So you're trying to kill me," Arty stated dryly.

Jim smiled and kissed him on the forehead. If he'd told him the war was over it would have been very different, but after more than a year together, Jim knew Arty would take the news of Hitler's death calmly. Until he saw or heard for himself that Germany had unconditionally surrendered, the war was still on.

"Is there anything else I need to know?" Arty asked.

"Other than I love you? Nope."

"You're sure?"

"Yeah." Jim narrowed his eyes. "Why?"

Arty frowned at him. "No reason." He just knew there was more, but perhaps he shouldn't push it. After all, if Jim was withholding information from him, it would be for health reasons, so he was likely safer not knowing. He let it go and instead asked, "What else is going on in the big wide world?"

Jim was noticeably relieved to be let off the hook and they moved on to discussing recent events—Mussolini's death, Italy's surrender, the Americans and Soviets advancing on Berlin—and agreed it certainly looked like the end really was in sight. When they'd finished discussing the war, Arty casually dropped in a question about the accident, for he knew only what he remembered, and Jim immediately tensed.

With gentle reassurance that he wasn't going to bleed to death, Arty was able to glean that the pilot died, but his navigator had survived. They had been taking the bomber up to Lincoln—one of twelve replacement craft for those lost on recent missions—when three of the engines cut out. The pilot managed to restart one on his approach to Minton, where he had intended to make an emergency landing. There was no way of knowing if the pilot would have been successful had the runway been clear, but thanks to Arty's quick thinking there were only two fatalities and three casualties, including himself.

"Who else died?" Arty asked.

"Corporal Allan?" Jim said, unsure of the man's name as they'd never met.

"Reg Allan—Charlie's right-hand man?"

Jim nodded. "Yeah, that's him."

"What a shame. Poor Charlie. How's he taking it?"

126

Jim shrugged. "Your guess is as good as mine."

Arty decided not to say anything further, as he still needed to have that conversation with Jim about telling Charlie the truth, but now wasn't the time. Once he was out of hospital, whenever that might be...

The nurses were on their way back with the patients from their impromptu celebration, and Jim vacated the bed.

"I'd better go," he said, straightening the cage and blankets. "I'm on duty in half an hour."

Arty nodded drowsily; it was the longest he'd stayed awake since the accident and only made possible by Jim's ministrations. "Thank you," he murmured.

"Always welcome," Jim replied, chancing another quick kiss before he strolled out of the ward, acknowledging the happy, exhausted patients with a lazy salute.

Arty watched until Jim was out of sight, and shut his eyes. *Not gangrene.* That was something. Of course it was just his bloody luck to get this close to the end of the war without injury and then cripple himself. But at least he was still alive, unlike the Lancaster's pilot and poor Reggie Allan, and he hadn't lost his sight or his mind. These were surely things to be thankful for.

***

Over the days that followed there was a constant stream of good news, with German troops surrendering to the Allies, and the liberation of concentration camps, cities and countries right across Europe. It gave the patients plenty to talk about, for which Arty was glad, because Jean had only been in to see him once since his outburst, and it was brief and awkward. He needed to say sorry, but it was still too raw for both of them. Charlie also came to visit a couple of times, the second of those interrupted by Jim's arrival, cutting Charlie's usual twenty minutes in half.

On the evening of the seventh of May, after a day of hopeful whispers, Thomas Cadett, a correspondent of the British Broadcasting Corporation, reported that he had seen '...the formal acknowledgement by Germany's present leaders of their country's complete and utter defeat by land, in the air and at sea.' The deafening cheers could have razed the hospital to the ground, and nurses and patients hugged each other, laughing and crying in celebration. Through it all, Arty could do nothing but keep telling himself, *don't get worked up, stay calm.*

Bright and early next morning—Victory over Europe Day—Jim bounced into the ward with a wheelchair.

"Good morning, darlin'," he called loudly, attracting the glares of the other patients. Arty looked up at him in disbelief. "What?" Jim said with a grin.

"It's bad enough that you're stuck with an invalid. Don't be getting us sent to prison and all."

"No one's gonna be worrying about a couple of—"

"There's no need for that sort of thing today," one of the men across the way complained.

"What's it to you, gramps?" Jim said, gesturing to Arty, who was trying his hardest to hide behind the leg cage. "This man here is a hero."

"He's not the only one," someone else pointed out.

"Absolutely," Jim agreed. "You're all heroes in my book. Every last one of you. Soon y'all gonna be demobbed, go back to your wives and kids, and I'm real happy for ya." Jim glanced back at Arty, who shook his head, silently beseeching Jim to shut his mouth. He just smiled and said, "I'm not ashamed of my love for you, Arty. Why should I hide it, today of all days?"

"Sergeant Johnson," Matron interjected. "If you're intending to take Sergeant Clarke on a jaunt, I recommend you hop to it."

"Yes, Ma'am," Jim said.

She gave him a stern nod and continued to watch him for a moment before a smile almost broke. She fought it and sighed in exasperation. "Here. Let me give you a hand."

"Very kind of you," Jim acknowledged. The matron stepped to the other side of the bed, and Arty saw a look pass between the two of them that he couldn't interpret. He let it go unchallenged, for the time being, and did his best to assist them in dressing him. Once he was fully clothed, he shuffled to the edge of the mattress, where Matron helped him to sit up while Jim carefully swung Arty's legs over the side of the bed in which he had lain for a month. Jim put his arms under Arty's.

"Hold on to me," he instructed.

"I could try to stand—" Arty began.

"No, you most certainly could not!" Matron scolded.

Arty grumbled under his breath, which made Jim chuckle.

"Grab on, pardner," he said.

With no other choice, Arty compliantly looped his arms around Jim's neck and became weightless as he was lifted from bed to chair.

Matron nodded, satisfied, and handed Arty a urine bottle. He stared at it in horror.

"I'll take you to the men's room if need be," Jim offered.

"No. It's all right."

Jim took the bottle from him and handed it back to Matron. She clicked her teeth, disgruntled, and shrugged at Arty.

"Thank you, Matron," he said.

She offered him another of her stern nods and added, "I'll walk you out, make sure Sergeant Johnson doesn't get you into any more mischief." Her nostrils flared and the corners of her mouth twitched. Jim laughed and scratched

129

his head, doing a fairly convincing job of acting bashful. Arty rolled his eyes, not convinced at all.

Taking control of Arty's wheelchair, Jim set off, with Matron walking at his side or going ahead to open the ward doors and any others along the way. Not a word was spoken until they were out in the grounds, where the delighted shrieks of children at play carried on the warm May breeze, and the air around them exuded a joyful peace.

Jim stopped alongside a jeep he had borrowed to take Arty back to the base for the VE Day party. He lifted Arty out of the wheelchair and up onto the seat, helped him to get comfortable and covered his lap with a blanket. Matron collapsed the wheelchair, and Jim put it in the back of the jeep.

"Be careful, Jim," Matron warned.

"Don't worry, I will," Jim assured her.

"I'm not talking about your driving."

"Yeah, I got that."

Arty watched in astonishment as Jim and the hard-nosed matron embraced.

"And don't bring him back too late," she called, moving towards the hospital entrance.

"I won't," Jim promised. He climbed in beside Arty, started the engine, and slowly moved off.

***

"...enough?" Jim asked.

"Hm?" Arty had been watching the world whizz by and only half heard the question. He gave Jim an enquiring look.

"Are you warm enough?"

"Oh! Yes, I'm fine. Changeable, isn't it?"

Jim laughed. "You could say that. Didn't you hear the storm last night?"

"Can't say I did. Does Captain Taylor know I'm coming?"

"Everyone at Minton knows you're coming. Didn't I tell you? You're a hero."

Arty returned his gaze to the road ahead. "I did what any one of us would've done."

"Maybe, but don't say I didn't warn you." Jim turned out onto the lane up to Minton, slowly accelerating to a steady twenty-five miles an hour. Arty shifted position and grimaced. "Too fast?" Jim asked.

"No. Just...stop worrying. I'm perfectly fine."

Jim reached over and squeezed Arty's hand. "Sorry," he said. The road had quite a few bends, and Jim attempted to take them one-handed, but eventually had to relent. He released Arty's hand and gave him a quick smile.

"You and Matron," Arty said.

"We go back a way."

"I gathered. How d'you know her?"

"From the Palais. Remember the girl I was dancing with that first night at Minton?"

Arty thought back, trying to recall. "You pretty much danced with every WAAF that night, love."

Jim chortled. "You got a point there. Daphne and I were dancing when you went outside and I followed you."

"Daphne...ah, yes. Corporal Buchanon. I thought you meant you were dancing with the matron."

"Not at all. Daphne and Molly—sorry, Matron Reagan—are, shall we say, confirmed spinsters."

"Oh." Arty didn't have much to say to that.

"Mol knows about us."

"Hm, yes, well, if she didn't before I landed in hospital she certainly does now," Arty griped. Jim grinned sheepishly, and Arty shook his head. "Please tell me not everyone at Minton knows."

"Good God, no. I mean, I don't give a damn, but I know you do, so…" Jim turned off the lane into the base, acknowledging the two men on gate duty with a smile and one of his lazy salutes, before driving past the main barracks to the mess hall. He stopped the jeep and pulled on the brake.

"So?" Arty prompted.

"So…" Jim frowned thoughtfully, planning what he wanted to say. Whatever it was, Arty had the feeling he wasn't going to like it. "Maybe we should tell 'em."

"Jim—"

"Or not." Jim took Arty's hand again. "It was only an idea, darlin'. I hate we gotta spend today pretending we're just pals. Charlie's spoiling for a fight as it is, but like I say, it was an idea. Don't get all worked up on me and bust somethin'." Jim made a feeble attempt at a smile. Arty squeezed his hand.

"Right, Jim Johnson. How about this? You stop fretting about every little bit of excitement finishing me off and—"

"You're asking for the impossible. You know that?"

"As are you, but I'm prepared to give it my best shot if you are. However, I need to talk to Charlie first."

"I understand. He's your buddy."

"More than that, Jim. Charlie's mad for Jean. He always has been, which is why he can't stand the sight of you."

"Aw, jeez. I've seen 'em flirt, an' all, but I thought it was a bit of fun. Why didn't you say?"

"I was planning to talk to you about it before the accident, because I don't know how he'll take it. We've been friends for six years, Charlie and me, but he's always assumed I like the fairer sex just as much as he does. I could've put him straight, I suppose, but…" Arty turned to Jim with a smile and a helpless shrug. "Until I met you I never had any intention of doing anything about it."

"So, either I made an honest man of you, or I'm a bad influence."

Arty laughed. "A bit of both. Are you all right with me telling Charlie?"

"Sure," Jim agreed, though Arty could see it still bothered him and waited for him to say more. Jim smoothed his chin and frowned heavily. "Trouble is, you tell a lie so long it just keeps building on itself, and I been trying real hard to make it look convincing for your sake. If Jean takes up with Charlie everyone's gonna think she's easy."

"I know," Arty agreed. "But she went into it with eyes open. In fact it was her idea, so I'm not too worried about Jean, or not on that score. She's tough as old boots, that girl."

"She sure is. So it's Charlie we need to think about today." Jim nodded. "All right. Just good pals, huh?"

Arty smiled. "I love you."

"I love you too. And if you need me there when you talk to Charlie, just say the word."

"Thanks, but it's probably best if it's just the two of us. I'll try and snatch a minute with him later." A group of airmen and women wandered past the jeep, all of them laughing and joking. Arty watched and smiled. How good it was to see everyone again, and looking so happy. "We should probably go in."

"Yeah. Let's do it." Jim climbed out of the jeep and collected the chair from the back on his way around to Arty's side. He leaned in and put one arm under Arty's knees, the other behind his back. Arty grabbed on and Jim hoisted him with ease, sneaking a kiss as he gently lowered him into the wheelchair.

"I saw that, Sergeant Johnson," a voice called from behind him. Arty peered around Jim and grinned broadly.

"Morning, Jean."

133

"Good morning," she replied, giving Arty a warm hug and a kiss. "You look so much better, Arty."

"I am," he said sincerely, keeping hold of her a little longer and whispering, "I'm so sorry, Jean."

She patted his back and released him, her eyes glassy but she smiled through. "Forgiven and forgotten. Come on, let's get you inside." Jean looked up at Jim and winked, which worried Arty a little. He had the impression they were scheming something, and if that proved to be the case, he'd be having it out with them both later.

Chapter Sixteen:
VE Day, 1945

When they entered the NAAFI, Arty had to choke back his tears. The place was packed to full capacity and all of them turned and applauded, raising their glasses in his direction. He was completely astounded by the reception, not to mention perplexed. After all, what was he but a wounded ground technician? Thankfully they quickly resumed their drinking and chatting, a few chancing a brief hello and promising to come back *after*. After what? That's what Arty wanted to know, but whenever he looked at Jim and Jean, they weren't looking at him.

This continued for a further half an hour, at which point Captain Taylor banged on a table to get everyone's attention and the room instantly fell silent. "Thank you, all," he said. "I'm not going keep you from the festivities for long, however, I'd like to formally welcome back Sergeant Robert Thomas Clarke, Minton's longest serving airman."

The room buzzed briefly with mutterings of *welcome back*. The captain looked directly at Arty.

"Sergeant Clarke. Were it not for your quick thinking and evasive action, we would have lost many more lives, not just on the day of your tragic accident, but throughout your time here at Minton. Your conduct is, without exception, exemplary, and this year, on Monday, the twenty-sixth of March, you demonstrated gallantry, risking your own life to save another. The young airman in question, along with the five others you were training that day, successfully joined their crews and flew in several missions, contributing to the victory of the Allies. They sent this message to wish you well."

Captain Taylor withdrew a letter from his breast pocket and shook it open. He cleared his throat and adopted an overly formal stance as he began to read aloud.

> Sarge. Sorry we can't be with you today. We were hoping to come down to Minton and take the Wellington out for a spin...

The captain paused while everyone laughed and groaned at the joke, which was in appallingly bad taste but funny nonetheless. Arty chuckled away, holding onto his belly, just in case.

> ...Unfortunately our group captain is even more of an old fart than Taylor.

The room erupted. Taylor took it on the chin and, once they'd settled down again, read through the final part of the letter.

> Joking aside, we're glad you're all right, Sarge. We just wanted to thank you for everything you did for us. Our eyes have seen the glory and we lived to tell the tale— It's all thanks to you, Sarge. Have a spectacular day and get well soon.

The applause exploded, and Arty put his hands over his face, wailing like a baby. He felt the warm comforting pressure of Jim's palm on his shoulder, and he laughed through his tears.

"Come on, darlin'," Jim murmured, "the captain ain't done yet."

Arty gave his eyes a quick wipe and moved his hands away. Captain Taylor advanced and drew to attention in front of him.

"Sergeant Clarke, it is my privilege today to award you this medal, for your distinguished service to His Majesty's Royal Air Force."

The captain leaned down and pinned the medal to the flap of Arty's shirt pocket and then stepped back and saluted. Arty returned the salute as best he could in his chair, and once again the NAAFI filled with the sound of clapping and cheering. People came over to shake Arty's hand or hug him, offering their congratulations and moving to make way for others. All the while Arty was aware of Jim's concerned, watchful gaze, but there was nothing to worry about, for whilst Arty was touched by the reception and delighted with his Distinguished Service Medal, he thought the whole affair was a little over the top when he'd only been doing his job.

When things settled down a little, Charlie came over with a couple of pints and handed one to Arty.

"How are you doing, Art?"

"All right, I think," he said, still a tad overwhelmed by the attention. He took a large mouthful of beer, swallowed and moaned in pleasure. "I needed this." He drank some more and nodded his thanks at Charlie. "How are you?" he asked.

"Getting along," Charlie replied curtly. Jim and Jean were standing together just a few feet away but out of earshot. Charlie nodded at Jim. "Nice of him to go and fetch you today." The remark was cutting, but before either of them had a chance to say more, the rest of their friends came over to join them.

Arty put tackling Charlie on the back burner and focused his efforts on being jolly. He was, in fact, in good spirits, but the other men were uneasy around him, not knowing what to say or where to look. To them, Arty Clarke, ace technician and dancer, was no more, but Arty wasn't giving up that easily. He was under no illusion about his condition. He'd nearly died; he'd have to relearn to walk, and he'd likely never dance again. But he was still alive, the war was over, and he had a life ahead of him with the man he loved. Paralysed or not, Arty refused to follow in the fated tyre marks of Sir Clifford Chatterley, remaining 'strange and bright and cheerful' whilst Jim romped in the woods with the gardener. No, that would not be Arty's future.

Arty and Charlie's friends hung around for a while, becoming more at ease the more beer they consumed. Arty didn't much fancy his chances with Matron if he were to return to the hospital drunk, so he gracefully declined the offer of another drink. The men wished him well, and went back to propping up the bar, leaving Arty at the mercy of the WAAFs, who came over in pairs and threes, admired his medal, giggled at his jokes and moved on. All the while Charlie sat there looking miserable, and it was a good hour before they were on their own again.

"What's up?" Arty asked.

"Not a lot," Charlie replied, frowning into his beer.

"Hm," Arty sounded doubtfully. "I think I might know what it is. We need to talk, Charlie."

"About?"

"Jim and Jean."

Charlie shrugged. "Not much to say, is there?"

"Actually, there is. Look, can we go outside?" Arty set his pint on the table in anticipation. Charlie followed suit and pushed Arty's chair towards the door. As they passed Jim, Arty gave him a nod to confirm all was well.

"Will here do?" Charlie asked, stopping a few feet from the door.

"Bit further away, if you wouldn't mind."

Charlie obliged and steered Arty to the end of the building, put the brakes on and stepped around in front of the chair. He sparked up a cigarette and leaned against the wall, facing Arty without looking at him.

Arty clasped his hands in his lap, squeezing them tightly together as he tried the rally the words into a sensible order, for whilst he'd been thinking about telling Charlie for some time, he hadn't really considered the nitty-gritty of what to say, and he was stumped. The prospect of losing his oldest friend, particularly over something that had no bearing on their friendship, was once again making a coward of him, but there was no getting out of it. It had to be done, for all their sakes.

"There's no easy way to tell you this," Arty began. He waited for confirmation that Charlie was listening. It came in the form of a fleeting glance. Arty continued, "First off, Jim and Jean are not engaged to each other."

"They've broken it off?"

"No. They were never engaged to start with, nor even together."

"Funny, that, seeing as they sent each other love letters every week for God knows how many months."

"Yes, well the thing is, Charlie, those letters—"

"I have it on good authority," Charlie interrupted.

"You mean Betty from Jean's office?"

Charlie's cheeks reddened, and it made Arty laugh, easing a little of the tension, which was as well; his legs were aching, and he could feel the blood pulsing in his groin.

"Betty wasn't lying to you about the letters," Arty confirmed, "but…she may have been slightly misled."

"The letters were forgeries?"

"Oh, no. The letters were real, but Jean was corresponding with Jim on someone else's behalf."

"Whose?"

"Mine."

Charlie's eyes widened, and he swallowed so hard Arty heard the gulp. Charlie took another draw on his cigarette and held the smoke in for a good half a minute. His face started to turn purple and he let the breath go. "You—" he said, the realisation cutting his words dead. He dropped the cigarette and shoved his hands in his pockets.

"I'm sorry I deceived you, Charlie. I think the world of you, and I don't want to lose your friendship, but I'd rather that than get in the way of your happiness."

Charlie nodded mutely, still staring past Arty. If he'd been on his feet, Arty could have forced him to look him in the eye, made him promise not to do anything drastic until he'd had time to digest the news. As it was all he could do was watch his friend and hope for the best.

A few minutes passed in this stalemate, and then Charlie moved past Arty, turned the wheelchair around and pushed it back towards the NAAFI. "I appreciate you telling me the truth," he muttered.

"I owed it to you," Arty said.

They returned to their table, where Charlie wordlessly passed Arty his pint and turned away. He was angry, Arty could see that, and it was understandable. Arty would have felt just the same if he'd discovered Charlie had been intentionally deceitful.

"Want another?" Charlie asked, waving his now empty glass at Arty. His own glass was still half full, and he shook his head.

"I'm all right, thanks."

Charlie strode away to the bar. Arty pinched the corners of his eyes and stifled a yawn: the day was not yet half over and he was already exhausted. He opened his eyes again and blinked a few times to clear them, catching sight of Jim in his peripheral vision. Jim gave him a questioning thumbs up, and Arty returned it. Charlie had taken the news better than he'd anticipated; only time would tell if they were still friends, but it looked promising, as Charlie now returned with his full pint and sat down again.

"So Jean's single, I take it?" he asked.

Arty smiled to himself; everything was going to be all right between them, in time. "Yes, she is," he confirmed. "I can also tell you she likes you and she knows how you feel, but she's an independent woman."

"Yeah," Charlie agreed with a frown. He smoothed the glass with his hand. "That was the part I couldn't work out—why she'd gone with Johnson after telling everyone she wasn't interested in love and marriage." He laughed quietly and shook his head. "It makes perfect bloody sense now. Or not sense, because…" He finally looked Arty in the eye. "It's a sickness, isn't it?"

Arty shrugged. "So they say. Though if it is, I've had it all my life."

"You can get treated for it, I've heard."

"Yes, but it's not like measles, or a broken leg, is it? It's more like…I don't know. Being born with brown hair instead of blonde."

"You're telling me you were born that way?"

"Well, I certainly didn't choose it, but I'm not sorry, not any more. I don't want to be cured. And in any case, the treatment is nothing more than a hair tint, if you know what I mean. It only conceals what's underneath."

Charlie's face gave away the hard thinking going on in the background. "Forgive me, but it's all new to me, this," he said and returned to silently pondering while he drank his third pint, at the end of which he wandered off to buy another. He returned with one for each of them, although Arty was not yet done with his first.

"How did you know?" Charlie asked. "That you were a…" He tilted his head to imply 'one of them'.

"Well, I—"

"What I mean is I'm not going to wake up one day and realise I'm one too?" Charlie asked.

Arty chuckled. "Somehow I doubt it. How d'you feel when you see a beautiful woman?"

"You know…" Charlie tutted at himself. "No, you don't, do you? I, er…how to explain? I might notice her shapely figure, or her pretty eyes, the curve of her lips, or maybe the way she moves, or speaks—all of those, really."

"Right," Arty said. "And the same's true for me."

"But not with beautiful women."

"Precisely."

Charlie returned to thinking and supping until another pint was finished and immediately went in search of a refill. This time his trajectory was prone to veering off course, but he made it to the bar and stayed there a while, chatting to other airmen. Jim came over to Arty and sat in Charlie's seat.

"How you holding up?"

"Fine. Charlie's getting hammered."

"You told him?"

Arty nodded. "He's taken it well, actually, other than getting hammered, of course."

"He's not alone in that today." Jim glanced over to where Charlie and his friends were laughing loudly and eyeing up the WAAFs. Charlie looked over to where Jim and Arty were sitting and met Jim's gaze head-on with a glare. Jim turned back to Arty and raised an eyebrow.

"I can see this coming to blows," he said.

"Don't involve yourself," Arty warned.

"I'm gonna do my best not to, but if he starts something…"

"Jimbo!" Charlie shouted.

"Great," Jim muttered to Arty and then turned in Charlie's direction.

"Want a drink?" Charlie called.

"Sure, thanks," Jim accepted. "Jimbo. Jeez. Guess it could've been a whole lot worse."

Arty laughed and shifted uncomfortably. "Sorry, but I need to relieve myself."

"No problem, darlin'." Jim wheeled Arty out to the toilet block and stopped the wheelchair next to a cubicle. Arty held onto Jim as he walked him into the cubicle, unfastened Arty's pants and lowered him onto the toilet. Once he was satisfied Arty was securely seated, Jim stepped outside and pulled the door to. A couple of other men came in and used the urinals; Arty was having to concentrate hard to pass water, but he eventually managed it and called Jim back in so they could repeat the procedure in reverse.

When they returned to the NAAFI, Charlie was once again sitting at the table with a three-quarters-full pint glass, two full pints next to it.

"Yours, gents," he said, his voice noticeably slurred.

Jim picked up one of the glasses and tapped it against Charlie's. "Thanks, bud."

Charlie watched with the intensity of a would-be poisoner as Jim tipped the glass to his lips. Jim swallowed down his beer and smiled warmly at Charlie. "Think I'll leave y'all to talk awhile," he said, excusing himself to give Arty and Charlie space to speak further.

When Jim was far enough away, Charlie grumbled, "I still don't like him."

Arty nodded. "Fair enough."

"Sorry."

"It's fine."

"It's not. He's your…whatever he is, and I'm your best friend."

"If you don't like him, you don't like him."

Charlie frowned heavily. "No. It won't do at all," he said.

Arty was too tired to get into more deep and meaningful conversation. Indeed, much as it pained him to say so, he was looking forward to returning to the peace and quiet of his hospital bed. As it turned out, Charlie was too far gone to pursue the matter, and so Arty did the rounds to say goodbye and Jim drove him back to the hospital. Matron was off-duty, so the nurse helped Jim get Arty back into bed, gave him a dose of pain relief and it was 'lights out'.

The next day, when Jim came to visit, Arty was still a little the worse for wear, but not so much that he missed the black eye Jim was sporting.

"Don't ask," Jim said, holding up his hands.

"Did you hit him back?"

Jim laughed, wincing at the same time. "You should've seen Socks and Soot this morning…"

Arty shook his head in dismay.

Chapter Seventeen:
June, 1945

It was two months after the accident before Arty was able to stand without assistance. Some of the feeling had returned, but his upper-leg muscles had wasted considerably; for his own safety, Matron would only let him out of bed if she or Jim was there, and for a maximum of two minutes at a time. Arty fought her as hard as he dared, which was to say he muttered under his breath and smiled innocently if she caught wind of it. Walking to the sink at the end of the ward was the next goal he'd set his sights on, determined to do away with the indignity of bed baths. And he really was determined, conquering the walk to the sink in less than a week and setting his next objective: walking the corridor, and after that the hospital grounds.

"I think we should work on our jive," Arty informed Jean one afternoon as she accompanied him to the hospital gate and back. She kept her gaze averted, evidently trying her best to hide how little hope she and everyone else had for Arty ever walking without sticks again, let alone dancing. He continued, "It's a good energetic dance for youngsters like us," but the more he said the more distressed Jean became, so he changed the subject and asked how everyone was back at the base. She had little new to tell him, but she did so just the same.

The next time Jean visited, she was accompanied by Charlie, and Arty was glad. He'd been overdoing it and Matron had ordered bed rest for a few days, which, to his visitors, would look like he'd taken a turn for the worse. From his prone position in his hospital bed, Arty watched the flicker of anxiety in Jean's eyes, and Charlie was also back to being on edge.

The following week Jean and Charlie again visited together, the pair of them acting very cagily. They took Arty out for lunch, but it was a dreadfully sombre affair, as neither was particularly talkative.

When Jim came to see him that evening, Arty asked if there was something going on, but Jim knew nothing, so Arty put it out of his mind. They had other things to worry about: Jim and the rest of the American airmen at Minton were waiting for their transport back to the States for demobilisation, which the US Army was processing as quickly as they could, but there was no knowing how soon they would get to Jim's group, nor how long it would be before he returned to England once he'd demobbed and been home to see his parents. He hadn't seen his mother and father in four years, and he was looking forward to and dreading it in equal measure.

When Jean and Charlie visited together a third time, Arty had worked out exactly what was going on, and he decided to play ignorant. Jean asked for a wheelchair so that the three of them could go and sit in the grounds. Arty protested—he could walk that far—but Jean shot him a stony glare so he shut his mouth and got in the chair.

Finding a secluded corner of the hospital grounds, Jean stopped the wheelchair next to a bench and then fussed unnecessarily, checking Arty's knees were covered with a blanket, asking if he was comfortable, whether he would prefer a less sunny spot, a better view, more of a windbreak, and so on. When finally there was nothing left to delay, she sat on the bench, and took his hand in hers.

"You know how important you are to me?" she began. Next to Jean, Charlie had his head bowed; he was leaving the talking to her. "And also to Charlie," Jean added.

"I've never doubted it," Arty assured her.

"What I'm about to say…it has no bearing on us. What I mean is, we're still dancing partners, or if we're not, it's…" There was no tactful way to say what Jean was trying to.

"Come on now," Arty comforted. "How long have we been friends?"

"Seventeen months."

"And whether we're dancing or not, we're still friends. Your happiness matters more to me than almost anything else."

Jean closed her eyes, but the tears still squeezed their way out. Arty shifted so he could wrap both of his hands around hers.

"Look, Jean, I know you hate it when I crack jokes about it and truthfully, I doubt I'll ever dance again. I can't deny that the thought depresses me, but I'm not going to let it get in the way of living, and nor should you. If I do ever dance again, it will be a long way into the future, and I certainly don't expect you to wait for me. So, if you want to dance with Charlie…"

"But that's what I'm trying to say," Jean interrupted. She opened her eyes again and turned to Charlie, who was absently tapping a cigarette against his thigh. "You're no help at all," she said, exasperated.

Charlie lit the cigarette and gave it to Arty, accompanied by a wan smile. Jean sighed loudly and took the cigarette from him, drawing in deeply.

"All right," she said over the smoke, "I'm just going to say it, Arty, and hope that you're not too upset. Charlie and I are engaged to be married, and we wanted to tell you first, because you are our closest friend. It makes no difference to our continuing to dance together. That is all."

"That is all?" Arty repeated, amused. He leaned forward and stared hard at Charlie, and kept staring until Charlie looked his way. "You'd best give me one of those cigarettes."

"I just did," Charlie said, nonplussed. He put his hand in his pocket and Arty laughed at him.

"Charlie. I don't smoke."

"Oh, yeah."

Arty pointed accusingly at Jean. "This is the woman who told me she wasn't looking for a husband."

"Yes," Charlie agreed. "She told me that too."

"What have you done to her?"

"Me? I'm innocent in all of this. Ask Jimmy."

"Why?" Arty asked suspiciously, shifting his attention back to Jean. "What's Jim got to do with it?"

"He was…worried," she hedged cautiously. "About you coping when he goes back to America, so he, well, we…have been discussing arrangements."

"Come again?"

"Jim asked Charlie and me if we would look after you while he was away, and we were trying to get ourselves organised."

Arty could feel the anger rising within, which was foolish. He would be discharged from hospital soon and it hadn't even crossed his mind that he would need assistance. In fact, he hadn't given the immediate future any thought at all, because right at that moment the prospect of being separated from Jim, never mind him being so far away, was unthinkable.

Containing the indignant child within, Arty asked tightly, "What did you decide?"

"I'm sorry, Arty. You're cross, aren't you?" Jean said, lowering her eyes in remorse.

"I don't think it's too much to expect a say in what happens to me, so yes. I am cross."

"We thought this way would cause you less distress. I know from Sissy that going to stay with your mother and father—"

"Sissy's in on this too?"

"Keep your voice down, Art," Charlie beseeched.

Arty snorted in disbelief. "Keep my voice down?" He took in air a few times, intending to fully convey how appalled he was by what they'd done, but each time words failed him. How could they possibly have imagined it would cause him less distress?

"Please don't be angry, Arty," Jean pleaded. "We were only thinking of you."

Arty nodded. "I know, and I'm really not angry with the two of you. But Sissy? And Jim?"

"You're being very unfair to them," Charlie said.

"I thought *you* didn't like Jim."

"I didn't, but that was before I got to know him, and..." Charlie looked to Jean before he continued. "I'm ashamed to admit it, but I picked a fight with Jim, and he made mincemeat of me, but that's by the by. We got talking and I suppose...I just hadn't realised how important you are to him. We had a few drinks, and Jim got chatty, telling me about his dream of the two of you opening a workshop together in London, and I thought, he's going to hop it back to America and you'll never hear from him again.

"So he was telling me about how he'd work around whatever you needed—whether you fully recovered or didn't recover at all—he had it all sussed out. Still I was thinking, it's all blarney, this. And then the next day he took Jean down to London to look at a plot of land."

Arty looked at Jean, amazed. She nodded to confirm it and continued from where Charlie had left off. "It's at the back of Dalton Place. Sissy mentioned it last year. One of Antonio's friends had a house there, but it was bombed in The Blitz and demolished. He was more than happy to sell the land."

Arty blinked in astonishment. "You mean Jim's already bought it?"

Jean nodded her head in a 'so-so' motion. "Jim and I bought it together. We thought with Sissy's plan to move to Italy—" Arty took in air sharply. Jean wrinkled her nose. "She didn't tell you? Oh, darn it."

Arty flopped back in his chair, his anger dwindling to hopeless confusion. It was all too much to take in. "Right," he said. "To clarify, my sister is moving to Italy, to be with Antonio?"

"Yes."

"And you and Jim have bought a plot of land with a view to building a workshop."

"Correct."

"You and Charlie are getting married."

"We are, yes."

"When?"

"We're going to wait until Jim comes home."

"Home? West Virginia is his home."

"Comes home to you, Arty!" Jean was getting annoyed with him. "The plan is for the four of us to rent Dalton Place from Antonio. Charlie and I will take the upstairs, you and Jim the downstairs. Charlie's already got a job on the

150

railways, and I'm going to look after you until Jim comes back." Jean folded her arms and nodded resolutely.

Arty looked at Charlie and asked, "Anything you want to add?"

"Jim and I discussed me going in on the workshop too, but that's as far as we got."

"I'll be having words with him about this."

"Well, here's your chance," Charlie said, pointing across the hospital grounds.

Jim was on his way over to them, but as he got closer, Arty saw his expression and his heart sank.

"Hey," Jim greeted bleakly.

Arty looked up at him. "When?"

"Tomorrow morning."

"So soon?"

"I'll be back before you know it."

Arty looked from Jean, to Charlie, to Jim, and smiled. "At least you know I'm in safe hands."

PART THREE: 1946

Chapter Eighteen:
January, 1946

In the quiet solitude of the early morning, Arty set down the book he had been reading and gazed out at the icy haze of fog around the lone street lamp. The gales of the previous few days had blown themselves out, leaving in their wake the sort of bitter frost that made one's fingers and toes feel as if they could be snapped off as easily as old twigs, but Arty wasn't cold. In Dalton Place, with its luxurious central heating and vast hearths in every room, it was almost impossible to feel the cold at all.

Back in 1930, Antonio Adessi had bought the three-storey house for a very good price, and the first thing he'd done was install the heating; the second thing he'd done was transport his entire library and art collection from his home in Florence. The third was to appoint Arty's sister as housekeeper, which was why Arty felt such an affinity for the house and, ultimately, was how Jean, Charlie and Jim had won him round when they took over his convalescence without his knowledge or involvement.

Whilst Arty's memories of Dalton Place were vivid and all-consuming, in reality his visits had been few and far between. Yet there was such wonder and magnificence within those walls, when viewed through the eyes of a child, and it had left a permanent mark on his soul. The sculptures, mostly vulgar, shapeless forms he could not identify, had impressed his younger self far less than the vast oil paintings of large, curvaceous women with skin like porcelain, which would enchant him for hours, while he considered who the subjects were, conjuring life stories for them in his mind. It would have been an interesting experiment to see how he perceived those sculptures and paintings now.

However, it was the library that had captured Arty's heart, for it was in that dim, brown, cluttered first-floor room he had discovered himself. In that room, amongst the words of scholars and artists, Arty had found others like him: men who loved men. And it was in that room, in the passionate heat of a chill October night, he and Jim had consummated their relationship.

Alas, Adessi's library had returned to Florence with him, and whilst the excessive hotness of Dalton Place spoke of how unbearable the English winter had been for the Italian, Arty doubted his sister was having the same trouble adjusting to the warm Florentine climate, particularly now she was reacquainted with her much-loved books. He missed Sissy dearly, but he did not begrudge her for following her heart. If six years of war had taught the world one thing, it was, alas, not as Arty had once believed. The Allies had won; they had liberated Europe. It was hard to claim that war solved nothing in the face of all the evidence. No, what six years of war had demonstrated beyond doubt was that somehow, some way, regardless of the death and destruction, life goes on, or as D H Lawrence once so eloquently wrote, 'We've got to live, no matter how many skies have fallen.'

There was little D H Lawrence in Arty's own library, which, in contrast to Adessi's, was quite meagre and staid, consisting of the books he had owned as a child, plus the few Sissy had gifted him over the years. Following his discharge from hospital, he had stayed with his parents for a few weeks, making it clear from the very start that he was moving to London, much to his mother's apparent relief. She was not the nurturing sort and had flown into an immediate panic, thinking she would have to spend the rest of her days supporting her invalid son. By the time Jean sent word that Dalton Place was habitable, Arty's mother had already helped him pack his belongings into two trunks, which his father helped Charlie to lift into the back of the van he had borrowed, and so began the next chapter of Arty's life...or almost.

Arty checked the time—not long to go now—and glanced down at the cover of his most recent acquisition: the book Sissy had given him for Christmas, entitled *Reflections in a Golden Eye*, by Carson McCullers. It was a slim volume, for which he was glad; he found it flat and depressing, but it had at least filled the sleepless hours of this final night of waiting: Jim's ship was due to dock mid-morning and by the evening they would be reunited. Arty shivered in anticipation and laughed quietly, not wishing to disturb Jean and Charlie, sleeping in the room above.

Glancing around his and Jim's bedroom, Arty finally allowed himself to anticipate what it would be like to share his nights with Jim. The double bed had felt too big and empty for him to appreciate its warmth and comfort; now, as he looked across from his window seat, he could almost see the two of them cuddled up, reading a book together, not that Jim was especially fond of books, but he had read to Arty in the hospital. And he'd written that ridiculous letter; thinking about it made Arty want to read it again, and he carefully eased himself to his feet, taking a moment to get the blood flowing properly before doing his best to tiptoe across the room—not the easiest thing to accomplish with no feeling in the tops of his feet.

Avoiding the creakiest floorboards, Arty reached his side of the bed and sat down, smiling as he remembered Jim's remark in his last letter about oiling the bedsprings. The bed didn't squeak, but apart from the night in the old library— now Jean and Charlie's kitchen—he and Jim had never shared a bed. Arty really hoped they would be testing it to its limits tonight. Or perhaps even before then. Jim's train was due in at four-fifteen—would it be too early to go to bed? Arty covered his mouth to stifle his embarrassed chuckle at the brashness of his thoughts.

So that Jim's letters were always close at hand, Arty kept them in his bedside cabinet, and he opened it and took out the entire bundle, fanning it across the bed. The seven months since Jim returned to the USA for demobilisation had been the longest and loneliest months of Arty's life, and from Jim's letters it was clear he was feeling it too. Since the previous summer, Jim had been back in West Virginia, waiting for his paperwork to be processed, and all was far from well. Jim's younger brother, Joshua, who was a civilian and thus under no obligation to go through demobilisation, had remained in London with his girlfriend, leaving Jim at their father's mercy and, by Joshua's account, the man had little to spare. He drank heavily and daily, and though neither brother ever used the word, it was clear their father was violent and lashed out at his wife and sons.

Knowing this, and also that Jim's mother had let slip about Jim to his father, caused Arty no end of worry, but there was nothing he could do. Molly—the matron who had cared for him after the accident and whom he now considered one of his dearest friends—kept ticking him off for worrying over things that were beyond his control. Not only was it pointless, she chastised, it was also dangerous to his health. Arty tried to argue that his blood vessels were all healed and he could worry as much as he jolly well liked, but Molly ignored him. It was true, as far as any doctor could tell: whilst the atrophy in his upper-leg muscles was a permanent debility and the drop foot could be a real nuisance, in all other ways Arty was back to full health. Indeed, he was confident that once the workshop was up and running he would be able to undertake the lighter jobs, and dared to believe that one day he would dance again.

Of course, Arty never wrote of his worries in his letters to Jim, instead updating him on progress with the house, his hopes for the future and reassurances that he loved and missed him. Nor did Jim mention any of the trouble going on with his father, but Arty sensed it in the words Jim chose. Although the two of them were the same height, Jim was so much bigger than Arty—broader at the shoulders, wider at the hips, more muscular, larger hands, thicker hair, a big laugh and that glorious deep baritone drawl. When he spoke he used big words—not long words, or clever words with complex meanings—but words that were open and confident, conveying his love, or his anger, or his joy. Jim was a strong man, not afraid to show his emotions, and when he entered a room, everyone felt his presence, but it was never threatening. He was a jolly, happy soul and peaceable, yet able stand up for himself if need be, as Charlie could testify.

And so it was that through those thirty-one letters, Arty could trace the ups and downs of Jim's every waking moment. The good days were littered with *I love yous*, sentences that started 'I'm so excited about…' and hilarious observations of the mundane, or tall tales of practical jokes he and his friends played on each other, where everything was 'real funny'. The sad days still had plenty of *I love yous*, but the excitement was absent, in its place 'I cannot wait…' and 'Today I missed…'. Then there were the letters written on the bad days, filled with factual accounts of what Jim had been up to—'fixed this', or 'helped out with that', and so on—and it was those letters that tore at Arty's heart, because the only time Jim contained his emotions was when they had the potential to overpower even the mighty-happy Jim Johnson.

That was how it had been when Arty was in hospital, and looking back to those first few weeks after the accident, Arty could only marvel at the patience Jim and their friends had shown him. So many times he had succumbed to dark, bleak thoughts, wishing he had died when the Wellington crushed his legs. Some of it was down to the excruciating pain and the accompanying frustration of learning to walk again. Mostly it was because of the burden he had become to those he loved, and the indignity of having other people tend to his personal care. All of it was selfish, he realised now, even though he'd tried to convince himself he was only thinking of Jim, or Jean, or whomever might be put under duress by his existence.

In that respect, his mother's aloofness had worked in his favour: rather than bathe and toilet her grown-up son, she had paid a woman called Gitel Kohn to come in and do it each morning. Gitel was a Jewish refugee whose husband had died in a concentration camp, and she spoke very little English, her favourite phrase being *nu gay shoyn*, which Arty assumed meant 'hurry up', as she usually shouted it when he was taking too long doing whatever he was doing. He couldn't complain or grumble, or, at least he could, but there was little point when Gitel understood barely a word he said. She didn't pander or fuss, she just did what was required and went on her way. In spite of the language barrier, the two had got along well, and when Arty departed for London, Gitel had been there to see him off; it had been a tear-free but nonetheless emotional farewell.

And so Arty had moved into Dalton Place, determined to be self-sufficient, and the adjustments to their living quarters made it possible for him to quickly recover his independence. Originally built for multiple occupancy, the building's three floors were identical in layout, each consisting of two large and two small rooms. Prior to it becoming Adessi's London residence, the house had been served by one outside toilet; however, Antonio had lived on the first floor, hence that was where he had put the bathroom. The kitchen and dining room had been located on the ground floor, which he'd used for entertaining guests and displaying his art collection, whereas the second floor had been little more than storage space for those pieces he had grown tired of, because, as Arty had always said, the house was far too big for one.

Now Dalton Place consisted of three self-contained apartments, one on each floor, and all equipped with a bathroom, kitchen, bedroom and sitting room. The apartments were modest, but of a good size, and Jean's mother, in a conspicuous display of her delight at Jean finding a husband, had given her a substantial sum towards the refurbishment. Once Jim was home it would be straight on with planning Jean and Charlie's wedding, and then getting the workshop up and running, or else they'd have nothing to live on.

Once Jim was home…

Arty sifted through the letters and found the one he knew would put a smile on his face to see him through the next twelve hours. Jim Johnson, attempting to write in the style of D H Lawrence: appalling, amusing, adorable.

My darling,

For some time now I have been filled with a restlessness that threatens to take over my very sensibility. It seeks out the very source and core of my innermost, closing in, like the soft, loose passion I sought and found that one sweet night with you.

I have feasted a thousand times on that memory, died a thousand deaths and in each I see you, as clearly as if you were lying right beside me, your sleek, slender body flushed with the colors of the rising sun, the sunset and all the seconds between.

Arty, I guess you know what I'm trying to say by now. I can't get you off of my mind. You complete me, if you get my drift. Maybe I shouldn't be telling you that.

We'll be together soon, though not soon enough. Until then—

All my love,
Jim

Chapter Nineteen:
January, 1946

As the train pulled into the station and drew to a stop, Arty's excitement mounted to the point where he thought he might be physically sick. The doors opened and passengers began to pour forth onto the platform. Arty frantically scanned the length of the train, terrified he might not spot Jim in amongst all those people. What a foolish notion that was, for the second he came into view everything else instantly ceased to exist. There was Jim and there was Arty, and an empty platform in between. Arty started moving towards Jim, at first taking firm, steady steps, each coming faster on top of the other, until he was limping at speed whilst muttering to himself to slow down. The space between them shrank and shrank and finally they were yards, feet, inches apart. Jim dropped his bag and threw his arms around Arty, sobbing into his ear.

"Oh God, it's so good to see you. I missed you so much."

"I missed you too," Arty cried back, otherwise left speechless by the wonder of being in Jim's arms again, trying to sniff back the tears and at once inhaling the familiar scent of the man he loved: the man who loved him. Everything that was ever wrong was suddenly so perfect and right.

"I'd kiss you, but I think they all might stare," Jim said, slowly releasing Arty but not quite letting go. Jim's gaze met his and then shifted up, down, side to side, as he took in Arty's features; Arty was doing the same, almost as if each needed to remind himself of what the other looked like, though it was more to satisfy a hunger born of seven months deprived of that which sustained them.

When they eventually harnessed the willpower to release each other, the platform was empty, with just the guard waiting for them to pass through the gate.

"Thanks so much," Jim acknowledged, receiving a curt nod from the guard.

"He's still watching us," Arty said out of the corner of his mouth as they reached the far side of the station concourse.

"Yeah. Trying to figure what a handsome guy like you sees in a hick like me."

"Yes, Jim. That's exactly what he's thinking."

"You know it." Jim laughed.

Having walked from home to the station, the walk back was a bit much for Arty, especially when he was trying to save himself for later, so they hailed a taxi. They pulled out onto the street, and Jim was instantly enthralled by all the work that had been done since he was last in London: the city was still in ruins, but clearance was well underway.

At the next junction, the cabbie glanced back at his passengers and grimaced out a toothless smile. "How are ya finding civvy life, fellas? Tough, innit?"

Arty nodded vaguely. Returning to life as a civilian hadn't really affected him the way it had others. In particular, the air crews were having quite a hard time trying to find their way in the world. Many had gone straight into the RAF with no trade behind them, although with all of the construction work and the efforts to get Britain's industries back up and running, the technicians and engineers were set for a good few years.

"It's good to be alive," Jim said belatedly. The cabbie peered over his shoulder and chuckled.

"Oh, blimey. A bloody Yank. Thought you lot would've had enough by now."

"England's a great country. Beautiful scenery," Jim looked Arty's way, "so much to see and do." He winked. Arty smiled and turned away.

"Yeah. It's not bad, is it?" the cabbie agreed. "So you come back for a girl?"

"Pretty much," Jim replied.

"You ain't got none over you way?"

"Oh, there's a few. But you got the pick of the crop over here."

The cabbie nodded smugly.

For a while, the journey progressed in silence, but as they reached the turning to Dalton Place they got caught in a traffic jam, granting the cabbie the opportunity to further interrogate Jim, not that he seemed to mind.

"So you got a job lined up, have ya?" he asked.

"Kinda. I'm going into partnership with a couple guys, including Arty here. See over yonder?" Jim pointed to the empty plot of land across from where they were idling in traffic. "We're setting up shop as mechanics."

"Oh, right. Interesting. I tell ya what, it'd be well worth asking around the cabbies. We're always on the lookout for a reliable mechanic, ya know what I mean? Fast, cheap, knows what they're doing. So what were ya? Navy?"

"Air forces."

"Both of ya?"

"Yes, sir."

"Well. Might I say, sir, it is indeed a privilege to have you in my cab. Your lot saved our lives, you did, flying low and chucking fags and candy our way. Got us through the war, that. We've got bugger all now, mind you."

Arty turned back and caught Jim's gracious smile. Even though the compliment was quite general in nature, it had still turned his cheeks a rather delightful shade of pink. Jim glanced in Arty's direction and quickly faced front again. Arty started to laugh; he couldn't help it, because he'd seen the twinkle in Jim's eyes. There was only one thing on his mind at that moment, and it wasn't accepting thanks on behalf of his fellow countrymen.

Another couple of minutes passed, in which Arty considered telling the cabbie to let them out where they were. They were within walking distance of Dalton Place, although he was also enjoying the build-up. Of course, Jim expected Jean to be there, waiting to greet him; he'd be preparing for the frustration of hours of catching up before he got what he'd hinted at in his saucy letter. However, Jean was going straight from work to visit friends, giving Arty and Jim time to themselves, and Arty had it all planned out—just as soon as he got Jim through that blesséd front door.

It wasn't much longer before the taxi made it to the house. Arty shoved a few bob into the cabbie's hand and told him to keep the change.

"Thanks, gov. Much appreciated," the man said.

Arty gave him a swift nod of acknowledgement and marched to the front door, key in hand. He heard the double toot of the taxi's horn as it pulled away, heard the click of the Zippo as Jim lit up, smelled the rich, familiar tobacco, felt the warmth of Jim's presence. He twisted the key and pushed the door open, giving Jim just long enough to clear the threshold before he grabbed his face with both hands, pushing the door shut with his hip at the same time, and he kissed him. None of that trying out a little peck like he might give his mother, or Sissy, or Jean. Seven months he'd waited, and he was going to get his fill of Jim Johnson.

Jim's bag slid from his shoulder and dropped. It may even have hit the floor. Right at that moment all Arty was aware of was the warm, wide palm against his back, the press of Jim's chest to his, the taste and smell of Jim filling his mouth and his nose. Arty devoured Jim, stole his breath and gave it back again, refused absolutely to stop even for Jim to extinguish the cigarette in his hand. Or maybe it was a pipe. Arty neither knew nor cared, he just...needed this. This kiss, like their very first in the hangar at Gaskell, was desperate, a promise of so much more to follow. But unlike that first kiss, the promise now was of a lifetime of kisses, of passion, of having Jim in his bed; a lifetime together, in love. *Oh yes—* Arty's feet might no longer have it in them to dance, but his heart knew every single step.

And then, just like that, the moment was rudely stolen from them by the one rival Arty had for Jim's affections. Only slightly disgruntled, Arty let go as, for the second time that day—which was no mean feat, bearing in mind he'd only left his train half an hour ago—Jim sobbed unabashedly, and it set Arty off too.

Jim fell to his knees and scooped up both cats, hugging them tightly to his chest. The two big toms put up no fight whatsoever. "Why didn't you say you brought them with you?" Jim asked.

"I thought I'd surprise you."

"You did that, all right," Jim said, laughing and crying at the same time. He sighed and kissed first Socks, and then Soot, on the head. "Every time I wrote I wanted to ask, but I was afraid I wouldn't like the answer." Jim looked up at Arty, tears streaming, yet he had the biggest, most brilliant smile on his face.

"I'll introduce you to Silky later," Arty said. At Jim's enquiring frown, he added, "She followed the boys home a few months back and decided to move in."

"Fellas! You got yourselves a lady?" Jim asked the cats, who purred in response. Always the more independent of the two, Soot decided he'd had quite enough fuss and jumped from Jim's arms, whilst Socks snuggled closer, pushing his head up against Jim's chin and growling loudly. Jim continued to stroke the cat and carefully stood up, leaning sideways into Arty. Jim's laughter was breathless and delighted.

"I'm here," he murmured, kissing Arty again, and again.

"Yes, you are," Arty replied between the kisses, attempting to wipe the tears from Jim's face. "And already Socks has stolen you from me."

"Yeah. He has, but he's fickle."

As proof of point, Socks decided he'd also had enough and pushed his front paws against Jim's chest—his way of asking to be released. Jim crouched slightly so that Socks could hop down to the floor, and straightened again. He took Arty into his arms.

"Can I show you how much I missed you?" he asked.

Jim's voice sounded against Arty's parted lips and he let out an involuntary groan. He pushed back against the hardness of Jim's body. "I have a fairly good idea," he said.

Jim gave another quiet, breathless laugh. "Where's the bedroom?"

Arty pointed past him, and Jim backstepped, allowing Arty to steer him down the hallway and into the bedroom.

"You oiled the springs?" he asked, still on the move.

"Mm," Arty sounded, refusing to break the kiss. Pausing long enough to shut and lock the bedroom door, he continued to walk Jim backwards across the room, until his legs contacted the end of the bed and his knees buckled. Arty pushed him onto his back and climbed on top of him.

"Careful not to put any strain on—"

"Don't you dare!" Arty warned. "You've only just walked through the door."

"Sorry, but are you sure you're up to—"

Arty used his mouth to silence Jim and grasped the advantage, reaching down to unbutton Jim's coat, and then unbuttoning his shirt, far too eager to get to bare skin to worry about fully removing either article. He sat back to get a better view, and Jim grabbed him by the wrists, flexing up as if to kiss him, but Arty had already seen it: the mark Jim was trying to conceal. He tugged his wrists free of Jim's grip and reached down, pulling back the blue-plaid shirt fabric and gently tracing with his fingertips the red welt that ran from Jim's navel, around his side and continued out of sight.

"Your father?" Arty uttered, already knowing the answer.

"It's only skin-deep."

"Jim, I—"

"Shhhh." Jim sat up, with Arty straddled across his lap, and pulled him close. "Truly, it's all surface. He's dead to me. Please let it go. Can you do that?"

Arty delayed a moment before nodding. It would take some effort to neutralise the gut-wrenching, ugly anger bubbling inside, but if it was what Jim wanted, he would do his best to never show it or mention it again.

Jim took the opportunity to wriggle out of his coat and shirt, uncovering his broad, muscular shoulders. Arty smoothed his palms over the taut, tanned skin, and his mind filled with all kinds of lustful thoughts, for the time being pushing aside his fury at Jim's father's brutality. Jim began to unfasten Arty's shirt, all the while gazing deep into his eyes.

"What are you afraid of?" he asked.

Arty tried to shrug it off. "Do you like the wallpaper?"

"It's real nice," Jim said, quickly dismissing Arty's attempt at distraction. "Talk to me. What are you afraid of?"

Arty bowed his head. "That I'm not the man I was last time you saw me undressed."

"Darlin', the last time I saw you undressed you had a knee the size of a pumpkin."

Arty conceded the point with a wry chuckle. "I'm doing really well, aren't I? All those able-bodied men out there, and—"

"*You* are all I need," Jim murmured, lifting Arty's chin so he could kiss him. "Now let's get these damn clothes off."

Arty slid from Jim's lap, watching steadily while Jim unfastened and removed both his trousers and the long johns underneath.

"It's mighty warm in here, ain't it?" Jim observed, kicking off his socks.

"Yes, it is. Jean insists on keeping the place like a furnace for my benefit."

"Then there's no need—" Jim stepped towards Arty, unclipped his braces and pushed his shirt over his shoulders, letting it slide to the floor "—for these." In a flash he unzipped Arty's trousers, and gave him a gentle push so that he fell onto the bed, flat on his back.

"I could've taken them off myself," Arty protested half-heartedly.

Jim whipped away Arty's trousers and kissed his way up, from Arty's ankle, to his knee, all along his thigh to the leg of his underpants. "Can you feel that?" he asked. Arty nodded soundlessly, quite overcome by Jim's boldness, for now he was studying the sheathed outline of Arty's penis. It was painfully turgid, aching for Jim's soothing touch. Too long had he needed it.

Jim glanced up briefly. He had such a wicked grin on his face it made Arty wonder what he was planning, not that he cared particularly, so long as ultimately it brought about their mutual satisfaction. Jim's fingers slid under the waistband of Arty's underpants; Arty put his head back and closed his eyes, focusing on the sensation of the fabric dragging down over the pulsing flesh, followed by hot breath and a touch so gentle it could almost have been imagined. He lifted his head again and cautiously opened one eye.

"You're kissing me...down there?"

Jim smiled and carried on. For a brief moment, certainly far less than a second, the word 'germs' entered Arty's mind, but the increased, all-encompassing, *hot* pressure rendered him defenceless. Already the sensation was building to the point of no return, and he gasped, unsure whether the urge to yell *stop* was strong enough to counter the desire to beg Jim to just keep doing what he was doing forever more. Jim made the decision for him; he withdrew, finished undressing Arty and lay beside him, running the tip of his index finger around Arty's lips.

"I been dreaming about doing that," he whispered. His eyelids were drooping, or lilting; Arty couldn't decide.

"You're tired," he said.

"Yeah, but I ain't ready for sleeping yet. How are your legs holding out?"

"Fine, so long as you don't expect me to do the jive."

"Aw, gee. That's exactly what I had in mind."

Arty laughed and rolled Jim onto his back, climbing on top of him again, but now they were naked, the sensual contact was more than either could stand. Arty reached over to his bedside cabinet, somehow flung the door open, and searched by touch for the tub of petroleum jelly he had bought under instruction. Jim's eyes widened.

"Is that for you-know-what?"

Arty nodded. "Matron's orders," he said very solemnly, and both of them burst into laughter. Jim's cheeks turned pink again.

"Well, I guess if anyone would know about these things..." he reasoned.

"That's what I thought," Arty agreed, unscrewing the palm-wide lid and setting it aside. "Although it'll make a heck of a mess of the bedspread."

Jim's eyebrows rose. "I never had you down as the decorative type, Arty Clarke. Wallpaper, bedspreads—did you stitch the drapes too?"

Now Arty blushed, because he had, in fact, hemmed the curtains. "They were too long," he justified.

"Uh huh?" Jim teased.

"When all those dirty thoughts have been dealt with, you might just appreciate how hard I've worked to turn this apartment into a home for us."

"Hey..." Jim reached up and cupped Arty's cheek with his hand. "I'm sorry, darlin'. It's been hard on you too, I know that. So, I guess..." He released Arty and scooped a large dollop of petroleum jelly out of the pot, watching Arty intently, seeking his permission—as if there were any chance of it not being granted.

Arty leaned across to set the pot on the bedside cabinet, and before he could move back, Jim's hand was between his thighs, slowly smearing the jelly over places that were even more sensitive than usual. How fortuitous the accident had not numbed him there, though he would have given himself to Jim regardless. Perhaps, considering Jim's prone position, Arty was taking, not giving, but either way the end result would be the same.

With the clear grease on his hands, Jim was struggling to get a firm grip on himself and had to leave Arty to make the adjustments. His legs were aching a little, but he refused to be thwarted. He lifted and aligned their bodies, recalling acutely the exquisite pain of their first and only time. Hoping for more of the 'exquisite' and less of the pain, he slowly lowered his hips and felt a hot jab of discomfort—nothing compared to all he had endured in hospital. Lower still, with the slippery jelly easing their joining, Arty's body accepted Jim, expanding to accommodate, welcoming, becoming whole.

"Sweet Jesus," Jim hissed. For a moment his eyes rolled in his head, and Arty felt triumphant. No matter now the damage inflicted on his body. How insignificant was the mourning of his waltzing days, and how quickly those seven months diminished in the immediacy of this connection. Arty's hips rose and fell of their own accord; he was a finely-tuned engine, sleek and smooth, superior and indefatigable with Jim at the controls, giving it more throttle, and more still, until he was soaring high above the clouds. He needed more, and he took it.

"Allow me." Jim's voice came into focus, and his hand firmly grasped Arty's by-now throbbing penis. He tugged to the tempo Arty set, ever-quickening, barely sustainable, with Jim's body rising to meet his and finally turned rigid but for the pulsating that Arty felt within, and then without, as his own orgasm was torn from him, and it was tremendous, long-lived, worth every second of waiting. Better still, until that moment, as the sensation dwindled, he'd spared not a thought for Lady Chatterley's many absurd crises.

"Damn D H Lawrence," he said, laughing at himself.

Jim laughed too, a drowsy, deep rumble. "I figured he'd show up sometime," he said. Without prompting, Jim held Arty by the hips and assisted his movement so that he could...*dismount*, he supposed. He collapsed onto the bed and rooted out the small towel, kept from when his body had been overwrought with infections and fevers. With a clumsy care, he wiped away the worst of the sticky greasiness, threw the towel to the floor and nestled close to Jim. Reunited with his lover, Arty was finally at peace.

Chapter Twenty:
January, 1946

That first night Jim was back in England he was fit for nought: after he and Arty had welcomed each other, they slept until seven o'clock, when Arty heard the communal front door close, followed by Jean and Charlie's not-so-hushed voices. Arty lay still and silent, or as still as he could when he was shivering, naked and in a tangle of limbs. He placed a light kiss on Jim's cheek and quietly spoke his name. Jim stirred with a groan and folded his arms around Arty, pulling him close.

"Jean and Charlie are home," Arty whispered.

"So soon?" Jim said, stretching but otherwise doing little to suggest he would be getting up from the bed any time soon. Arty tickled his back, which made him wriggle and grin; still he didn't shift.

"You at least need to go and say hello," Arty reasoned.

Jim took a deep breath, released it as a reluctant sigh and…stayed put. Arty poked him in the side, prepared to do it again if need be, but the effect was immediate. Jim rolled away and sat on the edge of the bed, his back turned. Arty cringed, for now he realised he had just poked the welt he wasn't allowed to mention—the welt he could now see was caused by a whip and extended diagonally across the full width of Jim's back.

Oblivious, Jim stretched again and yawned. "All right, you win," he said, wearily rolling to the side of the bed. "But first I need to wash up."

"I can run you a bath," Arty offered.

"We got a shower?"

"Yes."

"I can have a bath another day. Which way to the bathroom?"

Arty got up and fetched his and Jim's dressing gowns—he had purchased a full wardrobe of clothing on Jim's behalf—and led him to the bathroom, where he set the shower running for him. On his way back to the bedroom to wait out his turn, a knock came at the door to the apartment. Knowing it would be Jean, Arty answered it.

"Good evening," Jean greeted, eyeing his attire. She raised a pencilled eyebrow and grinned. "He got home safely, I take it?"

Arty grinned back at her. "Oh yes, he did. He's just having a wash. Shall we come up to you when we're ready?"

"Perfect." Jean gave him a swift embrace and stepped off towards the stairs. "There's no rush," she called back over her shoulder.

Arty gave her a stern look and she winked at him before continuing on her way. Arty closed the door and returned to the bedroom, wondering if he'd always feel so self-conscious about people knowing what he and Jim got up to. There again, it was only Jean, and hadn't she been the instigator in all of this? Perhaps it was no more than after so long apart, being reunited had heightened all of his emotions, because he was feeling overly affected by everything. Silky's kittens were due any day, yet it had not occurred to him that anything could go wrong. Now his mind insisted on revisiting the loss of Socks and Soot's brother, and he was once again in mourning for the tiny boy who didn't make it.

After seven months of waiting, the last week of which he'd spent constantly fretting over gales and other unfavourable conditions reported in the shipping forecast, Arty was emotionally drained. He had long ago been ready to embark on their life together. Planning all of the things they would do was what got him through their time apart, first at Minton, then in hospital and finally when Jim was waiting on his immigration papers. Now the much-anticipated elation was being tempered by the requirement that he forget about Jim's father's parting gift to his son. Even if Arty hadn't promised to let it go, it would do no good to raise the matter again, for it was one of the unspeakables, the stuff Jim simply could not give voice to, which, Arty rationalised, was no bad thing.

Corporal R. T. Clarke is a thinker and a dreamer—Jim's words from the first time he caught Arty daydreaming echoed often in his mind, for what Jim had said was true: Arty had always been a thinker and a dreamer. Chasing butterflies, absorbing himself in tales of romance and adventure, learning to dance…were it not for the war he likely would have followed his father into academia, pursued the life of the 'well-to-do intelligentsia' with which D H Lawrence had been so enamoured, and to which Antonio Adessi belonged. In those circles, being homosexual was not a norm as such, though it was accepted as part of the nature of man and, to a lesser extent, woman. It occurred to Arty that where reason was granted the opportunity to prevail, little significance was placed on how one might behave in private.

Perhaps, then, given time and the social insurance scheme the government was instituting, reason might eventually prevail over society as a whole, for it was very difficult to think grand thoughts with an empty belly and nowhere to call home. Or perhaps it was just wishful thinking, more Arty Clarke pipe dreams, but how wonderful to imagine that the conversation he and Jim would be having with Jean and Charlie that evening might one day be in preparation of their own marriage. Who would they invite? Jean and Charlie, of course, Sissy and Antonio, Molly and Daphne, Joshua and his girlfriend Louisa, Jim's mother—what story would they tell Jim's father? And who would bear the brunt of his wrath then?

He had been so deep in thought that only when Jim cleared his throat did Arty notice he was no longer alone. Jim remained just inside the doorway, his usually neat blonde hair darker for its wetness and sticking out in all directions from being vigorously rubbed with a towel. His eyes, ringed by fatigue, studied Arty with a deep, probing intensity that had clearly seen past the heroic shield of indifference he had almost succeeded in raising. Jim shrugged and offered a defeated smile.

"Go take a shower, darlin', and I'll tell you what you need to know."

Arty walked over to Jim and took his hands. "You don't need to tell me anything."

"I do, for you to let it be." Jim kissed him on the forehead, his lips lingering awhile, his warm breath lifting Arty's hair and setting off new shivers of desire. "Go shower," Jim repeated, "then we'll talk."

"All right," Arty agreed. He stepped past Jim, out into the hallway. "Your clothes are in the four-drawer chest."

"*My* clothes?"

"I hope they fit. Charlie said you and he were a similar size, so I took his word for it."

Jim squared his shoulders and stood tall. "Charlie's shorter than me."

178

"An inch, if that."

"And…scrawnier," Jim added with a grin. Arty raised his eyes and continued on his way. "But you're mine," Jim added as an afterthought.

"Yes, I am," Arty called back as he shut the bathroom door. He opened it again. "You still here?"

"Yeah. Why?"

"Just checking." Arty smiled to himself. *Jim's home.* He left the door ajar and turned the shower tap.

***

Arty returned from the bathroom with renewed resolve, strengthened further by Jim's caginess, which betrayed the mental anguish he was going through just thinking of his father, let alone talking about him.

"Arty…"

"No, love. It's all right. I can let it be, but at least let me help you heal." Arty went to his bedside cabinet and took out a small, round tin. "Take off your shirt."

"I just put the thing on," Jim protested, though he was already unbuttoning it. Arty approached, his fingers coated in pink ointment. Jim eyed him nervously. "What's that?"

"Germolene. It's antiseptic," Arty explained as he lightly applied it along the mark on Jim's chest. "Arm up," he instructed. Jim complied.

"Smells like root beer."

"Root beer?"

"You ain't heard of root beer?"

"Can't say I have. Is it nice?"

"Kids seem to like it, though it's too sweet for me. I'd rather have a real beer. Never thought I'd say this, but I missed English beer."

"There's a pub up the street. We can go for a pint, if you like. Not now—once you're rested. There you go. All done."

179

Arty moved away and replaced the lid on the tin of Germolene.

"Thanks." Jim put his shirt back on, avoiding eye contact. Now they were in a room with proper lighting, all of the other marks on Jim's back were obvious, and he would have known Arty had seen them.

Once Arty was dressed, he held out his hands to Jim and pulled him up from the bed. "Are you ready?" he asked.

Jim frowned. "You really ain't gonna say nothing?"

Arty considered for a moment. "I'll just say this: by helping you heal, I don't just mean slapping ointment on your cuts and bruises."

"I don't understand."

Arty kissed Jim's chin, nose, lips. "I mean, Jim Johnson, the scars are in here." He smoothed his hand over Jim's hair.

"I told you, he's dead to me."

"Yes, you did, and however you choose to grieve for him I'm right beside you."

In spite of the tears welling, Jim held Arty's gaze. He smiled and whispered, "Thank you."

Arty sighed in mock frustration and grabbed Jim around the head, pulling him close and delivering a noisy kiss to his ear. "Shall we go and see Jean and Charlie?" he suggested.

Jim nodded against Arty's shoulder. He slowly withdrew and allowed Arty to lead him by the hand from the bedroom, along the hallway—

"I love you," Jim said.

"I love you too," Arty replied.

—out of the door to their apartment and up the stairs. Arty knocked on Jean and Charlie's door; Jim sniffed the air a couple of times. "Mm. Something smells good."

"Ah, hell. It never even crossed my mind. I bet you're famished."

"I am a little. You eaten?"

"Not since…" While Arty was pondering, the door opened.

"Hello, hello," Charlie said, holding out his hand for Jim to shake and then drawing him in for an embrace and a slap on the back. He released him and both men gave each other a nod. "How was the crossing? All right?"

"Yeah, not bad at all. You're looking well, Charlie."

"Likewise. Come in." Charlie walked back along the hallway, and Jim and Arty followed. "We're in here," Charlie said, veering off into the sitting room, where Jean quickly swiped at the mantelpiece with her sleeve and spun on the spot to face the men.

"Jim." She crossed the room at the same time as he did so that they met in the circle of light being cast by the lampshade above, where they hugged warmly. "It's wonderful to have you home," she said tearfully. She took a step away and kept hold of his arms while she studied him. He smiled.

"Believe me, it's good to be home," he said, glancing back at Arty.

A tingle ran down Arty's spine, and he suppressed a gasp. Though the evidence was right in front of him, he kept having to remind himself that Jim was really here; not a dream, not wishful thinking, but in the flesh and large as life—and with a very empty belly, which was rumbling loudly. Arty shifted his attention to Jean. "Were you about to have dinner?" he asked.

"We've already eaten? Haven't you."

"Er, no," Arty said, his face heating up as his mind flashed back to what Jim had been doing earlier.

Jean gave him a knowing look, and he started to sweat. She laughed. "There's plenty of leftovers. Rabbit stew and dumplings," she said, already on her way out of the room. "Do you want some, Arty?"

"Please," Arty called after her. "I'll come and give you a hand." He didn't wait for a response and quickly followed her to the kitchen, closing the door behind him. Jean put the pan of leftovers on the stove to warm, brushing her hands together as she turned back and looked at Arty expectantly.

"Do you remember me telling you what Joshua said about their father?"

Jean nodded and moved to the table in front of the window, where she sat and lit a cigarette, and waited for Arty to join her. "What about it?" she asked.

"He's…" Arty frowned and leaned back, watching the smoke drift up and fan out across the ceiling. He sighed. "Don't get me wrong, Jean, I've had my fair share of clips 'round the earhole from my old man, although it was Mum we had to watch out for—you'd think you'd got away with it and then she'd catch you with a backhander on your way past."

Jean smiled. "Oh, my mother was just the same, and she'd always follow it up with a remark about us being lucky Dad wasn't around, or we'd have been getting it with the belt, not that she needed a belt. Her hands were tough as old leather as it was." Jean laughed and Arty joined in. She didn't talk much about her family: her mother wasn't short of money, although her father was dead before Jean was old enough to remember him, and her brother had died from tuberculosis. She'd never mentioned how old he was, but the stories involving him stopped long before adulthood and telling them always left Jean quiet and thoughtful, so Arty didn't like to ask.

"How bad is it?" Jean asked.

"He's been lashed with a whip, quite a few times. He doesn't want to talk about it, which I completely understand. He must be worried sick about leaving his mother."

Jean put her cigarette in the ashtray and went to stir the pan. "He'll tell you when he's ready."

"Maybe," Arty said doubtfully. It wasn't how Jim was, but with both sons now living in London, Arty could see their mother joining them at some point in the not-too-distant future. By Jim and Joshua's accounts, she was a tough old bird, and now there was little to keep her in West Virginia. Indeed, from the stories Joshua told, it sounded like she gave as good as she got, so they might yet end up harbouring a murderess.

Jean brought him back from his thoughts by setting a plate of steaming-hot stew in front of him. She called through to Jim, who arrived a few seconds later, still looking just as tired, although his eyes widened enthusiastically at the sight of the food. He sat opposite Arty and tucked right in, shovelling several spoonfuls of stew into his mouth before he mumbled his thanks to Jean.

"No thanks needed. See you when you've finished." She left them and returned to the sitting room, the sound of the radiogram momentarily drifting through to the kitchen when she opened the door.

"Charlie was about to show me his Bing Crosby records," Jim explained.

Arty groaned. "You'd best have a few hours left in you."

Jim just smiled and continued eating. He was positively voracious, and he'd cleared the bowl before Arty was even halfway through his, at which point he watched Arty eat, whilst licking his lips hungrily, or salaciously, Arty couldn't quite decide, but it made him laugh. He pushed the bowl across to Jim, who ungraciously accepted and emptied it in less than a minute. Arty shook his head in wonder.

"Didn't they feed you on the ship?"

"Yeah, but not much. And anyway I used it all up earlier, so I figured I ought to refuel." Jim grinned mischievously.

"Hm. We'd best get on with it," Arty said. He took their empty bowls over to the sink, and he and Jim went through to join Jean and Charlie.

"What do you think of the place, Jim?" Jean asked, handing him a glass with a half-inch of golden liquid in the bottom. Jim sniffed it and nodded his approval.

"Bourbon?"

"A gift from your Joshua," Charlie said.

"That'd explain it. Cheers." Jim held up his glass and waited for the other three to do the same in celebration of both his safe return and Jean and Charlie's pending nuptials. When the toast was made, Jim answered Jean's question with a vague, "I'll let you know what I think of the place tomorrow, when I can see a little better."

Jean affectionately brushed her hand down Jim's arm. "We just wanted to welcome you home, Jim. We know you're shattered, and the wedding arrangements can wait."

"Nah, don't you worry about me. When's the big day?"

"We were thinking late May," Jean said. "But that's all I'm telling you tonight. Drink your whisky and get to bed."

Jim laughed and mock-saluted. "Yes, Ma'am," he said, letting his arm fall from the salute to Arty's shoulders. Jean made eye contact with Arty, and they both smiled.

Soon after that, Arty and Jim bid good night to Jean and Charlie, with a tentative arrangement in place for the four of them to head over to the prospective workshop site the following day. Arty fed the cats, which wasn't the easiest task with Jim's arms around him, and Silky wasn't impressed by Jim at all, although he was all compliments for the smoky-grey tortoiseshell with her fine, sleek coat and polished jade eyes. She ate her dinner and slinked past him into the hallway, where she loitered outside the sitting room, mewing loudly for someone to open the door. Jim went and opened it for her and she shot him a killer glare.

"Hey, girlie, you already got two guys. This one's mine."

She hopped up onto the armchair and set about cleaning her face, taking furtive glances his way.

"Once she gets to know you she's very loving," Arty said on Silky's behalf.

"She's doing what any pregnant lady would do."

"Yes, I suppose. Right, come on, you. Bedtime." On those words, Arty grabbed Jim with one hand, switched off the lights with the other and led the way to the bedroom. No horseplay: between exhaustion and relief, they needed nothing more than to cuddle up under the cosy blankets, safe and no longer alone.

So began their life together.

Chapter Twenty-One:
January–April, 1946

Now Jim was back, the workshop progressed very quickly indeed. The plot of land, once occupied by a large townhouse and substantial grounds, was more than big enough for their needs, but money was tight. Arty had borrowed a significant sum from his parents to fund the construction of a corrugated aluminium workshop with an inspection pit and just enough space to work on two vehicles at a time. He was glad he was able to contribute financially; he still had a long way to go in his recovery, which meant Jim would be doing most of the work for the time being. Arty planned to help out wherever he could, but they weren't banking on his labour: at such time as the business could sustain two wages, Charlie was going to leave the railways and join them.

They weren't expecting miracles, of course. London was still on its knees, and the few people wealthy enough to own private cars were in no hurry to return to a city in ruins when they had the luxury of remaining in their country homes. The bus company had its own mechanics, although the taxi driver's tip-off proved to be a good one, as Jim found out when Arty sent him to distribute the flyers he'd made. Poor Jim was gone for hours, and he returned home so drunk it was the next day before he was sober enough to explain that nearly every cabbie he met wanted to share their hip flask and their story. It was good for building relations, so Jim couldn't really refuse even though he wasn't much of a drinker. Arty found it highly amusing, but kept his laughter to himself—mostly—and instead spent the day looking after Jim as if he had a fever rather than a hangover.

***

At first, the jobs coming in—almost all of which were taxis, thus had to be done at lightning speed—were few and far between, and the workshop was bitterly cold. It made Arty's legs ache, but they needed to keep the place manned, so he brought an old eiderdown over from the house. It was just like the old days back in the disused hangars, wrapped up together, talking about anything and everything—politics, Jean and Charlie's wedding, the late return of soldiers whom everyone had assumed were lost. Charlie's older brother had returned from Belgium the previous spring, and he was doing well, all things considered. Alas, there had been no news from Arty's Uncle Bill in over two years, and they had long ago accepted he wasn't coming home, but there was that tiny, impossible glimmer of hope found in stories like the one Jim told of the two men from his hometown.

Having grown up together, George and Roy enlisted with the same unit and the two GIs were inseparable. Jim had always known they were more than good pals, and when George was captured by Japanese troops, Roy also surrendered. They were taken to a POW camp in December 1944 and escaped in February 1945. Unaware that their camp had been liberated just days after their escape, the two men trekked across Japan, taking shelter in derelict buildings, until they found a sympathetic farmer who let them stay in his goat shed but refused to help them any further. They survived on goat's milk, 'stolen' from the goat every night, resulting in rage and confusion from the farmer every morning when he discovered his goat was dry, and he never did work out why.

Eventually George and Roy made it to the border and found passage back to the USA, arriving a good three months after everyone else, fully expecting to be welcomed as heroes, although it was safe to say they were no more *compos mentis* than the poor Japanese farmer whose goat they had repeatedly milked dry. Nonetheless, they deserved better than the mocking reception that greeted them. They were honest young men, but they weren't astute enough to even understand what the war was about, let alone that their commitment to each other would result in a 'less than honourable' discharge: the dreaded blue papers that denied them their GI rights.

Jim was livid and powerless to assist without jeopardising his own situation. He had already mentioned in his letters to Arty that he had joined an association set up by a handful of homosexual veterans who had been served blue discharge papers. Jim didn't care about the dishonourable discharge, but nothing was going to get in the way of him being with Arty, and so he'd waited until he reached London before writing to George and Roy, telling them to get in touch with the association.

Jim, like Arty, had always been politically minded. It was a commonality they'd discovered in the early days of their relationship, when they'd spent hours discussing the war, the decisions their respective governments were making, their beliefs about equality, and so on. On almost all counts their opinions coincided; all but one, in fact, although Arty concluded it was more cultural than personal.

When the American airmen first arrived, it was like hot air blasting through the cool stoic ranks of the RAF. For where the British struggled to squeeze out a polite 'how do you do?' and talked of 'missing Mother dreadfully', the Americans offered hugged declarations of 'I love ya, buddy' and cried unabashedly over everything from missing their families to losing a girl.

All considered, Jim wasn't so different. He wanted to be open about his homosexuality, and he was prepared to take whatever punishment came from being so, but for Arty's benefit he kept quiet and reined in any public displays of affection.

In truth, since the accident, Arty had slowly been coming round to Jim's point of view, although the change in his thinking began in earnest the day he told Charlie. What Arty had expected at best was that Charlie would keep it to himself and their friendship would be ruined. Indeed, even imagining Charlie might respect him for his honesty had seemed overly optimistic a year ago. It took a while, but Charlie had accepted it, and he and Arty were as close as they had ever been, with the rivalry between Jim and Charlie mostly effected in jest, although they did almost come to blows when the kittens were born. It all came down to a misunderstanding of intention: Arty and Jim had decided they were keeping the kittens, which Charlie interpreted as meaning neither could go through with disposing of them, and he offered in good faith to take care of it on their behalf. Arty had never seen Jim so angry, and he was all for giving Charlie a reminder of the pulping he got the last time.

After a few days of silent seething and ignoring each other, the two men made their peace, although Silky showed no appreciation whatsoever for Jim's valour, leading him to joke glibly that the cat was even more vicious than his pop. Arty cringed inwardly and said nothing; it was the first time since returning to England that Jim had mentioned his father. He didn't ask after him in letters to his mother, nor did she report back on his well-being or lack thereof. Likewise, whenever Joshua visited or they went over to his and Louisa's place, any conversation about home steered well clear of talking about their father. To all intents and purposes, Jimmy Johnson Senior was already dead and buried.

Joshua and Louisa were just two of the many visitors they had to Dalton Place. Molly and Daphne would call in whenever they were in town, and Jean had become pally with a few of the girls from the accounting firm she had been working for since the previous autumn. Having run her own office, Jean found it tedious being told what to do by someone who knew far less than she did. He was in charge simply because he was a man, and discussions could get very heated when all of the women descended on Dalton Place at the same time. Some of Jean's co-workers had lost jobs elsewhere when the men came home, and their present employer was under pressure to sack them, but he couldn't afford to pay men, so for the time being their jobs were safe.

The end of the war had brought to the forefront many aspects of life that had previously gone unquestioned, and the conversations at Dalton Place would often carry on late into the night, covering everything from the appalling treatment of black GIs in the USA, a lot of whom were served blue papers for no other reason than the colour of their skin, to the expectation that women on both sides of the Atlantic would readily return to their home-making duties now their husbands were home. If Molly and Daphne were involved, the discussion would veer towards the treatment of homosexuals, during which Jim listened quietly rather than risk breaking his promise to Arty, but it couldn't go on. Before the war, Jim had been a union man, and it was not in his nature to sit back and quietly accept injustice. He was used to fighting on other men's behalf for better treatment, fairer pay. Now he wanted to fight for himself, and he was left prostrate by his duty to protect Arty.

After one particularly late night, when Molly and Daphne had finally gone home, Arty sat on the end of the bed and leaned down to take his socks off, all the while aware of Jim's restless pacing. The evening had involved a rather distressing discussion of homosexual POWs being made to serve their full prison sentences, with no reduction for their time as Hitler's guests, and even Arty was outraged.

"I'm gonna make cocoa," Jim said, heading for the door. "I ain't gonna sleep well tonight. You want some?"

"Please," Arty confirmed to Jim's disappearing form, and as he listened to him banging around the kitchen, he realised he had about five minutes to reach the biggest decision of his life: stay silent, or stand up and be counted.

As things stood, no one batted so much as an eyelid at the pair of them sharing an apartment. It was quite ordinary for men to share the cost of rent and no doubt many shared a bed simply because needs must. And whilst Arty had vowed never to deny what he and Jim had, no one had asked the question. However, the second Jim spoke out, or became involved in any kind of political activity, the rumours would abound and everyone would know the truth. If Jim was *that way*, then so was Arty, but he didn't care what people thought. He loved Jim with all his heart. He admired him, and he was proud of him—how patiently he cared, how hard he worked to turn his ambitions into reality, how handsome, and kind, and honest—to Arty, Jim was perfection itself. Jim was prepared to sacrifice his freedom to fight for what was right: to start another war. *Yet we are already among the ruins. How many more skies must fall?*

Arty had barely survived the last war, and he was terrified—not of losing his liberty, but of losing Jim. It was a no-win situation: force Jim to suffer a life of silence and watch as he slowly lost his spirit, or release him from his promise and risk incarceration and a life apart.

"Are you praying, darlin'?"

Arty startled and opened his eyes. He laughed quietly. With his palms pressed together and eyes closed in deep contemplation he could see how it would have looked like he was praying. "I've been thinking," he said.

"About?" Jim left a cup of cocoa on Arty's bedside table and walked around to his own side of the bed. Once again, he was avoiding Arty's gaze.

"I'll stand by you," Arty said. Silence followed, and Arty swivelled to face Jim. "If you want to fight, I will be there, at your side."

"I promised you."

"And I promised I'd never deny us. But that's exactly what I've been doing."

"We're partners, Arty."

"We are," Arty agreed, "and yet it's always you making the compromises. I think it's about time I met you halfway, don't you?"

Jim ran his hand through his hair and studied Arty for a moment. "You realise if people know about me, they'll know about you?"

"I don't care about that. I love you, Jim. I'm honoured that you want to share your life with me, especially after the accident. I wouldn't have blamed you for walking away, but you didn't. And you ask for so little in return. I'm scared, I'll admit it, but not so scared that it gives me the right to stand in your way."

"I can try to—" Jim began, but Arty glared at him. Jim shrugged. "I'm just trying to keep you safe."

"I know." Arty smiled, grateful for Jim's continued attempts to protect him, although not so much for his stubbornness. It was hard enough to see this through without being given a dozen escape routes. "What better way is there to keep me safe than by changing the world?"

"Jeez, Arty. When you say it like that it sounds impossible."

Arty laughed. "Not for you, love."

"I appreciate your vote of confidence," Jim said. He chewed his lip pensively for a moment and then sat down on his side of the bed. "I figure there's more folks like me and Mol out there who wanna put their shoulder to the wheel, but how do we find 'em? That's the thing. I guess we start with Molly's contacts, and then? I don't know. Friends of friends, maybe, or people who went to jail, or..." Jim continued to gabble at speed, thinking aloud whilst he untied his shoes, undressed and put on his pyjamas, pausing every so often to ponder on something he was saying. Meanwhile Arty also changed into his pyjamas and climbed into bed. By the time Jim's monologue was winding to a close, Arty's cup was empty.

"...and we're gonna need a place to meet. Could be a problem." Jim got into bed and took Arty's hand. "Are you really all right with this?"

Arty sighed in exasperation. "I wouldn't have said it if I wasn't. And I know somewhere you can meet."

"You do?" Jim looked at Arty doubtfully. Arty nudged him with his elbow.

"Hey! Who found the hangars? And, might I add, in less than a week."

"Yeah, all right. So where'd you have in mind?"

"Upstairs."

"I thought you and Jean were planning to rent it out."

That was true: when Jim was still in America, Jean and Arty had discussed sub-letting the top-floor apartment to bring in a little extra income. However, Jean had suggested it would be better to leave it empty and make it appear that

Jim lived there, just in case any trouble came their way. Arty hadn't mentioned it to Jim, knowing he'd be against the idea but would have gone along with it for Arty's sake. The apartment, therefore, was still empty.

"I'll talk to Jean about it after the wedding," Arty said. "I don't think she'll mind." In fact, knowing her as he did, he was confident she'd be all for it, once the wedding was out of the way.

***

In the final run-up to the day, Jean and Charlie alternated between attending the local church and driving up to Jean's home parish to hear the banns being read. It only took a couple of hours to get there by car, and so Jean drove there and Charlie drove back. When it came to the wedding itself, Jean's mother invited the four of them to stay with her for the weekend, and she could easily accommodate them: the McDowell residence made Dalton Place seem like a tiny hovel. However, the cats were now accustomed to being looked after, and everyone they knew in London was going to the wedding, so they weren't sure what to do, until their next-door neighbour, Mrs. Greene, overheard them discussing it and offered to keep an eye on the cats for them.

"That's very kind of you," Jim said.

"We don't want to put you to any trouble," Arty countered. What he meant was he didn't want Mrs. Greene rooting through the apartment, in case she put two and two together.

"Oh, it's no trouble at all." Mrs. Greene smiled and patted Arty on the arm. Keeping her hand there, she leaned closer and added, "Makes no odds to me what you do in your own home, son." She gave his arm a squeeze and released him. "So there's seven of the little so-and-sos, is there?"

"Er…yes," Arty confirmed, blinking in shock.

"Right. What I'll do is, the day before the wedding, I'll call round. You can show me where everything is and give me a key. Bob's your uncle." With that, she waddled back home, went inside and shut the door.

Arty turned to Jim and stared at him, speechless. Jim laughed and slung his arm around Arty's shoulders. "Guess so long as you ain't causing trouble, folks around here really don't care."

"No," Arty said with a doubtful frown. "I guess not."

Chapter Twenty-Two:
May, 1946

Waiting in the atrium of Mrs. McDowell's fine country home, Arty was reminded less of D H Lawrence and more of Jane Austen. The house was splendid, with almost too much sunlight cascading through every window, bleaching every surface to a dazzling pastel hue. Upon the walls were mirrors, so many mirrors, in fact, that there was no direction one could turn in order to avoid one's reflection. Arty caught a glimpse of himself in the ornately etched oval glass to the left of the front door; he straightened his waistcoat and tugged his cuffs down past the sleeves of his morning suit. The grandfather clock chimed a quarter to the hour: bride's prerogative or not, Charlie would soon be having kittens of his own.

"How do I look?"

Arty turned to the sound of Jean's voice, watching in awe as she slowly descended the wide staircase, one hand keeping a tight grip of the banister rail, the other obscured by a swathe of white satin skirt draped over her arm so that she didn't trip, revealing slender legs, the top of one pale stocking top also in view. Not that it mattered: the others had already left for the church, and Arty had seen Jean's legs plenty of times during the past two years.

Reaching the atrium, she stopped a few feet away and adjusted her skirt. The gown was stunning, with a heart-shaped bodice encrusted with small pearls, the V accentuating Jean's narrow waist, although it wouldn't be narrow for much longer.

"You are the most beautiful woman in the world, Jean," Arty said most sincerely, aware of the quiver in his voice that gave away how emotional he was. Jean met his gaze, her eyes shiny with brimming tears, and he smiled. "No tears today, my wonderful friend." He crooked his arm and held it out for her to take, which she did, and they departed, arm in arm, through the wide front door.

"Am I late enough, do you think?" Jean asked as they carefully stepped down from the porch onto the path.

Arty nodded. "I'd say so."

"Good." Jean grinned mischievously.

The chauffeur was waiting by the open door of the enormous wax-sheened Bentley. He took off his hat and bowed to Jean.

"Thank you," she quietly acknowledged.

Arty held up the train of her wedding gown while she clambered indelicately over the Bentley's high sill and attempted to turn and sit down without creasing her skirt. Once she'd organised the yards of fabric into a heap on her lap, Arty climbed in beside her, trying not to show any indication that he was in pain. It was nothing sinister, just the usual ache in his legs made worse by having been on his feet all morning. The chauffeur closed the door; a moment later he appeared in the driver's seat and glanced over his shoulder.

"All set, Madam?"

"Yes, I think—" Jean gasped. "My bouquet!"

Arty groaned. "Where is it?" he asked, already halfway out of the car.

"On the draining board."

He went back to the house and collected the bouquet, which he had helped Jean to choose because she said she knew nothing about flowers; he'd opted for dusk-pink tea roses nestling against a backdrop of tiny white gypsophila. He lifted the flowers to his nose and inhaled deeply, momentarily intoxicated by the sweet scent of his favourite bloom, his mind filling with memories of summer days long past, chasing butterflies around the garden of his childhood home, while Sissy sheltered in the shade of her parasol, supposedly minding him from behind her book. She'd been invited to the wedding, and she was honoured, but made her apologies; it was only a few months since she had made the arduous trip across Europe to be with Antonio, and she was not keen to make it again.

"Are you sure that's everything?" Arty asked Jean on his return to the car.

"Yes," she confirmed with a smile, taking the posy from him. Once he was seated, she hooked her arm through his, musing aloud, "Let's hope Walter hasn't lost the rings."

"Funny you should say that. I was thinking the same thing about Charlie."

Jean squeezed Arty's arm and gave a tiny squeal of excitement. "I'm so glad we're doing this together," she said.

Arty took her hand in his. "Me too."

For the rest of the short journey to the parish church, they shared memories of their time at Minton, in particular the nights at the Palais, watching the USAAF airmen show off, concurring that Jim was one of the worst offenders. Fortunately for him, he had the moves to pull it off, and he was so charming he rarely offended anyone. In fact, out of all the Minton personnel there was only ever Charlie who disliked him, but that was all water under the bridge now. If business continued to grow at the same rate as it had so far, within the month Jim and Charlie would be working side by side again, and it was apparent that they were both, secretly, looking forward to it. For all of their past antagonism, each knew they could rely on the other and, though neither would admit it, they had a great deal in common.

The Bentley rolled to a smooth stop, and Arty peered through the church gates. "It was a very proper wedding. The bride was elegantly dressed; the two bridesmaids were duly inferior…"

Jean glanced past him and spotted Jim and Betty—her fellow WAAF wages clerk and maid of honour. Jean laughed. "Jane Austen," she identified. "Alas, I only have Betty."

"But her mouth is big enough for two. What do you think they're talking about?"

"No doubt she's telling Jim he had a lucky escape."

"Yes, probably." Arty agreed. "Are you ready, Mrs. Tomkins-to-be?"

"As I'll ever be," Jean said. Arty released her hand for a moment to get out of the car, and took it again, holding steady whilst Jean stepped out onto the pavement. Once she was happy her gown was hanging correctly, she held on to Arty's arm and they walked up the path to the church doors. With a soundless nod, Jim returned inside to let the vicar know the bride had arrived. Jean and Betty embraced quickly, and Arty told Betty how lovely she looked. He meant it too: her maid-of-honour dress was in the same hue of pink as the tea roses and a wonderful complement to her brown-black hair and dark complexion.

The organist began to play. Jean took a deep breath, grabbed Arty's arm once more, and they moved off, with Betty following behind and holding the short train of Jean's wedding gown. Ahead of them, Charlie and his older brother, Walter, were standing in front of the altar, both in matching morning suits and for once looking very much alike. They were dissimilar in looks and stature, with Charlie being the taller and broader of the two, but they shared the same stance and expressions of nervous anticipation. Beyond them, the vicar was a statue in starched white vestments, a fixed smile on his face as he followed over the rims of his half-moon spectacles the bridal party's slow-march progress. Naturally, the three of them were in step, taking the mandatory pause as each foot passed the other.

Finally they arrived at the altar and the service began. At the appropriate point, Arty symbolically gave Jean to Charlie and then took his seat between Jean's mother and Jim. Someone lightly squeezed his shoulder; he looked behind him and nearly fell off the pew in surprise.

"Sissy! What are you doing here?" he hissed.

"Attending a wedding," she whispered, flicking her fingers in his direction, just like she used to when he was a little boy rather more interested in the ladies' ridiculous Sunday hats than the vicar's boring drone. Arty turned to face front again, briefly making eye contact with Antonio, sitting to Sissy's left. He didn't seem in the least bit impressed by the Church of England service of holy matrimony Sissy had forced him to attend.

All in all, the ceremony was unremarkable, which was as well; both Jean and Charlie had been fretting about stumbling over their vows, though neither did. The hymns were rousing—'Praise My Soul The King Of Heaven' and 'All Things Bright And Beautiful'—and whilst Arty had heard Jim singing along to some of their records at home, it was nothing compared to the way he sang in church, with an almost opera-like quality to his deep, rich baritone. It left Arty in a glorious daze, wondering how it was possible that he could fall even more in love with the man he already loved so completely.

From the chilly recesses of the church, the wedding party and their many guests spilled out into the sunny grounds, liberated at last from the restrictive silence and able to greet each other properly. Many of those who had served at Minton hadn't seen each other in almost a year, and the reunion was joyous and, in some quarters, raucous. Walter was, on the whole, performing admirably as best man, intervening whenever someone hogged Charlie's attention for too long, and keeping up a cheery banter in between. The Tomkins men's sadness for their lost younger brother was their constant companion, even though they endeavoured to hide it whenever their parents were nearby.

"There's some of your little guys," Jim said, pulling Arty from his observations. Jim nodded to the floral borders of the church gardens. "Holly blues, right?"

Arty smiled. "That's right." He watched the small butterflies flit amongst the forget-me-nots, their pale blue wings affording an effective camouflage, and soon both insects disappeared from sight.

"And small white?" Jim identified, pointing to another.

"Close," Arty said. "See the green colouring to the underside of its wings?"

"Uh huh?"

"The small white doesn't have it, so that one is a green-veined white."

"Green veins. Got it." Jim nodded and frowned thoughtfully. It made Arty chuckle.

"You don't have to pretend any more," he said.

Jim's frown became a grin. "Your legs all right?"

"Just about. I could do with a sit down though." Arty switched his weight from one leg to the other, for what it was worth. Between walking up the aisle and sitting on hard pews, followed by coming up on half an hour of standing around, he was in significant discomfort.

"You got a couple hours to rest before tonight," Jim said.

"True enough," Arty agreed vaguely. They were returning to the house with the newly-weds, along with Joshua and Louisa, to wait out the time between the ceremony and the wedding reception. However, rest was not on Arty's agenda, and he was starting to feel a little anxious, although if it did go terribly wrong he could always blame Jean, even if this time the idea had been his own.

"Arty," Sissy called as she made her way over. She hugged him fondly and moved straight on to Jim, bombarding him with questions and giving him no time whatsoever to answer. Arty was somewhat startled when Antonio also hugged him, particularly when he followed it up with a loud kiss delivered to each cheek. Flustered and with face burning, Arty watched Antonio greet Jim the same way, whilst Sissy laughed loudly. "Oh, dear brother of mine. How much you have yet to learn."

Antonio released Jim and shrugged at Arty. "Ten years in London, I go home and I forget." His dark eyes twinkled with fun, and Arty chuckled. Antonio Adessi was a handsome man, with thick, steel-grey hair and olive skin that was surprisingly smooth, given his age and all he had weathered over the past few years. He was perhaps as much as twenty years older than Sissy, certainly in his mid-fifties, but he had forgotten nothing; he was making it clear he had no issue with Arty and Jim's partnership, which meant Arty could safely invite Sissy and Antonio to join them.

"We're going back to the house for afternoon tea. Will you come?" Arty met and held Sissy's gaze, imploring her to agree.

"We'd love to," she accepted graciously, and with a modicum of suspicion. "But you'd better come with us in the car, or we won't know where we're going. When do you want to leave?"

"Now, ideally. My legs are sore. I'll just let Jean and Charlie know."

"I'll tell them," Jim said. "You go get in the car." He was gone before Arty could draw breath to protest.

"Are they getting no better?" Sissy asked, as she, Arty and Antonio set off along the churchyard path towards the road.

"They're better than they were at Christmas," Arty replied, keeping his eyes on his goal: his sister's pre-war Triumph Dolomite that she had refused to sell, instead renting a garage to store it in until such point as Arty learnt to drive. The truth of it was he never went anywhere that meant he needed to drive. Since the accident he had avoided going to dances, and there was a pub within walking distance of Dalton Place, so if he fancied some company that was where he went.

As much as Arty enjoyed watching others dance, he was afraid that doing so would force him to accept his lot, and he had affected what he thought was a fairly convincing veneer of indifference. On the few occasions that Jean and Charlie had been out dancing, they'd asked if he wanted to join them, and he'd always dismissed the offer with some quip about not wishing to be the fifth wheel. Before Jim came back, telling them *thanks, but no thanks* hadn't been a problem, but no matter his insistence, Jim refused to go out dancing and leave Arty home alone.

Tonight, however, there would be no getting out of it. It was the wedding reception of their two best friends: the end of a long and complicated courtship, and a new beginning. There would be much dancing and Arty refused to spoil anyone's fun. No envy, no bitterness; already he was preparing himself, strengthening his conviction to remain happy, for Jean and Charlie's sake, and for Jim. With so many WAAFs in attendance there would be no shortage of partners to assist Jim in showing off his jitterbug prowess, and Arty was looking forward to watching him in action again. It had been too long. *It will be fun*, he repeated to himself, as Jim opened the car door and climbed in beside him.

"Were they all right?" Arty asked.

"Yeah," Jim confirmed. "Are you?"

Arty nodded cheerfully. "Yes. I'm fine."

Jim frowned at him, his disbelief apparent. Sissy started the car and moved off. "What's on your mind?" Jim asked.

"Oh, you know. This and that," Arty said cryptically. He waited for Jim to light his pipe, and put his hand on Jim's knee. Jim smiled away behind the merry little puffs of smoke.

They were first to arrive back at Jean's mother's house, where Jim headed straight for the bathroom, whilst Sissy fussed Arty into a chair and made a pot of tea, lecturing him all the while about talking to his doctor.

"I'm sure he can give you something for the pain."

"I can manage, thank you, Sissy."

"Day to day, maybe, but on a special occasion, like your best friends' wedding?"

"I don't want to depend on medicine for the rest of my life. You know how it muddled my brain in hospital."

"I'm not suggesting you take it all the time, Arty. It's not fair on Jim—"

Arty raised his voice, cutting Sissy short. "It has no bearing on Jim. He worries whether I'm in pain or not."

"And do you tell him?" Sissy demanded. "When the pain is as bad as I know it is today?"

Arty opened his mouth to retort, but Jim was on his way downstairs. "*That* would be unfair to him," he hissed under his breath.

Sissy folded her arms and glowered. Arty shook his head and laughed. "What?" she snapped.

205

"You look like our mother."

"Attack me, why don't you?" she grumbled jokingly, although Arty could see she had taken offence, and it was only Jim's arrival that stopped her from saying anything further.

"How are we all?" he asked, resting his hands on Arty's shoulders. Arty peered up at him and smiled.

"Sissy says I'm to tell you whenever I'm in a lot of pain."

"You don't need to. I already know."

"I was only telling him to talk to the doctor," Sissy protested. "He could take something when it's at its worst."

Jim nodded, as if he were mulling over her suggestion. "We'd have to make up the couch for when D H Lawrence comes a-visiting."

Arty felt himself turn red and started to laugh.

"What's this?" Sissy asked.

"The morphine they gave me in hospital made me, er…imagine things that weren't real."

"And you imagined D H Lawrence?"

Arty nodded.

"Doing what?"

"Reading his stories to me, of course."

Sissy rolled her eyes. "Of course."

"Look, Sissy, I'm perfectly fine, really I am. With Jim's physical therapy—"

"That's what you're calling it these days, is it?" Sissy's remark sent both men into fits of laughter. She watched them for a moment and then bustled over, hugging them both at the same time, which meant Arty's face was squashed against her midriff; he blew hot air out of his mouth, ruffling the front of her frock. She released them at the same time as the front door opened, and Jean and Charlie burst through it under a rain of rice. Joshua and Louisa were the culprits and followed them in. Jean turned back, holding up her hands to say 'stop', and the pair did as requested, still silently laughing as they came through to join the others in the kitchen. Jean and Charlie continued straight past, out into the gardens.

No more than ten seconds later, the front door opened again, this time to admit Molly and Daphne.

"Lovely day," Molly remarked.

"Absolutely glorious," Daphne concurred, as they, too, made a beeline for the gardens. Arty glanced up, catching Jim's bemused frown, and quickly turned away, stifling his laughter.

Joshua met Arty's gaze for a moment before briefly shifting his eyes to Jim, and then in the direction Molly and Daphne had taken. Arty gave him a thumbs up.

"What's going on?" Jim asked, watching his younger brother's gestures to Louisa. Before he met Louisa, Joshua had never used sign language, but he was now fluent. "I wish he wouldn't do that," Jim griped.

"You'll find out soon enough," Arty said.

"You're in on it?"

"More like *they* are in on it," Arty corrected.

With a final nod to Louisa, Joshua started towards the door to the gardens, beckoning the others to follow. Arty rose to his feet and held his hand out to Jim, who narrowed his eyes, but nonetheless took the offered hand and allowed Arty to lead him outside.

"I thought you needed to rest," he said.

"After we're done here."

"What *are* we doing here?"

Arty didn't answer and continued towing Jim by the hand, along the path through the middle of the lawns, past the greenhouses, finally coming to a stop under a rose arch.

"Where did they all go?" Jim asked, his question immediately answered by the reappearance of their closest friends and family: Jean, Charlie, Molly, Daphne, Joshua, Louisa, Sissy and Antonio. Jim looked around the gathering, his mouth hanging open in bewilderment.

Charlie stepped forward and clasped his hands together. Clearing his throat dramatically, he said, "Dearly beloved, we are gathered here together—"

Jim's mouth widened into a huge smile as he looked Arty right in the eyes, trying and failing to glare angrily.

Charlie continued, "We are gathered here together in this company, to witness the union of this man," he pointed at Jim, "and this man," and then at Arty, "in..." Charlie looked to Jean, who shrugged. "In good old-fashioned marriage."

Charlie gave a self-satisfied nod, and it dawned on Arty that his friend was a little bit drunk, or emotional, or possibly both.

"Do you, Robert Thomas Clarke, take Jimbo to be your awfully wedded husband?"

Arty tried hard to keep his face straight as he answered, "I do."

"Goodo." Charlie nodded some more. "And do you, James Johnson, take Arty to be your awfully wedded husband?"

"I do," Jim said, working so hard to suppress his laughter that he was grinding his teeth.

"Marvellous," Charlie said. "Now, I have here..." He patted his chest, paused, had a sudden thought, and fished in his inside pocket. "Hold that." He passed Arty a spanner. "Told you I'd bring it back, didn't I?"

Arty stared at the three-quarter-inch spanner in amazement. "You bugger!" he said.

"Ah! Here we are." Charlie held out his hand, palm up, on which there were two gold bands, and all of a sudden Jim became very serious.

"Arty, I...er..."

Arty smiled and took Jim's hand. "When I asked Jean to help me work out the size of ring to buy, she didn't say a word about you having already done exactly the same. I don't know what you were waiting for, Jim. You've had me since…well, that first time I saw you across the Palais Dance Hall." Arty took one of the rings from Charlie's palm and waited for Jim to hold out his left hand. Arty slid the ring onto Jim's third finger and said, "With this ring, I thee wed."

Jim gripped Arty's hand and made a very strange noise, making it difficult to discern if he was crying or laughing. He pinched the corners of his eyes and took a few deep breaths, the last being the deepest. He released it slowly and moved his hand away from his face, offering Arty a tearful smile. "You got me good this time. Gimme the ring."

Without looking, he held out his hand to Charlie, who duly passed over the ring. Jim took Arty's hand in his.

"I guess you already know the rest of it—for better, for worse, in sickness and in health, and so on?"

Arty nodded solemnly.

"Just checkin'," Jim said, gently sliding the gold band into place with the words, "With this ring, I thee wed."

A brief pause followed, before Charlie decreed, "I now pronounce you husband and husband. You may now kiss the—" he paused as if to check he was right "—groom!"

Arty and Jim both smiled as they leaned in to each other and kissed, no longer aware of their friends and siblings standing nearby, clapping and cheering, nor of the pair of brimstone butterflies and their perfectly timed flypast.

PART FOUR: 1947–1954

Chapter Twenty-Three:
1947–1948

Edward Lucien Tomkins, so named after the two uncles he would never meet, was born January, 1947, on the day after they were snowed in, which turned out to be rather fortuitous, as Molly had been staying with them in between shifts at the hospital, thus she was on hand to deliver the baby. Having stocked up in advance with oil for the central heating, they were largely unaffected by the power cuts, making Dalton Place one of the warmest and brightest homes in the city.

Other than little Eddie's arrival in the blizzards, the year progressed quietly. The business—which the locals had dubbed 'Wingy's Workshop'—steadily grew; Antonio offered them first refusal on Dalton Place, and for a very good price. The trouble, however, was that Jean and Arty were stubborn as mules, for they both felt an obligation to contribute financially to the purchase, but Jean no longer brought in a wage and Arty refused to draw one from the workshop. He tried to build up his strength by attempting increasingly heavy tasks, but it would leave him in so much pain he could barely walk, and it could take days for him to recover. Until he could do his share of the work, Arty could not justify taking the same pay as the other two men, and so he and Jean revisited the possibility of renting out the top-floor apartment, or maybe even selling it, but quickly realised it was no longer an option. One day Eddie would need his own room, as would his younger siblings, not that Jean was planning on having more babies. There again, she hadn't planned on having Eddie.

There was, of course, one other potential solution, but whenever Arty brought it up in conversation, Jean changed the subject. Her dream to run a dance school was the very first thing she had shared with him, and he knew that he was the reason she refused to pursue it. Short of doing to her what she and Jim had done to him—finding and renting a space without her knowledge—there didn't seem to be any way of getting her to turn her lifetime ambition into a reality. And so the four of them, plus one, saw in another New Year with some dreams fulfilled whilst others languished.

January of 1948, thankfully, brought no snow, although it rained long and hard enough to flood the workshop inspection pit. Each night, Jim and Charlie squelched home, wrung out their socks and hung them on the radiators to dry in a steamy monochromatic parody of Christmas Eve. Ignoring Arty's terrible warnings of trench foot, the two men trudged to work next morning, returned home in the evening, took off their boots…and so on, and so forth. All in all, it was a damp, dreary month, with only two high points: Eddie's first birthday, and the much-anticipated publication of a book that made Lady Chatterley's lovers seem positively demure.

Alfred Kinsey's tome, entitled *Sexual Behavior in the Human Male*, had already been causing a furore in the USA, and Jim's desperation to read it far surpassed his patience in waiting for it to arrive. Indeed, it was the cause of Arty and Jim's first real argument, which began when Arty jokingly remarked that Jim didn't even like books, to which Jim retorted that he liked books of merit and substance, inferring that Arty's passion for literature was worthless. The storm circled for a couple of days, sucking in all manner of flotsam concerning Jim's continued worries for Arty's health, and Arty's feelings of inadequacy.

Many unkind words were spoken, and the reconciliation reopened wounds that each had believed healed, yet it afforded a necessary, though far from welcome opportunity to talk frankly about their fears, the biggest for Arty being the sense that his disability stopped Jim from living a full life, to which Jim replied simply that Arty was his life.

"I'm hardly knocking on death's door," Arty protested.

"Not yet, you ain't."

"Meaning?"

"You push yourself too damn hard."

"I'm just trying to do my fair share."

"You're trying to prove a point."

"Because you worry over nothing."

"Darlin', if you can't do the one thing you love more than any other, then I ain't worrying over nothing."

Jim's words cut deep, and Arty hated him for them—for reminding him of what he had lost, and for the seven months alone, and for all of the small, inconsequential things that loom vast and ugly when spite and fury rule the senses. But what he hated most of all was that Jim was right. The day Arty could dance again would be the day he was fit enough to work. His rage spent, he fell in defeat, and into Jim's waiting arms.

"When that book gets here it's going straight back where it came from," Jim said through his all-American tears.

Arty kissed him, and the storm rolled away, leaving in its wake a night of passionate peace making and a new resolve to share their worries rather than attempting to carry the burden alone.

215

By the time the book that started it all finally arrived, Arty was just as excited as Jim. As soon as the grumbling postman who delivered the exceedingly heavy package was out of sight, Arty went over to the workshop to tell Jim.

At lunchtime, Jim called Molly to let her know and then opened the package, leaving the books on the table while he ate, just so he could look at them. Arty had never seen Jim quite so enthralled and it made him chuckle, watching him flick through the pages, trying not to read because he'd promised Molly he'd wait until the evening.

Evening came, as did Molly, and dinner went uneaten, with the two of them instantly consumed by the eight-hundred-page report on Kinsey's research. They were sharing the same copy, so Arty read the other one, carrying it back and forth to the kitchen whilst he furnished a constant supply of tea. Were it not for Molly leaving to work a night shift, she and Jim would likely have read through till morning—ne'er had a bookmark been so reluctantly inserted.

By the following bedtime, Arty had read Kinsey from cover to cover, whereas Jim and Molly were still only halfway through, not helped by them pausing every few pages to discuss some finding or other, although Arty read quickly under ordinary circumstances, and the subject matter had him sprinting through the pages, desperate to gobble up every last word. It also forced him to concede Jim's point, for now he understood: just as he had once referred to his feelings as an 'abhorrence', so too did fictional stories treat homosexuals as if they were an abomination almost always destined for a tragic demise. There was no hope in that. It was…worthless.

In Alfred Kinsey's work—and this was no work of fiction, but research of some scientific merit—Arty did find hope, if not of the same kind Jim and Molly had for a sexual revolution. Evidence that homosexuality was rife among American men would strike at the heart of the establishment, and fear was a dangerous instinct. However, if governments could be persuaded that homosexuality was an 'inherent physiologic capacity', then surely there was no purpose in their continued attempts to rid men of it?

To Arty, it seemed like a practical direction for Jim and Molly's group to take, not that he had ever been especially involved. The group met every other Thursday, and had done so for the past eighteen months, and whilst there was much to be said for the sense of belonging it gave to its two dozen or so members, they didn't seem to be making much progress of the kind Jim had anticipated, and he was profoundly frustrated. Jim wanted to take a stand and get out there, fighting for their rights, whereas Molly's approach was far more subtle, and she had achieved what she'd set out to. They now had a small yet strong network of lawyers, doctors, academics, senior policemen and other professionals who were well clued up on the law and on standby if the worst happened.

Arty could see both sides, and in the longer term they would work together in formidable tandem. Jim and Molly were organised, enthusiastic, and each complemented the other wonderfully. Nevertheless, four years with Jim Johnson had transformed Arty's intellectual theorising and daydreaming into a more radical pragmatism, and he had to admit he was guilty of egging Jim on.

When Molly and Jim finally relented on their second night of reading, mostly because neither could see the words any more, Molly went off to work her night shift, and Jim settled on the settee, patting his thighs by way of prompting Arty to lift his legs. At least three times every week, Jim gave

Arty's legs a firm massage. Whether it was helping at all Arty couldn't say, but he wasn't about to complain.

"So what'd ya think?" Jim asked, once they were settled.

"Of Kinsey's findings? I think there's hope for the future, but I'm not sure society is ready for it yet."

"All the more reason for us to keep making a noise."

"Maybe." Arty groaned and slid a little further down the settee. "Mind you, I've had it if you end up in prison. Who's going to rub my legs?"

Jim laughed. "It won't come to that. Not with the people we know."

The truth was, for all of Jim's outspokenness, he stopped short of doing anything that would draw attention to them personally, because Arty needed him. Since their argument, Arty had withdrawn from physical labour and instead took care of the administrative side of things—logging work, ordering parts, banking the day's takings, going to the post office for Jim and Charlie's stamps, and so on—but that only kept him occupied for an hour or so at best, and it didn't tax him in the slightest.

It was also damn cold in that workshop, and so Arty had started to spend more time in Dalton Place, keeping Jean company, now she was 'stuck at home' being a housewife and mother. And what a job that was! Between washing nappies and bibs, doing the cleaning and cooking, and then washing the nappies and bibs all over again, poor Jean never had a moment to herself. Coming from a well-to-do family, she had been looked after by a nanny, and now she understood why, although it was just one of her many annoyances with how unequal things were between the haves and the have-nots, and men and women.

The welfare promises were slowly but surely coming to fruition, and de-rationing had begun, making life more tolerable for those in greatest need, none of which tamed Jean's fury that once she'd married, she lost every last bit of her independence.

"If I'd known, I'd have carried on living over the brush," she complained at an astonishing frequency. "Clearly the man had no regard for women whatsoever."

The man in question was the late John Maynard Keynes—the economist whose ideas had been influential in bringing about the improvements they were seeing all around them: new houses, hospitals and schools, help for the unemployed, state pensions. Arty thought it was a great achievement, which only added to the high esteem in which he already held Keynes, courtesy of Antonio's anecdotes, passed on through Sissy, who went into a period of extended mourning when Keynes passed away.

Keynes had been Sissy's idol; he was everything she admired in a man: a gifted economist, openly homosexual, but he also loved women. She declared that had she met Keynes before Antonio, she would have thrown herself upon him in a spectacularly embarrassing fashion. Curiously, Antonio wasn't in the least bit perturbed by this news.

Jean was not quite so enthralled, for the entire system Keynes had inspired relied on women staying at home and men going out to work. A woman didn't need to earn as much as a man, because she didn't have a family to provide for. Why did a wife need to pay the same national insurance when it was her husband's responsibility to look after her? Charlie, who often arrived home in the midst of one of Jean's rants, kept his head down and his mouth shut. Whether he agreed with her or not, he preferred the quiet life.

The more Arty heard, the more certain he was that their time was yet to come. There were bigger battles to be fought before homosexual rights could have their day and, in spite of the initial excitement about Kinsey's report, nothing happened. There was still a long way to go in recovering from the war, and the destitute cared little for women's laments or men's private proclivities. In time, perhaps things would change, although it was by no means certain that the change would be for the better.

Chapter Twenty-Four:
September, 1949

There was a letter Arty kept writing. It began:

Dear Mum and Dad,

At the grand old age of…

The first time, he had been twenty-five years old, for he had written it in hospital, when his death had seemed imminent. He'd tried again at twenty-six, when he and Jim married each other under the rose arch on a gloriously sunny day in May, then at twenty-eight, when he'd dared to believe that Kinsey's research would offer irrefutable evidence to sway his father, ever the academic. The first letter he had neither sent nor destroyed, in case its possession was somehow tied to his fate. The second letter he'd shown to Sissy, who talked him out of sending it, and eventually he had thrown it on the fire. The third letter he didn't finish: it would take a better man than him to summarise eight hundred pages into around a hundred words. That, too, went up the chimney.

Now, on the eve of his thirtieth birthday, as the glow of the low autumn sun faded from gold through copper into cherry, becoming one with the mahogany of the bureau beneath the blank page, Arty started the letter once more:

Dear Mum and Dad,

At the grand old age of thirty, I believe it's time I told you the truth about the kind of man your son grew up to be.

He stopped writing and read it back. How absurd his words seemed. He hadn't 'grown up to be'; he had always been. He screwed the paper into a ball and threw it at the unlit hearth, where it hit the back of the fireplace and bounced out again. Seemingly leaping from nowhere, Soot pounced on the paper ball, causing it to tumble across the Axminster. Arty put his pen down and watched absently as the cat batted and chased his makeshift prey all around the room.

His birthday had nothing to do with it, or not in any direct sense. It was because of Jim's father. In early spring, Jim's mother had written to both sons, telling them their father was gravely ill, but before either of them could arrange passage back to the States, he made a full recovery. In summer, when it happened a second time, Joshua flew from the new airport in Heathrow to New York, and from there drove down to West Virginia: a day and a half of travelling to find that once again Jimmy Johnson Senior had pulled through.

"Third time lucky, Mom says," Joshua reported on his return to London a fortnight later. Another fortnight had since passed, during which Arty had been consumed by morbid thoughts, mostly concerning his parents' mortality, but also, at times, his own. It was not that he believed he was nearing the end; far from it. He ate well, he exercised

222

and rested regularly, he and Jim were still deeply in love, and they had a good life together. However, whilst Arty was happier and healthier than he had been in years, his parents were already in their seventh decade; regardless of what Sissy thought, he felt a compulsion to tell them before the sand stopped pouring through their hourglasses.

The whistle of the kettle came into focus, followed by the dainty clink together of china cups on saucers, and Arty smiled to himself, the frustration of his failed letter writing instantly diminished by the mundane reminder that telling his parents was of little real consequence. Nor were his intentions entirely honourable. *I want to shout it from the rooftops—this is the man I love and don't you tell me I can't.* Jim's words, uttered almost five years ago, were on perpetual standby in Arty's mind, a constant reminder that he had entered this partnership, this common-law marriage, with eyes open.

Jim appeared at his side and set two cups down on the desk. "Did you quit?" he asked.

Arty peered up at Jim's gentle, knowing smile. "I did," he confirmed. "Soot is taking care of it."

Jim stooped and wrapped warm, strong arms around Arty, and together they watched the cat at play. Arty nestled closer, rubbing his cheek against Jim's, knowing their thoughts were as one: remembering the two young cats they adopted and raised, hour upon hour spent in silent observation of hunting or play, chasing balls of hay, and the recent loss of Socks, hit by a car a few months ago. They'd lost one of Silky's first brood the same way, another defected next door to Mrs. Greene, and Silky's second litter found new homes—all but one, who was the image of his father, with the same white belly and three white socks, thus was christened accordingly.

Soot tired of his game and slinked off to the bedroom, where his offspring and nephew would be snoozing in their favourite spots. Silky preferred to sleep in the sitting room, and she had taken one of the armchairs as her own. Not even Matron Molly was brave enough to take on the feisty grey tortoiseshell, who hissed and spat at any human foolish enough to go near, other than Jim, whom she would glare at spitefully but honoured their pact of mutual respect, and Arty, whom she adored and reluctantly shared with Jim.

"Let's go sit," Arty said, slowly rising from the hard-back chair. Jim released him, and they each picked up their cups of tea and retired to the settee.

"Sounds like you got important business on your mind, darlin'."

Arty laughed quietly. "I have. It's about tomorrow night. I know I said I didn't want to celebrate my birthday, but it occurred to me...we could go dancing."

"The four of us?"

"Yes."

Jim frowned and rubbed his chin, deep in thought. He nodded slowly and said, "It's a great idea, and I know you're trying to do the right thing..."

"I have to, for Jean, and for you."

"We been here before, ain't we? You don't have to do this for me."

"When did you last go dancing?"

Jim pretended he had to think about it, but they both knew it was at Jean and Charlie's wedding reception, over three years ago.

Arty continued, "I've been thinking about it for a while now. I might not be able to dance any more, but I haven't forgotten how. I'm going to propose to Jean that we open a dance school together." Arty paused, expecting Jim to argue, and then added, just in case, "Before you say it, this isn't about the money."

Jim laughed and raised his hands in a wide shrug. "Now what makes you think I was gonna mention money?"

Arty rolled his eyes and moved closer so that when Jim lowered his arms, one fell around Arty's shoulders. "It really isn't about the money," he said.

Jim turned and kissed Arty's cheek. "I know," he murmured against the skin. "You're the most incredible, kind, brave man, Arty Clarke, doing this for Jean and for us. Whatever you decide is good by me. I'm with you all the way, d'you hear?" Arty nodded. "And if you wanna dance tomorrow night, then you just go right on ahead, and when you're done I'll sling you over my shoulder, carry you home and take you to bed."

Arty laughed. "I'm holding you to that."

"I mean it," Jim said. "'Specially the last part." He gave Arty's thigh a slow squeeze and started working his way up.

With a heavy sigh of both relief and contentment, Arty leaned against Jim and nuzzled into his neck, breathing him in. "Thank you," he whispered.

"Welcome," Jim replied.

Chapter Twenty-Five:
September, 1949

During the war, the dancing at Hammersmith Palais was integral to maintaining people's morale across the city. The sirens would be sounding, Jerry would be dropping bombs all around, and still the good people of the Palais danced on. Four years later, the atmosphere inside the grand building was just as spectacular as ever it had been, although, in spite of the faster dancing and a more jazzy feeling to every number the band played, everyone was so much more relaxed. To regular attendees the changes might not even have been noticeable, but Arty and Jean hadn't danced at the Palais since March of 1945, when they had lost out to a London couple in the waltz, yet had won the prize for the quickstep, which they rarely bothered to practise. To them, the difference in the place was remarkable.

Being there again, Arty felt the same rush of nervous excitement he'd always felt, not just prior to a competition, but any time he went dancing. He'd fully expected it to vanish the second he arrived, but he was determined he was going to get out there, even if it was for only one dance and he would suffer for the next week. After so long without dancing he'd be stiff as a board anyway, so what difference would a little muscle fatigue make?

Once they'd found a table with a good view of the dance floor, Jim offered to buy the drinks.

"White wine for me, thanks, Jim," Jean replied.

"All right, a white wine, and...Arty?"

He was thinking about it, so Charlie jumped in first. "The usual for me. I'll come give you a hand."

Jim nodded in acknowledgement. Now he was just waiting on Arty, who shrugged, still not entirely settled on a drink.

"I'll just have a double brandy and ginger," he said. He usually drank beer, but Jim didn't pass comment, instead setting off with Charlie for the bar and soon obscured from view by the swirling dancers. How strange it was to see men in suits rather than uniforms, although the women's ballroom gowns were as stunning as ever.

Jean lightly tapped Arty's arm to get his attention. "Do you remember 'The Woodchopper's Ball'?"

Arty nodded and laughed as the memory filled his mind of wartime nights at the Palais, when the poor caretaker was sent up onto the roof to keep lookout. If there was a raid, he'd come back down and flash his torch at the bandleader, and all of a sudden the band would start playing something loud, like 'The Woodchopper's Ball', and the drummer would be banging the hell out of his kit, drowning out the sound of the sirens and explosions. The poor caretaker was charged with deciding whether they needed to head for the shelters or they could keep dancing, the safety of hundreds of people in his hands, and he was only young. Then again, they were all young: some of the Lancasters' pilots were barely twenty years old and their crews were younger still.

Jim and Charlie returned with the drinks, and both remained standing with eyes trained on the dancers. Jim rested his hand on Arty's chair, gently stroking with his thumb back and forth across Arty's shoulder. Arty shivered at the touch; what he wouldn't have given to dance with Jim tonight, but at least he'd get to see Jean dance. Maybe she'd even dance with Jim: they did a stunning jive, although Jean preferred the slower dances, particularly the waltz and the rumba.

The next dance was a foxtrot, and Charlie led Jean onto the floor. They had been out together no more than a half-dozen times since Eddie was born, but Joshua and Louisa were minding him for the evening. Louisa doted on Eddie, who, at thirty months old, was able to communicate almost as well in sign language as he did in spoken English. He was bright as a brass button and always smiling, such a happy, well-behaved little lad. Nevertheless, Jean and Charlie were clearly relishing this rare night away from their son, and their dancing was astounding. It was a shame they weren't competing, because the intimacy of their bond as husband and wife spilled over into their movements and their timing: tonight they danced as one.

Jim bent down to talk into Arty's ear. "You know watching those two?" His breath disturbed Arty's hair and he let out an involuntary gasp. Jim chuckled quietly. "Man, I love I can do that to you."

Arty smiled and felt his face heat up. He cleared his throat in a poor attempt to regain control of his impulses. "What were you going to say?"

"Charlie might not have your gracefulness or that neat little sway of the hips you got going on, but they're quite something, ain't they?"

"Yes, they are. When they come back, I'm—"

A loud, female voice interrupted Arty mid-sentence: "Jim Johnson? Good God. It's not...surely... It is you! Fancy seeing you here."

A tall, red-haired woman swooped in and flung herself on Jim, leaving a lipstick kiss mark on his cheek.

"Good evening, Dot. Lovely to see you. How are you doing?"

"Better for seeing you, Jimmy boy. I thought you went home to the States."

"Yeah, I did, and then I came back." Jim turned and gestured to Arty. "Dot, this is my friend, Arty. We share an apartment."

"Hello, Arty," Dot said. Arty stood to greet her and was rewarded with a crimson kiss mark to match Jim's.

"Arty, this is Group Officer Dorothy Carter. We worked together at RAF Tillbrook."

"Lovely to meet you, Ma'am," Arty said, briefly eyeing the woman's attire: an ankle-length, emerald-green gown, split on one side to the thigh, and a boned, strapless corset, showing an undignified expanse of milk-white bosom.

"Just Dot these days, Arty," Dot said, offering a pleased smile in acknowledgement of his visual appraisal before she turned her attention back on Jim. "Are you jitterbugging tonight?"

"I could be persuaded," Jim said with a flirtatious wink. Arty raised his eyebrows.

"Then I might just have to stay around and persuade you a little harder," Dot flirted back, fluttering her long eyelashes.

Arty felt his hair bristle and silently chastised himself. He couldn't dance with Jim, so what point was there to being jealous of Dot's request and Jim's agreement to it?

"I'm just going to get a drink," Dot said. "I'll be back shortly." With a quick wave of the fingertips, she left. Arty watched her all the way.

"I can tell her if you like," Jim said.

"Pardon?"

"Dot. I can tell her about you and me. She already knows about me."

"Does she?" Arty was surprised, because she was behaving very suggestively.

"She does. What d'you want me to do?"

Arty shook his head. "Don't worry about me. I'm just being foolish."

"You trust me, right?"

"With my life. And it's not that I think she'll try anything on, especially if, as you say, she knows you're not interested. But…" Arty gazed wistfully at the dancers, kicking and sliding and swirling together, free-flowing and romantic as spring water rippling over smooth pebbles. He turned back to Jim and smiled sadly. "I wish we could join them."

"One day we will."

"High hopes, Jim Johnson."

Jim laughed. "You betcha."

The foxtrot was coming to an end, and those not dancing applauded and cheered for their friends. Ever a cunning move on the part of the Palais, dancers were judged by their peers, so the more friends they brought along the better their chances. Jean and Charlie had only danced for fun, but nonetheless received a few cheers and compliments on their way back to Arty and Jim.

"I'm going to ask her soon," Arty muttered quickly before they arrived. "I desperately need her to agree."

"I'll follow where you lead," Jim said.

"Then I'll need more brandy."

"How did we do, fellas?" Charlie asked.

Arty tilted his head from side to side. "Your turning box needs a bit a work, but not bad for an amateur."

Charlie gave him a playful slap around the head. "My wife taught me everything I know."

"You're not supposed to do the woman's part."

"You may mock, Arty Clarke—" Charlie began, but stopped abruptly and picked up his pint, draining the glass in one go. He gave Arty an apologetic smile, although Arty wasn't entirely sure why.

"My round," Jim offered, but Charlie waved him away.

"You bought the last one," he said, turning to Jean and Arty. "Same again?"

Jean and Arty nodded in confirmation, and Jim and Charlie once more set off for the bar, crossing paths with Dot, who laughed loudly at something Jim had just said and then pinched his bottom as he continued on his way.

"Who's that?" Jean asked Arty.

"Group officer from Tillbrook."

Jean continued to watch her. "She's very…confident, isn't she?"

Arty laughed. "You mean she's a flirt?"

"Well, that too," Jean agreed. "How does she expect to dance in that frock?"

"I wondered myself. She's after jiving with Jim."

Jean let out a very loud *Ha!* It was accidental, because she wasn't that sort of woman, and she covered her mouth with her hand. When she had recovered from her astonishment at herself, she confided, "Before I knew Jim properly, I thought he danced with all the gals as a ruse."

"Oh, not at all. He'll dance with anyone."

"Yes." Jean chuckled. "So long as he and I get a dance tonight, I shan't complain."

Arty looked out across the dance floor and said, as if it were of no consequence to him whatsoever, "Interestingly, I was just thinking the same about you and I."

"You…" Jean stopped. Arty glanced back at her. "You want to dance?"

"I don't know if I still can, but I want to try."

Jean's eyebrows arched in worry. "What if—"

"No one ever dropped dead from a gentle waltz."

"But it's all so much faster than it used to be."

"I'll be fine," Arty assured her. She still wasn't convinced, but the bandleader had just announced the waltz was next, so there was little time to dwell on it. Arty carefully pushed up from his chair and stepped around the table, holding his hand out to her. "Will you let me, Jean? Will you allow me to lead you in our dance tonight?"

Jean delayed a moment longer and then placed her hand in Arty's. He led her onto the dance floor, and they turned to face each other on the bandleader's count-in. Jean still looked worried, but Arty just smiled and put his arm around her waist, his palm pressed confidently to her lower back as they stepped off together; in an instant, four and a half years were forgotten.

Not everything from those years was gone, of course, for so many incredible things had happened to both of them during that time, not least their commitment to the two men watching them right now; Arty spun Jean as they waltzed past Charlie and Jim, both appearing emotional and doing a shocking job of hiding it. Arty spun again and noticed Jim wiping his eyes.

"He's crying," he said to Jean.

"That doesn't surprise me in the slightest. How does it feel?"

"That my husband is crying?" Arty asked. Jean squeezed his fingers, and he winced and laughed. "It's wonderful."

"No pain?"

"None."

Jean peered sideways at him. He smiled briefly and released her into an underarm turn, signifying the beginning of one of their set pieces, which proceeded faultlessly, drawing the attention of other dancers.

"That's Clarke and McDowell," someone said as they swept by.

"We're famous," Jean gasped excitedly.

233

"So it would seem," Arty concurred.

"I didn't know we were famous."

"Why wouldn't we be? We're damned good."

"And so modest too," Jean observed with a laugh.

"If you've got it, flaunt it, I say."

"Oh, do you now?"

"I do now, yes." Arty had always been the less confident of the two of them, but his liberation was complete and the timing was perfect. "What do you think of us opening a dance school together?"

"Yes," Jean answered immediately, much to Arty's surprise.

"Oh!" he said.

"Oh?"

"I thought I'd have to convince you."

Jean threw her head back in breathless, joyful laughter as Arty spun her through three full rotations. "You already did, Arty. We're waltzing together."

"Yes, we are."

Chapter Twenty-Six:
September, 1949

"After the ball is over, after the break of morn. After the dancers' leaving, after the stars are gone…"

"Arty Clarke, *you* are drunk!" Jim said, laughing and shushing him unsuccessfully. They'd left the Palais to catch the last train home, but Arty had consumed far too much brandy and ginger ale to risk five minutes in a confined space, being jogged from side to side. Jean and Charlie needed to get back for Eddie and took the train, whilst Jim and Arty walked. Or, rather, Jim walked and gave Arty a piggyback.

Arty clung tighter and continued to sing, "Many a heart is aching, if you could read them all—" He nibbled Jim's ear, and Jim sighed in exasperation.

"Just you wait," he threatened.

"You haven't changed your mind then?"

"About…?"

"Taking Dot up on her offer."

Jim chortled. "Jeez. She's a real live wire. I thought Jean was gonna give her a knuckle sandwich."

"Me too," Arty agreed ambiguously, not sure if he meant he'd also wanted to punch the woman, or just thought Jean might. Much as it appalled him to have even thought it, she had thrown herself at Jim and commandeered his attention all evening. Arty's one dance more or less finished him off, and Charlie couldn't jive to save his life, so Jean was left partnerless and, short of knocking Dot out cold, there wasn't a thing anyone could do about it. Still, there was no point dwelling on it. Arty *had* danced with Jean and they were going to start a dance school together. It had been a perfect night and his spirits were high. "I'm not drunk, you know," he said.

"Not even a little?"

"Maybe a little. And I'll be walking like John Wayne for at least a month."

"Are you saying I'm a wide ride, or should I take that as a compliment?"

Arty didn't answer. They had arrived back at Dalton Place and once they were inside, he responded by giving Jim a long, passionate kiss, making clear his intentions, although his legs were already aching and stiffening.

"Maybe a hot bath before bed?" Jim suggested, as always picking up on Arty's pain, however hard he tried to conceal it, and it worked both ways. Since Jim's father's illness, Jim had been thinking about him a lot, Arty knew, but he stayed true to his word. Maybe one day Jim would want to talk about his father; maybe he wouldn't, but Arty wasn't going to force the issue.

Jim followed Arty into the bathroom and helped him undress while the bath was filling, and not because he needed assistance. Indeed, it took a great deal longer than if he'd left him to it, particularly as the hot steam made Arty's clothes stick to his skin.

"Too warm in here," Jim said, removing his own clothes, whilst Arty climbed into the deep water, ridiculously aroused, and slid beneath the surface. When he came up for breath, Jim was kneeling beside the bath. He leaned over and kissed Arty, at the same time smoothing the cool bar of soap over his chest, stomach, and down, creating circles of fine creamy foam. Jim released him from the kiss and combed through the soapy mess with his fingertips, turning Arty into an erotic portrait of swirls of dark hair and white suds.

"I'm gonna be real gentle with you tonight, darlin'," Jim crooned. "Real gentle."

Arty closed his eyes, too far into his mind to reply. Gentle or rough, he cared not. First, however, he had to get out of the bath, but when he eventually attempted to do so, his legs refused absolutely to comply.

"Whatever you do, don't mention this to Jean," he implored, making one last scrabbled effort before relinquishing control.

"My lips are sealed," Jim promised. Moving to the top end of the bath, he braced his arm so that Arty could grab on and, with some further assistance to make his knees bend, Arty finally got both feet on the floor. A quick rub with a towel and Jim took Arty to bed, where he rolled him onto his side and then lay behind him, moving with slowness and great care.

Arty rocked back onto Jim, revelling in the constant flow of hot kisses to the nape of his neck, the hot palm wrapped around him. It was long past midnight, but beyond the urgency of their desire they were in no hurry to finish. Arty turned his head as far as his position would allow, and sought Jim's lips. It proved to be impossible without breaking the connection, and the slow-build was almost too much; Jim sensed it before Arty could muster his plea. Jim tightened his grip and groaned an apology as instinct took over, the gentle swaying lost to the need for release. Arty shoved his face into the pillow to mute his cries, not of pain; of sheer ecstasy.

Drifting back to Earth, he ignored the little voice reminding him that they needed to get into their pyjamas, just in case they were called upon in the night. Jim's breathing had already deepened, his bare chest gently heaving against Arty's naked back, a soothing, hypnotic rhythm teasing him into sleep.

***

Arty tugged hard on the belt of his dressing gown, took a deep breath, and opened the front door. "Constable."

"Sorry to wake you, sir. We've had a report of a disturbance. May we come in?" The two policemen barely waited for Arty to move aside before they were standing next to him.

"I haven't heard or seen anything," he said curtly, not intentionally to aggravate them. It was hard to squeeze out the words without giving away his pain.

"We'll just take a quick look around and satisfy ourselves."

They strode down the hallway and Arty limped after them as quickly as his stupid broken legs would allow. They glanced into the sitting room, the kitchen, the bathroom and then walked straight into the bedroom, as if it were a public space, not a man's private domain. Arty was incensed by the violation, and there was not a thing he could do about it.

"Are you married, sir?"

"No, Constable. Why do you ask?"

"This is your room, is it?"

"Yes. The apartment only has the one bedroom."

"And you live here alone?"

"I do," Arty confirmed calmly, though his heart was racing and the pressure in his head was tremendous, the only positive aspect being that the combination of anger and fear was seeing off the pain.

"Has anyone else been sleeping in this bed?"

Arty bit back the urge to ask if the disturbance was caused by a little girl with long golden hair and a penchant for porridge. "No," he said.

"So you're the only one who sleeps in this *double* bed, sir?"

"My legs are restless at night, Constable. I need the space."

"Restless legs, sir?"

The questions were merely a means to delay their departure, and again, Arty was powerless to protest. "An accident in 1945."

The policeman nodded. "That will be all, sir. Sorry to wake you." As the two officers reached the apartment's front door, the one doing all of the talking turned to his colleague and stated loudly enough for Arty to hear, "We'll check the flats upstairs while we're here."

Arty watched from the communal hallway as they trod heavily up to first floor and banged on Jean and Charlie's door. It was flung wide open, revealing Charlie's angry scowl, Eddie's cries drifting down to where Arty stood.

"What's the meaning of this?" Charlie demanded.

At the same time, Jim descended the stairs from the top floor, stopped a few feet behind the two policemen and asked, "Is everything all right, officers?"

"You check upstairs," one of them said and entered Jean and Charlie's apartment. Arty held his breath, trying to listen to what the other officer was saying to Jim on the way up to the top-floor apartment, but he couldn't hear over the blood banging on his ear drums. He went back inside and shut the door. He wasn't the only one on edge: poor Silky was prowling the hallway like a caged beast. Arty gently scooped her up and went to wait in the bedroom. It was four o'clock in the morning, he was wide awake and he was livid—in part at his own foolishness for dancing and drinking and being so loud in public, because now it had brought them to the attention of the local constabulary.

That was the main source of his anger: after such a perfect night of dancing and intimacy, both he and Jim had been sound asleep when the first knock came at the door. Knowing what was coming, Jim went straight up to the top-floor apartment, where, thankfully, they'd made up the bed and left it in a state of disarray for this eventuality. There were even a few tins of food in the kitchen cupboards and, along with the kettle and teapot Jim and Molly's group used for their meetings, the apartment might just pass as someone's home.

But even before tonight, they'd known this would happen sooner or later, and Arty's previous meekness, his fear of being publicly shamed, was fading fast. If they arrested Jim they might send him back to West Virginia, where the law was just as harsh as in Britain, should he make it alive past the violent mob in his hometown.

Some forty-five minutes later, when the policemen finally left, Jim returned to Arty, utterly broken. He sat next to him on the edge of the bed, his hands covering his face.

"I'm so sorry, darlin'," he whispered hoarsely. "I am so, so sorry."

Arty put an arm around Jim's shoulders, and he toppled helplessly, shaking so violently it made Arty squeeze harder to try and make it stop. "Why are you sorry?"

"I lied to them."

"To protect us."

"I promised I'd never deny my love for you."

"You had no choice."

"All the bullcrap I've been talking, saying we gotta stand tall and proud…" Jim tried to pull away, but Arty refused to let go. As if in cahoots, Silky stretched her front legs over

Jim's knees and hooked her claws into the fabric of his dressing gown.

"You were frightened," Arty stated. Jim gave no response, yet Arty knew Jim's self-torture was nothing to do with failing to stand tall and proud, or denying his feelings. There were so many things he wanted to say, to offer comfort, make it all better, but none of them were worth expending the breath. Could they fight this? Unlikely. Now the police were suspicious they'd be back again. They'd need to find somewhere else to hold the meetings. Jim would have to move upstairs for real. But all of that was superficial; they'd find a way to cope, learn to live with it if they had to.

Jim gulped and sniffed, reaching down a shaky hand to stroke Silky's smooth grey fur. She purred her permission. Jim laughed sadly.

"I love you," Arty said.

"I love you," Jim echoed.

"We'll get through this, love, I know we will. Look how much we've already survived." *We've got to live…*

"I hear you." Jim took a long, deep breath and slowly released it. "I got to get up for work soon. What will you do with your day? You gonna talk some more with Jean?"

"Yes," Arty said. They were moving on. No more talk of Jim's 'denial', or the reason behind it. That was who Jim was, but it didn't stop Arty from willing him to hear in his heart the words he could not, *would not* say.

He can't get to you here. I won't let him.

241

Chapter Twenty-Seven:
January–May, 1954

Little Eddie was without a doubt his mother's son. Every Saturday morning, at the children's ballroom and Latin class, there he would be: seven years old and already in constant demand from the older girls queuing up for him to lead them in the quickstep.

"Look at him, will you?" Jean said with a resigned sigh as her son danced past, arms high above his head in order to reach his eleven-year-old partner.

Arty chuckled. "He's as bad as Jim. Never could refuse a pretty girl."

"Very true," Jean agreed. She rubbed her swollen belly. She wasn't very far on, yet she was already showing, due to her slender dancer's form. "I wonder if this little lady will be a dancer too?"

"Dancer or not, I'm sure *he* will simply adore all those pink dresses you've bought *him*."

Jean glared at Arty and he grinned. He secretly hoped the baby due in four months' time was, as Jean insisted, a girl. He wasn't sure why; whatever it was, he would love him or her just the same as he loved Eddie, who was now striding purposefully across the dance floor in Arty's direction. Jean had gone to change the record.

"One more dance and that's all for this week, children," she forewarned the pupils, who offered a collective grumble of disappointment, although many also came for individual lessons, so they had a few days to wait, at most.

"Uncle Arty, do your legs work today?"

"They're not too bad, Ed."

"Please will you dance with Mummy and show Sylvia?"

It was a request Eddie made often, eager to show off his mother and 'uncle'—the champions—in his attempts to impress the girls.

"Leave it with me," Arty said, "and I'll see if I can persuade your mum."

Eddie dashed off again, calling, "Thanks," over his shoulder as an afterthought.

For the first hour of the children's session, Arty and Jean took half of the room each and taught the boys and girls separately, before providing them all with a glass of milk and a biscuit, and then bringing them together for the second hour, at the end of which they could choose their partners for the last dance. Straight after the children's class came the teenagers, followed by Saturday afternoon at the Palais. The fashions were changing and, once again, the Americans were to blame.

Rock 'n' roll was fast and noisy, and the first time Jim played a record, Arty genuinely thought the stylus needed cleaning, which amused Jim to no end. Since then, Arty had become used to it and, whilst he couldn't say he liked it much, he could understand how appealing it was to younger people—in particular the dancing it inspired, which seemed to require only the ability to abandon one's inhibitions. However, for Arty's generation, and the parents of his and Jean's dance pupils, it was about far more than the dancing itself. It was about survival and camaraderie, reliving those moments of light in a long and dark period of their lives.

Jim was delighted that rock 'n' roll was taking off. It was his kind of music, and when they ventured to the Palais in the evenings, he would dance until he was fit to collapse. Alas, it was far too fast and energetic for Arty: he had built up some stamina during the many hours of teaching and demonstrating, but it still drained him. He alternated between work and rest days, finally able to appreciate the importance of the latter, no longer wracked with guilt about being 'lazy' and lounging for hours on the settee, only getting up to make lunch and dinner.

Competitions were held at Hammersmith Palais every Tuesday afternoon, and so the dance school's week ran from Wednesday to Monday, with private lessons during the daytime on Wednesdays, Thursdays and Fridays. The Beginner and Intermediate sessions were held on Wednesday evenings, the Advanced class on Monday, and then the children came in on a Saturday morning, with the option to attend the Palais in the afternoon. The arrangements were flexible enough to ensure Arty could take his rest days and Jean could be home for Eddie after school. When the baby was born, they'd have to make adjustments, but for the time being it suited everyone, particularly as Jim and Charlie were working six-day weeks just trying to keep on top of the jobs coming in.

The city was prospering and as a direct consequence so was the workshop. More ordinary people owned cars and bikes, and whilst most owners were able to tackle the day-to-day maintenance, few had the skills or the equipment needed to deal with specialist jobs. There was also government talk of bringing in a test of roadworthiness, and from Jim's stories about some of the old heaps he'd had to fix up, it was no bad thing, particularly if it brought more business their way. There were now two apprentice mechanics working with Jim and Charlie, which, in spite of six years' retirement from mechanical work, Arty was still struggling to leave behind. He'd trained so many boys back at Minton, and he missed it more than he cared to admit.

It was remarkable to think back and realise those boys weren't much younger than him, and yet in wartime just a couple of years had felt like a lifetime of experience. Eighteen-year-olds manning gun turrets on bombers—what a different breed they were to the eighteen-year-olds they saw at the Palais, all so arrogant and seemingly unaware of the cost of victory. For these boys, the war had been an adventure, an extended holiday out in the countryside. Now they were old enough to understand, and they would soon go off to complete their national service: two years' conscription in peacetime and they returned believing they knew what it was like to fight a war, to lose friends every day, to survive on meagre rations. To live a lie.

After the early morning visit from the police in 1949, life went on, albeit more cautiously. The political group disbanded, Molly and Daphne emigrated to Australia, and Arty and Jim moved up to the top floor, whilst Jean, Charlie and Eddie moved to the ground floor. It gave Eddie direct access to the garden, and most days Arty could take the stairs without too much trouble; however, the main reason was to give Arty and Jim a time buffer, should the boys in blue come calling again. And they did.

For five years, all had been quiet. Of course they knew of the raids and arrests taking place in men's clubs where most dared not even give their name, never mind take another man home with them. Some of their friends knew of men who were arrested in public toilets, having gone there with the express intention of finding other men like them, or, as the police would have it, 'engaging in acts of gross indecency'.

"Why do they refuse to see it?" Jim asked, so angry he almost punched a hole right through the newspaper when he read of the Chief Constable's pompous intention to 'rip the covers off all England's filth spots'. "What the hell's a man supposed to do? How can it be more moral to send in cops as *agents provocateurs* who expose and play with themselves, than it is for guys to get so lonely they're forced to go there in the first place?"

Then came a high-profile case involving a peer and a well-respected journalist. What hurt Arty and Jim the most was that the men who turned Queen's evidence against them were RAF airmen, but they all knew the drill. If the police hauled them in, they'd be interrogated until they cracked and confessed to whatever was necessary to avoid imprisonment. Judges claimed leniency when they didn't dole out a life sentence for 'buggery', or agreed to a suspended sentence if the 'offender' underwent treatment—aversion therapy, electric shocks, female hormones—to rid men of the desire to act on something the Chief Constable believed was 'made'. His evidence: an increase in the number of arrests since the war, indicating that British soldiers had 'picked up the disease and brought it home with them', as opposed to the truth. It was a witch hunt of homosexuals, and the Chief Constable was the Witch Finder General.

"If he's a queer, then why haven't I caught it then, eh?" Charlie spat bitterly after the police officers who marched Arty away from Dalton Place. Eddie was screaming in his mother's arms, Jean was crying, and Jim had flown back to West Virginia the day before, with Joshua. Their father was dead.

***

247

"Are you a homosexual, Mr. Clarke?"

"No."

"Yet you've never married."

"I prefer to live alone."

"With another single man in the flat below? Convenient that, isn't it, Mr. Clarke?"

"The four of us moved in together after the war. We've been friends for a long time, and it made good financial sense."

"We've arrested Jim Johnson."

Arty said nothing, because he knew it was an outright lie: Jim had telephoned that morning to confirm he and Joshua had arrived safely in New York.

"He's agreed to testify that you committed buggery with each other. However, if you—"

"I want my barrister," Arty said.

"Mr. Clarke, it's almost nine o'clock on a Wednesday evening. I'm quite sure your barrister has better things to do than waste his time on someone like you."

"Like me?"

"A queer invalid."

"Please get my barrister," Arty repeated, impressed by how calm he sounded, and also grateful Jim was out of the country.

"A war injury, was it?"

Arty clasped his hands together and squeezed, and squeezed.

"You'd have been better off dead. Same goes for all your sort."

And squeezed. The tirade continued, and Arty tuned out, introspecting, reciting stories in his head, listing the butterflies he had seen over the years, trying not to be joyous that Jim's father was dead.

When finally the police officer realised he wasn't going to rile Arty into breaking his silence, he threw him back in his cell. The next morning, Bernard Cohen, QC, caused merry hell with the bigwigs and Arty was released without charge. Such was the benefit of knowing who was in the underground of homosexual London, for they all had their price: freedom.

The harassment continued, with the police hauling Jim away the day he returned from the States. He and Arty hadn't even seen each other. Yet again, Bernard Cohen was called in, but his tactics failed, and Jim was held on remand until the magistrates' court could fit him in, along with the dozens of other men arrested for conspiring to engage in homosexual acts. The magistrates adjourned the case to crown court, and the crown court added Jim to the list of homosexuals awaiting sentencing; to call it a trial would have suggested justice might prevail, and it did not.

Every day Arty waited for the police to come for him. After all, if they had evidence to charge Jim, then surely it must incriminate him too? He was so desperate to see Jim, but as time went by, and Arty was still at liberty, it became apparent that Jim had protected him somehow, and one visit or letter would mean it was all in vain.

The day of the court hearing arrived; Joshua and Charlie sat in the public gallery, whilst Jim admitted his guilt and was sentenced to eighteen months' imprisonment for three counts of gross indecency. Once sentencing was passed, Joshua was allowed to see Jim, who passed on a message for Arty.

"How?" Arty asked, taking the letter from Joshua. "Did they leave you unaccompanied?"

Joshua smiled and pointed at his lips. "Read," he instructed. "I will make a pot of tea."

Arty took the sheet of paper from the envelope and unfolded it, perpetually amazed by the man who was his brother-in-law. The letter filled both sides of the paper, and it would be Jim's words exactly, remembered by Joshua until he could write them down.

Hey darling,

I don't have long, but I needed to get this message to you before they move me to the jail. First I need to tell you I love you and I miss you. God, I miss you so much, it feels like my insides have been ripped right out of me. You're all I can think of and being apart is killing me. But I've got to stay strong, for you if not for myself. I'm sorry I'm putting you through this. You deserve so much better.

You will read in the papers of how I am guilty of gross indecency with three men whose names I do not know. Please believe me when I tell you none of it is true. You are the only man I have ever loved and the only one I ever will love.

I made you a promise that I would never deny my feelings for you, but when it came to it I had to do it to keep you safe. It's the only thing that matters to me, and I will spend the rest of my life locked away if that's what it takes.

The judge says I've got to have treatment because I refused to admit being homosexual was a sickness. I told them it doesn't work. I was born this way, and I'm going to keep on fighting them.

What it means is I'm not coming home any time soon, but you mustn't feel bad for me. It's worth it to know you are free. Live your life, darling. Go on without me.

I'll never stop loving you, do you know that? Never. But if you can, then please, I beg you. Please stop loving me.

Forever yours,
Jim

PART FIVE: 1955

Chapter Twenty-Eight:
October, 1955

"OK?" Joshua asked.

"I'll say yes," Arty replied, holding up his thumb to confirm it. He would be in a few hours' time, when Jim walked through those gates. Joshua affectionately roughed up Arty's hair and gave him a smile that conveyed a thousand feelings and thoughts. It was one of his greatest gifts: the ability to communicate so richly with a simple look or touch.

Eighteen months ago, Arty's life had stalled. He'd read Jim's letter and his world imploded. Other than the pain in his knees, which had lasted for weeks, the day Jim was sentenced was still a gaping hole in Arty's memory, and were it not for Joshua refusing to leave him alone, Arty would have taken his own life, or what was left of it. It was the only way he could do what Jim had asked of him.

His knees—he had apparently fallen to the floor—had recovered quite well, and quickly, whereas his mind shifted to some kind of autopilot, and it seemed nothing could switch him back to manual control. He was glad, in a way, for it had been a tragic time. Jean's baby was stillborn and the doctors had to remove Jean's womb, leaving Eddie an only child. At the strange, quiet funeral, Arty gave the eulogy, and mourners thanked him for his touching words. He graciously accepted their compliments and their sympathy, though he himself remained entirely untouched. He had not known this child; it was not his loss to grieve, thus it was no hardship to be the lynchpin that day, ushering, and welcoming, and nodding sadly as he listened to countless morbid tales of how the same thing had happened to so-and-so's sister, or aunt, or maid of honour.

Death, it seemed once again, was everywhere, for Soot also passed away. At the grand old age of eleven years, he'd had a good innings, Arty reasoned. He pictured the three brothers, reunited in their old hangar in cat heaven, chasing balls of shimmering, golden hay and leaping on unsuspecting angel mice. It was a lovely thought; comforting, even. Yet the mirage was no more meaningful to him than the pointless fairy tales he had once loved so dearly. The loss was a constant itch he could not reach; he was paralysed, alone on the battlefield, and still the skies kept falling.

Joshua and Louisa broke off their engagement, their bond unable to withstand the strain of all that had been put upon it by Jim's incarceration, coming so soon after Jimmy Johnson Senior's death. In the back of Arty's mind had been the rather callous notion that Joshua's willingness to support him was entirely self-serving, for in that respect the Johnson men were quite alike. Nonetheless, it was a shame to see Joshua and Louisa—two people so extraordinarily well suited—torn asunder, but for the longest time Arty didn't have it in him to care, nor to feel guilty for it.

Then came the horrifying jolt that finally set Arty free, administered by his mother, over the telephone.

"I'm calling with bad news. Uncle Bill is dead." She said it as if she were telling of the demise of some distant, unfamiliar acquaintance.

"Pardon?" Arty asked, his voice rising shrilly; he was convinced he'd misheard.

"He had a heart attack yesterday morning, but the hospital—"

"Mother, stop!"

She stopped. Arty tried to turn what she'd said into something that made sense. "You told me you hadn't heard from Bill since autumn, 1943."

"Yes. That's correct."

"So... You didn't know he had survived until now?"

"That's not quite right, no."

"You knew he was alive?"

"Yes, we did, but—"

"You lied. All these years, you've been lying to Sissy and me. You let us believe he never came home from the war. Why?"

"We didn't lie. We decided not to tell you...for your own good. The thing is, Robert, he was...he brought shame on our family."

"How so?"

"He was captured by the Germans."

"And what? Became a double agent?"

"Nothing so glamorous, I'm afraid. Your uncle..."

She didn't need to say anything further; her reluctance to put it into words said it all, but Arty was not going to make it easy for her. After all he and Jim had been through, enduring what amounted to years apart, and the countless times Arty had tried to write to his parents—a letter that might have led to discovering the truth about Uncle Bill sooner—there would be no gentle reprieve for his mother.

"Go on," he prompted coldly. "Say it."

"Bill was...a homosexual. He was undergoing treatment—electric shock therapy."

"And that's what killed him."

"I don't think homosexuality—"

"The therapy, Mother," Arty snapped.

"Ah. Yes. Apparently his heart gave out."

257

For the second time in as many years, Arty fell to his knees for Jim, this time to give thanks to God that Jim had refused the treatment and chosen to serve his full sentence.

Arty hadn't spoken to his mother since, and the way he was feeling he never wanted to speak to her again. His desire to tell her he was homosexual was no longer about seeking her acceptance. He would not beg for it, apologise, nor justify his existence. She had discarded her own brother, in death as in life; Arty listened in solitude to the priest's mumblings of ashes and dust as Private William Norris was finally laid to rest: no reversed arms, no salutes and no Last Post for this war hero, because he *had* died in battle, and it was the cruellest and bloodiest of all.

That was three months ago, and Arty had returned to Dalton Place a changed man. All of his life he had been careful, diligent, like the caterpillar that feeds in preparation for what is to come, meticulously builds its cocoon and cautiously crawls inside. Sealed safely away from the world, the metamorphosis begins, and soon all that remains of the caterpillar is its core essence, the fundamental building blocks of the winged creature that will one day emerge and unfurl, patiently waiting those last few moments as its wings dry and begin to flutter. The transformation finally complete, the beauteous beast soars into the air, magnificent, victorious, and splendidly reckless in its singular, instinctive pursuit.

Arty could not stop loving Jim, but he had done everything else Jim had asked. No letters, no visits, nothing but an eternal purgatory, and it was time to break his silence, although he was sensible enough to not throw all caution to the wind.

As Joshua prepared for what would be the last prison visit, Arty made his request: "Please tell your brother I'll be waiting for him."

"I will. But he already knows."

"Tell him anyway."

Joshua nodded and hugged Arty fondly. "I've got a proposal for you both. I'll explain later."

Chapter Twenty-Nine:
October, 1955

From across the street, through a slender crack in the blackout paint covering the car's side window, Arty watched Joshua, who, in turn, stood outside the prison gates, watching the vast wooden doors. Arty couldn't see the doors from his location; he could see only the gates and Joshua. The designated hour had arrived; Joshua's stance changed. The gate swung open.

"Jim!" Arty cried, pressing forehead and palm to the cold black glass as the tears began to flow. Joshua and Jim were locked in a tight, silent embrace and stayed so for many minutes, affording Arty time to compose himself, for what it was worth.

At long last, Joshua and Jim released each other, and Joshua led his brother across the road, glancing back so he could read Jim's lips. Arty read them too.

"In the car?"

Joshua nodded and Jim broke into a sprint. Skidding to a stop, he flung the door open so quickly, Arty fell forward, only just managing to grab the back of the seat and not tumble out onto the road. Somehow he shuffled over enough to allow Jim to get into the car, shutting the door behind him, and then he was encapsulated in arms so strong he could not have broken free if he'd fought with all his might. The kisses, at once familiar, left no time to breathe, or speak, and no need for either. A shaft of light illuminated the dark rear compartment of the blacked-out Morris, and Arty and Jim sprang apart, squinting at the source. Joshua grinned at them and the shutter closed again. The engine roared to life. In the darkness, through touch, Arty wiped away Jim's tears and smoothed a hand over his stubbled crown.

"I love you."

"I love you. And I've missed you so much."

"Me too. Oh, Jim. You can't imagine..."

"Shh. All right, darlin'. I'm here now."

Arty sniffed and spluttered and dug the handkerchiefs from his pocket: he'd brought them one each, and he pressed the softer of the two into Jim's hand. "Did Joshua tell you we're going to stay with him?"

"Yeah, he did."

"I know you'd rather go home, but it's safer for us there."

"Hey, don't shoot me for saying this, but home is wherever you are, darlin'."

"Why would I shoot you for saying that?"

Jim laughed quietly, and they kissed again. Arty kept it going for as long as he could, dreading what he needed to tell Jim before they arrived back at the house.

"I've already moved our belongings, and the cats."

"It'll be so good to see them again."

"I can imagine. But...Soot..." Arty inhaled, the gulp of air almost choking him. *Our sons are dead.*

"I know," Jim said gently, cupping Arty's head, cradling him, rocking and shushing him, as the geyser of grief erupted. "Everything's gonna be just fine. I promise."

Whether the promise proved true or false, it was all Arty needed to confirm Jim had come back to him. Prison had not broken him. *His* Jim was home again, even if for the foreseeable future home would not be Dalton Place. But Jim was right: wherever they were *was* home, so long as they were together, and Joshua's suggestion that they move in with him gave them a far better chance of staying that way.

Joshua still worked for the United States government, and as such was afforded diplomatic immunity. Whilst it didn't cover Arty and Jim, it created an extra layer of protection, because the Home Office would avoid acting in any way which might sully international relations. The police wouldn't dare enter Joshua's home without a search warrant, and the courts would likely refuse to grant one. However, with fear of communism rife, the situation in the States was as dire as it was in England, with suspected homosexuals ousted from their jobs in government because they were deemed to pose a security risk. By offering Arty and Jim room in his house, Joshua was putting his neck on the line, and in accepting, Arty and Jim were, essentially, going under self-imposed house arrest.

When they arrived, Joshua's chauffeur drove the car straight into the garage so that Arty and Jim were not seen entering the premises. They had spoken little during the thirty-minute journey, content with the physical contact and the comfort it brought. Arty had so much he needed to say, and he sensed the same was true of Jim, but all of that could wait until they had properly reunited.

The silence continued as they followed Joshua up to the rooms that were their accommodation for as long as they needed it.

"See you at eight for dinner," Joshua said on his way out of the bedroom, where Jim had already flopped onto the plush king-size bed and was revelling in the softness of the mattress and the clean, white linen. He raised his arm and offered his brother a thumbs up.

"You're welcome," Joshua replied, wiping away a tear and then adding, with a wink to Arty, "Dumb hoofer."

Arty was too choked with gratitude to use words, but he knew the sign for 'thank you', so he signed it. Joshua smiled and looked Jim's way as he signed it back. The door closed and Arty locked it, taking a moment to get his thoughts in order before he turned around.

"Come on over here," Jim called. "This bed's sweet."

"I imagine an RAF bunk would be just as sweet after what you've been sleeping on."

Arty about-turned to find Jim had prised himself off the mattress and was in the process of getting undressed. He'd lost some of his bulk, but gained a lot of muscle, and he was as glorious a sight to behold as ever. Arty swallowed hard and his legs started to tremble.

"You need to sit down," Jim advised.

Arty cleared his throat self-consciously. "That's not the problem."

Jim, now naked, shrugged and smiled. "At least get undressed?"

"I thought you'd never ask," Arty said, fairly tearing his buttonholes as he ripped his shirt open and threw it to the floor. Trousers unfastened and pushed to his knees, he sat on the side of the bed to remove them, but before he had the chance to do so, Jim scooped him up and lifted him to the centre of the mattress, kissing him all the while. He carefully set him down on his back and finished undressing him.

"You do realise this is the third time we've been through this?" Arty observed from his prone position.

"You forgotten how to count while I been inside?" Jim joked. Kneeling on the edge of the bed, he moved Arty's feet apart and shuffled forward into the space between them, running his palms over the skin, from ankles, to shins, to

264

knees, applying the same firm pressure as always, since the early days after Arty's accident.

"I've forgotten about you being *inside*," Arty said, keeping his eyes trained on Jim's erect penis to avoid any potential— though improbable—misunderstanding.

Jim chuckled and lifted Arty's legs a little higher, continuing to massage his thighs, slowly, carefully, easing them up and apart. He shuffled closer, using his hips to hold the weight of Arty's legs whilst he worked his way along the insides of his thighs, diverting when he reached the top. He tended to his abdomen, hips, stomach and sternum, but could not reach higher than that from his present position, and so he worked his way down again, with the same slow, deliberate care.

Arty sighed in pleasure. He'd expected, after eighteen months of enforced celibacy, they'd both be so desperate for release they'd have jumped straight to it, but it was more than the physical act—the 'buggering', as the law so crudely referred to it. It was in every touch, every taste, the knowledge they shared of each other's bodies, spots no bigger than a sixpence where the brush of a fingertip was sufficient to ignite every nerve ending. And it was in the connection of their hearts and minds, the trust, faithfulness and sacrifice.

The joining of their bodies was no less erotic on this occasion than any other, but its significance seemed to elevate it to another plane. Three times they had been forced apart; three times they had come back together, and beyond the base carnal act there was a deeper connection sustained by mutual resolve. They would fight to protect their freedom, just as they had once fought to liberate Europe.

Also rather liberating was the realisation that they could not be heard and neither held in their cries of satisfaction, nor the tears that followed their release. They huddled

265

together in the midst of the enormous bed with its thick, giving mattress, the soft linen sheets adding their caresses to the kiss-whispers of love that eased them into sleep. It was not yet past noon.

They napped on and off for the rest of the day, filling the wakeful moments with more intimacy and a lot of talking.

"You know they tried again to force me to have the treatment?" Jim said. He sought Arty's hand and laced their fingers tightly together.

"Did they?"

"Yeah. I told 'em if my pop couldn't beat the queer out of me, then their amateur methods weren't worth a dime."

Arty lightly kissed Jim's cheek, both reward for his bravery and encouragement to continue.

"He never let a day go by without telling me how much he hated me. And he wanted me to leave, but I couldn't, not till my papers came through." Jim laughed as a better memory surfaced. "Mom wouldn't let him in the house, made him sleep in the stable for almost a week. Man, he was stinkin', and I don't mean of manure."

Arty joined in with the laughter. There were so many questions he had wanted to ask about Jim's father, born of nothing more than his desire to know everything about the man he loved. But the whole conversation was delicate and precarious, like the skin of a recently closed wound, and Arty couldn't chance it.

Jim unlocked his fingers from Arty's and turned onto his side, so that they were lying face-to-face. "Mom told Joshua she was planning to come visit."

"Joshua mentioned it. I can't wait to meet her."

"I don't know when it'll be. She's sold the land, did he tell you?"

"Yes. He said she's looking after the old couple."

266

"That's right. They're great guys." Jim's eyes flashed briefly with anger and then determination. "You know the journalist and that other guy ended up in jail with me?"

"I knew they'd gone to prison. It was all over every front page. He admitted to being a homosexual in court."

"Yeah. He's got guts. They beat the crap out of the three of us. But we got to talking. We're gonna do something, darlin'."

"Like what?"

"Same as before, but this time we're gonna get ourselves organised—get all the facts and figures, talk to doctors and politicians, make allies. Peter said the government are putting together a report."

"Peter?" Arty queried.

"The journalist. He's got nothing left to lose. He already lost his career, and the man he loved." Jim stared deep into Arty's eyes, the message clear. He was going to war, whatever the cost.

"What's he like?" Arty asked.

"Determined. Bitter. Intelligent. Brave."

"Handsome?"

Jim laughed with the wondrous booming joy of old. He hauled Arty in and kissed him hard on the lips, and again, and again, each time becoming softer and longer. A sigh passed between them.

"Well?" Arty said, poking Jim in the side.

"I don't know if he's handsome. Maybe, I guess. He ain't you, that's all I know."

Arty couldn't imagine a better answer to his question. "You know, D H Lawrence—"

"No way! Only six hours and he's already in the room. How'd he know where to find us?"

"It's relevant," Arty promised. Jim smirked. Arty ignored him and continued, "He wrote *Lady Chatterley's Lover* after the Great War. The copy Antonio owns was published when I was nine years old—"

"A hundred years ago?" Jim teased.

"It's felt like it at times, that's for sure." Arty paused so he could get the anger in check. It had simmered for three months, threatening to boil over when he and Sissy argued and she defended their parents' decision. It left Arty feeling bruised and betrayed—they'd never argued before—but it wasn't Sissy's fault, not really. The gentle touch of Jim's fingers on his cheek soothed and calmed him, but he needed a prompt to force the words out. Jim gave it.

"What happened?"

"My Uncle Bill came back from the war. I don't know how long ago, my mother didn't say. She only called to tell me he was dead, and when I pushed her for details..." Arty closed his eyes and clamped his teeth tightly together to suppress the yell of rage and frustration. Three months had not quelled his hatred in the slightest.

"Was he homosexual?" Jim asked.

Arty nodded. "Yes. The treatment killed him, and then they buried him in a pauper's grave."

"Oh, darlin', I'm so sorry."

"I have to hold my hands up, Jim. I'm complicit."

"You didn't know."

"If I could just have written that blasted letter—"

"You couldn't have saved him."

"But he wouldn't have died alone. I'm so afraid, Jim. So terribly afraid, because I can't live without you. I know, because I tried, and I can survive, exist, but not live. I know you've got to do this. It's who you are, and it's one of the many things I love you for."

"If you don't want me to, just say the word."

"No. That would be asking the impossible."

"That ain't never stopped you before."

Arty laughed. "You make a very good case. However, that wasn't what I meant. As D H Lawrence wrote—don't mock—" Arty pre-empted, but Jim's expression was most sincere.

"You know, you always said it so much better than he did."

"He wrote—" Arty stopped again, as what Jim had said registered. Whenever he tried to explain he felt so inarticulate, but perhaps Jim was right, and his own words would suffice. "What I'm trying to say is this. I don't imagine for one minute that the fight will be quickly won. Indeed, Hitler was a far less complex adversary than the one we face. But I've stayed silent far too long, Jim. We're in this together—you, me, Peter, Uncle Bill, those old guys in the mountains—all of us. We've got to live, no matter how many skies have fallen." He grimaced. "That last part was D H Lawrence."

"Yeah." Jim laughed. "I figured. So we're really doing this together?"

"Yes. Together."

"All right! Let's bring down the sky!"

"You know you're asking the impossible?"

Jim smiled and smoothed Arty's hair back from his brow, leaving a light kiss in its place. "With you at my side, darlin', nothing is impossible."

Epilogue:
Saturday, 29th July, 1967

Dear Mum and Dad,

It's been quite some time since I last put pen to paper and wrote you a letter. How strange to think that not so long ago all we possessed was the written word. How impoverished our communication used to be, and yet there is a permanence to this mode of correspondence that a telephone conversation lacks. Imagine if I were calling you now: you would listen, respond, the call would end, and you would promptly forget most of what was said.

I doubt you will ever forget what I am about to tell you, and it might at first seem as if I am a coward to inform you by this means, but how easy it would be for you to simply pass it off as a figment of your combined imagination. Better that, no doubt, than to believe it is the truth, for you have made your thoughts on this matter quite clear.

Today is a very special day for me. I'll bet you're looking at each other right now, utterly perplexed. After all, my birthday is still two months away, and it's not my wedding anniversary—May 25th, 1946, in case you're wondering, and yes, I married in secret. Not officially, you understand. Well, you don't understand, not yet.

You see, Mum, Dad, today is the first day of my life that I am not a criminal. You may already have heard the news. After all, you've always kept up with current affairs, but in your sleepy hamlet, where the worst that ever happens is apple scrumping, and even then only if the season is right for it, perhaps the passing yesterday of a bill concerning prostitution and homosexuality is of no consequence.

Lest there be any confusion, I am not a prostitute. Indeed, I have lived virtuously, for there has only ever been "The One" for me. We met, we courted, we fell in love, and we committed to each other in common law, till death us do part.

You know Jim as my friend, my flatmate, the man who, after my accident, had "nothing better to do" than sit at my bedside, day after day, and has taken care of me ever since, though you never could quite understand why. This, Mum and Dad, is why.

Jim and I have been together for twenty-three years. We first set eyes on each other at the Palais Dance Hall in Minton, began courting, and soon after, we fell in love. We are some of the more fortunate ones, inasmuch as we have each other. Our love is not a sickness, nor is it a crime we "choose" to commit. If that were so, then the eighteen months Jim spent in prison would have deterred us. The barbaric "treatment" Uncle Bill was forced to endure would have cured rather than killed him.

We have lived in constant fear and, for the past twelve years, in reclusivity. Now that the state has decreed us innocent, we can finally come out into the open, but there is still so much more to be done. We are not sick. We are not predators. We were not "turned this way" by inadequate mothers, or perverts who took our innocence. We were born this way, and the love Jim and I share is as sacred and real as your love for each other.

There is still so much more to be done. For now, we celebrate our victory. After the way things were left with Uncle Bill, I don't expect that you will consider it a victory, nor would I dare to ask that you try and be pleased for us. I just felt that it was time you knew the truth about the kind of man your son is: happy, healthy, and loved.

Love,
Robert

**

Arty ushered the gaggle of pupils into the first two rows of seats along the side of the dance floor. It was Saturday afternoon at Hammersmith Palais, and as always the chance to be 'real' dancers for a couple of hours had the children overexcited.

"OK, chaps, get your shoes on," Arty instructed.

"Oy, Mister. Can you do my laces?" A scruffy little boy with tie askew and blinking round green eyes peered up at Jim.

"Magic word?" Jim prompted.

"Pleeeeaaase?"

"All right." Jim beckoned with his hand. "Gimme the shoes."

The boy handed over a pair of tiny and heavily scuffed patent dance shoes.

"You like spaghetti, huh?" Jim tormented, picking apart the tangled mess of laces. The little boy giggled.

"Where's Mrs. Tomkins?" one of the girls asked. "She promised she'd be here to watch me and Lucy do the rumba today."

"She had a very special delivery this morning, Alice," Arty said.

The little girl's eyes widened. She spun to face her friends. For several seconds a hiss of whispers behind cupped hands passed around the group, ending at a tall, pigtailed girl, who announced knowledgeably, "Mrs. Tomkins is going to be a grandma." She stared at Arty, daring him to deny it. He fought back a smile.

"No, Sharon," he said. "Mrs. Tomkins *is* a grandma. Eddie's wife had a little girl this morning."

"What's she called?"

"What's her name?"

"Shush!" Arty raised his hands. "She hasn't got a name yet."

274

The girls gasped en masse and the whispering began anew.

Arty shook his head, exasperated. "Are those shoes on?" he asked sternly, and the entire row of children bent over to reach their feet. Arty glanced Jim's way, and they shared a smile. It was good to be out in the open together again. The dance hall band began to play and Arty clapped his hands twice. "Off you go then, everyone."

The children filed out of their seats and onto the dance floor, where couples of all ages were already quickstepping. Arty watched his boys and girls pair up and join the circle—all except one little girl, who stood pigeon-toed and forlorn.

"Oh, Mary," Arty said to himself. "Why's it always you?"

The little girl turned away from the dancers and walked, with downturned face, back to Arty and Jim. Tears ran down the shiny streaks on her cheeks, and she tried to step past without being seen, but Jim caught hold of her and scooped her up into his arms.

"Hey, sweetness. What you crying for?"

She lifted her shoulders in a small dejected shrug.

"Is it because…your shoes are pinching?"

She shook her head, her eyes never leaving Jim's face.

"Your plaits are too tight?"

She shook her head again.

"Oh, wait. I got it. You're sad for the other girls, because they're not as beautiful as you."

The girl frowned at Jim. He raised an eyebrow and nodded.

"Am I right?"

She gave him another shrug and rested her head against his shoulder, still gazing at him intently.

"All right. I got an easier question. Which dance do you like the best?"

"Cha-cha," she replied, her voice so quiet the words barely sounded at all.

"The cha-cha," Jim repeated, nodding sagely. "That's a great dance."

The quickstep came to an end, and the dancers paused whilst the band changed their music over. A foxtrot followed.

"What's your name, sweetness?" Jim asked, even though he'd heard Arty say her name before.

"Mary," she replied.

"Mary. A pretty name for a pretty lady. My name's Jim." He shifted her onto his hip so he could offer his hand. She put her dainty hand in his and they shook. "I'm very pleased to meet you, Mary," Jim said. She gave him the tiniest of smiles.

Arty had been watching Jim and Mary in awe. She was the shiest pupil in the junior dance class and if, like today, there was an odd number of children, she was always the one left out. Quite a few of the dance school pupils came from poorer families, and Jean and Arty helped out as much as they could, by keeping a stock of shoes, as well as dresses and suits, bought from older pupils as they grew out of them. But for all of that, the quieter children, like Mary, still stuck out like sore thumbs. She was always clean and well turned out, and she learned quickly, but she hardly ever spoke to the other children, and they made very little effort to include her if it wasn't forced upon them.

Jim didn't know any of this, for he'd had no involvement with the dance school before today. Since he'd come out of prison, he and Arty had lived an undercover life. In public, they were the business partners of Jean and Charlie Tomkins, so if they did happen to be seen together they had good reason, which was just as well. Their involvement in the Campaign for Homosexual Equality had kept them in the sights of both local law enforcement and the press, and the invasion of privacy would have been absolute, were it not for some rather cunning commuting on Arty's part. His official residence had always been Dalton Place, and he would return there after work each night, later catching trains and buses across London, to a designated tube station, where Joshua's chauffeur would collect him and take him back to the house.

After twelve years of living like a Cold War spy, Arty knew the London Underground better than most of its staff, and many of the staff also knew him. He was 'one of those queers in the papers', and, of course, they could all tell he was a homosexual. After all, what kind of man reads romance, is fascinated by butterflies and earns his living teaching children how to dance? The previous evening, for the first time in his life, he had the power to answer back: *Ah yes, but my common-law husband reads medical papers, enjoys boxing and fixes cars for a living. Now hop it, before I get him to fix you!*

He didn't say it out loud. Indeed, he thought it ludicrous that his pursuits should make him any less of a man. But that was a fight for another time. Tomorrow they were moving back to Dalton Place: no more fear of prosecution for daring to love each other, so long as no one stayed the night, incumbent feline company excepted.

"...is a thinker and a dreamer."

Jim's singsong teasing snapped Arty out of his trance.

"This fine young woman has agreed to dance with me. What d'you think of that?"

"That's very kind of you, Mary. He has a lot to learn."

Jim waved away Arty's words, and Mary beamed as Jim led her by the hand across the dance floor to a spot directly in front of the band. The music began and the two stepped off, chassis right, chassis left, moving on to short simple steps, because Mary was only eight years old and barely reached Jim's chest, but she was quickly finding her rhythm, and Jim was an exceptional lead, which was why all of the women wanted to dance with him. He could make the clumsiest, two-left-footed girl in the world float around the floor like a fairy princess.

More impressive still, on this occasion, was that Mary had been attending lessons for four years and had never shown any dancing ability, until now. Jim slid her down to the floor, threaded her between his legs, spun on the spot, swept her high into the air, and on they went, Mary's huge smile lighting up the room, whilst her classmates missed steps and tripped over each other, staring in shock and envy.

As the dance came to an end, Jim bent down to kiss Mary's cheek, and she threw her arms around him in a big hug. He reciprocated, staying crouched beside her for a moment, a conversation taking place between them that Arty couldn't hear from his location, but now he could see what Jim had already seen, hence he had taken her to dance in front of the band.

"Arty Clarke, you are a fool," he admonished himself, for it all made perfect sense now. In the four years he had known Mary, not once did it occur to him that she might be hard of hearing.

One of the other pupils—a boy named Eric—approached Mary and Jim, and tentatively held out his hand to Mary. She glanced at Jim, who nodded and rose to his feet. Jilted by his jive partner, he started making his way back to Arty, only to be waylaid by another girl, and another, and on it went, right through to the time when parents came to collect their offspring.

When Mary's mum arrived, Jim volunteered to talk to her about her daughter. At first the poor woman was mortified: her perfect child was no more, but Jim continued, the deep, soothing tone of his voice calming and reassuring Mary's mother, as he told her about Joshua and all he had achieved in spite of having no hearing at all, and whilst Jim talked, Mary watched, lip-reading and hanging on to his every word.

"Does that mean she can't come dancing any more, Mr. Clarke?" Mary's mother asked, her mouth made small and brows drawn high in worry.

"Of course she can come dancing, Mrs. Jones," Arty assured her. "She's a wonderful dancer." He looked Mary in the eye and repeated, "You're a wonderful dancer, Mary." He gave her a thumbs up, and she responded with a big grin.

"Thank you," Mary's mother said. "Thank you, both." She gave Jim's hand a tight squeeze with both of hers.

"Same time next week?" Jim said to Mary, who nodded enthusiastically and waved as she followed her mother towards the exit.

Mary and Mrs. Jones were the last to leave, and Arty sighed in relief. He loved teaching the little ones—he especially enjoyed bringing them to the Palais—but it was exhausting to keep an eye on them all, even with Jim's very welcome assistance. Now it was just the two of them, he flopped into the closest chair to watch the dancing. The afternoon free-for-all had ended and the competitive dancers had taken to the floor, currently practising the rumba in preparation for the coming week's contests. Arty shook his head in weary wonder.

"Do you know, love? At some point, Jean and I have taught all of those dancers."

Jim shrugged. "Doesn't surprise me in the least. You got yourselves quite a reputation."

Arty continued to watch the couples lilt and sway, his gaze slowly losing focus as his mind drifted. Eighteen years had passed since he had convinced Jean to follow her dream and open a dance school, and so many hopeful young dancers had come through their doors. Some had stayed for just the one session and decided ballroom and Latin wasn't for them. Others had hung around until the allure of rock 'n' roll proved too strong to resist. Then there were the fine young people out there on the dance floor who had stayed the distance, perfected their style, taken exams; turned professional. Arty was proud of all of them, and himself. And to think, he'd once been convinced he'd never dance again.

How easy it was now to let go of the bad memories, almost as if they had been swept away and subsumed by the swirling rainbow eddies of the dance's eternal ebb and flow. For Arty it had always been like this: reality paled, lost its ugliness in the face of all that grace and beauty. Even in war, just the simple act of giving oneself over to the music could soothe away every trouble.

"Where's your head at, dreamer?" Jim murmured close to Arty's ear, making him shiver and smile.

"Right here," he confirmed.

"Good to know." Jim brushed his lips lightly over Arty's cheek as he moved around in front of him. "You know, I pride myself on being a man of my word."

"Yes, you do," Arty agreed.

"And sometimes I make rash promises. Don't get me wrong. I mean every single one of 'em, but maybe…" Jim nodded to himself and smiled. "You're not the only dreamer around here, darlin'. So, I think, when it comes down to it, what I'm trying to say is, would you care to dance?"

For a moment, Arty stared at Jim's outstretched hand, completely dumbfounded—no power of speech, no muscle control—but only for a moment. With a deep breath for courage, he accepted Jim's hand and allowed him to lead the way, arriving in the centre of the dance floor at the exact same time as the bandleader gave a count-in of three. Arty started to laugh.

"You planned this, didn't you?"

Jim just grinned and put his arm around Arty's side, his large, warm palm against Arty's back.

"Lucky I know both steps, really," Arty grumbled, but it was all an act. With one hand on Jim's broad shoulder and the other gripping Jim's hand, they moved off and lifted, and sidestepped, and turned, and all around them the dancing stopped as people moved back to watch. No disgust, disapproval, or judgement, just sheer delight and admiration. And then they were clapping, every single one of them; clapping, and whistling, and cheering on the champions.

"This is incredible," Arty said, breathless from exhilaration rather than exhaustion. He was floating, flying free, and he was falling…ever more deeply in love. He wanted it to never end, and was tempted to wish, but fate had been very generous of late, so instead he just relished every moment of waltzing with Jim.

Alas, all too soon the waltz came to an end, and Jim pulled Arty into his arms. "Worth waiting for?" he asked.

"I'd say so," Arty said, glancing over Jim's shoulder. He raised his hand to catch the attention of the bandleader, mouthing *jitterbug* at him and receiving a nod of confirmation. The drummer clicked his sticks together four times in quick succession, and Arty stepped back so he could take in Jim's expression.

"Are you sure you're up to this?" Jim asked.

"With you leading me, love, I'm up for anything."

The End

Glossary

Armed Services
RAF: Royal Air Force
WAAF: Women's Auxiliary Air Force
USAAF: United States Army Air Forces
NAAFI: Navy, Army and Air Force Institutes (provide the recreational institutes for the British Armed Forces)

Other Abbreviations and Terms
NCO: non-commissioned officer
CO: commanding officer
POW: prison/prisoner of war
FIDO: Fog Investigation and Dispersal Operation
LMF: lacking moral fibre (stamped on the discharge papers of those who 'lost their minds')
VE Day: Victory Over Europe Day (May 8th, 1945)
Jerry: nickname for Germans commonly used by Allied soldiers and civilians during WWII

Ranks (1944–45; lowest to highest)
RAF / WAAF
NCO Ranks
AC2: Aircraftman/woman 1st class
AC1: Aircraftman/woman 2nd class
LAC: Leading Aircraftman
Corporal
Sergeant

Officer Ranks
Warrant Officer
Officer Cadet
Higher ranks were differentiated by gender; they are listed as RAF / WAAF equivalent.
Pilot Officer / Assistant Section Officer
Flying Officer / Section Officer
Flight Lieutenant / Flight Officer
Squadron Leader / Squadron Officer
Group Captain / Group Officer
Air Commodore / Air Commandant
Air Vice-Marshal / Air Chief Commandant
Air Marshal / no WAAF equivalent
Air Chief Marshal / no WAAF equivalent
Marshal of the Royal Air Force / no WAAF equivalent

USAAF

NCO Ranks
Private
Private First Class
Technician Fifth Grade
Corporal
Technician Fourth Grade
Sergeant
Technician Third Grade
Staff Sergeant
Technical Sergeant
First Sergeant
Master Sergeant

Officer Ranks
Second Lieutenant
First Lieutenant
Captain
Major
Lieutenant Colonel
Colonel
Brigadier General
Major General
Lieutenant General
General
General of the Army

WWII Planes
Vickers Wellington (RAF): a twin-engined, medium bomber
Avro Lancaster (RAF): a four-engined, heavy bomber
Handley Page Halifax (RAF): a four-engined, heavy bomber
B-17 Flying Fortress (USAAF): a four-engined, heavy bomber
Junkers Ju 88 (*Luftwaffe*): a twin-engined, tactical bomber

Also by Debbie McGowan

LGBTQ Romance and Relationships

Champagne (novel)
First Christmas (novella)*
Breaking Waves (novella)*
Crying in the Rain (novel)*
Hiding Out (novella)*/**
Blue Skies to Forever ~ co-written with Raine O'Tierney*
Checking Him Out (novel)**/***
Sugar and Sawdust (short story)**
Checking Him Out For the Holidays (novella)**
Coming Up (short story) ~ co-written with Al Stewart
Cherry Pop Valentine (short story)
Leaving Flowers (novel) ~ co-written with Raine O'Tierney
When Skies Have Fallen****

*Stand-alone stories from the world of **Hiding Behind The Couch**
Part of **Checking Him Out
***Part of the **Love's Landscapes Anthology**
(Don't Read in the Closet 2014)
****Part of **Love is an Open Road**
(Don't Read in the Closet 2015)
MMRomanceGroup.com

General

'Time to Go' in Story Salon Big Book of Stories

Sci-fi/Fantasy Light

And The Walls Came Tumbling Down
No Dice
Double Six

Checking Him Out Series

Checking Him Out (Book One)
Checking Him Out For the Holidays (novella)
Hiding Out (novella)
Taking Him On (A Noah and Matty novel)
Checking In (Book Two)

Hiding Behind The Couch Series

The ongoing story of 'The Circle'…
Nine friends from high school;
Nine friends for life.

The Story So Far…

(in chronological order:
novellas and short novels are 'stand-alone' stories, but tie in with the
series - think Middle Earth—well, more Middle England, but with a
social conscience!)

Beginnings (Novella)
Ruminations (Short Novel)
Blue Skies to Forever ~ co-written with Raine O'Tierney
Hiding Behind The Couch (Book One)
No Time Like The Present (Book Two)
The Harder They Fall (Book Three)
Crying in the Rain (Short Novel)
First Christmas (Novella)
In The Stars Part I: Capricorn–Gemini (Book Four)
Breaking Waves (Novella)
In The Stars Part II: Cancer–Sagittarius (Book Five)
A Midnight Clear (Novella)
Red Hot Christmas (Novella)
Two By Two (Season Six)
Hiding Out (novella)

www.hidingbehindthecouch.com
www.debbiemcgowan.co.uk

All available from www.beatentrackpublishing.com

CPSIA information can be obtained at www.ICGtesting.com
Printed in the USA
LVOW11s2303080616

491824LV00004B/124/P